The Templar Conspiracy

PAUL CHRISTOPHER

PENGUIN BOOKS

PENGUIN BOOKS

Published by the Penguin Group
Penguin Books Ltd, 80 Strand, London WC2R ORL, England
Penguin Group (USA) Inc., 375 Hudson Street, New York, New York 10014, USA
Penguin Group (Canada), 90 Eglinton Avenue East, Suite 700, Toronto, Ontario,
Canada M4P 2Y3 (a division of Pearson Penguin Canada Inc.)
Penguin Ireland, 25 St Stephen's Green, Dublin 2, Ireland (a division of Penguin Books Ltd)
Penguin Group (Australia), 250 Camberwell Road, Camberwell, Victoria 3124, Australia
(a division of Pearson Australia Group Pty Ltd)
Penguin Books India Pvt Ltd, 11 Community Centre, Panchsheel Park,
New Delhi – 110 017, India
Penguin Group (NZ), 67 Apollo Drive, Rosedale, Auckland 0632, New Zealand
(a division of Pearson New Zealand Ltd)
Penguin Books (South Africa) (Pty) Ltd, Block D, Rosebank Office Park,
181 Jan Smuts Avenue, Parktown North, Gauteng 2193, South Africa

Penguin Books Ltd, Registered Offices: 80 Strand, London WC2R ORL, England

www.penguin.com

First published in the USA by Signet, an imprint of New American Library,
a division of Penguin Group (USA) Inc. 2011
First published in Great Britain in Penguin Books 2012

001

Set in 12.5/14.75 pt Garamond MT Std
Typeset by Jouve (UK), Milton Keynes
Printed in England by Clays Ltd, St Ives plc

B-FORMAT ISBN: 978-0-241-95120-0
A-FORMAT ISBN: 978-0-241-95254-2

www.greenpenguin.co.uk

MIX
Paper from
responsible sources
FSC C018179
www.fsc.org

Penguin Books is committed to a sustainable
future for our business, our readers and our planet.
This book is made from Forest Stewardship
Council™ certified paper.

ALWAYS LEARNING   PEARSON

PART ONE
Overture

I

It was Christmas Day in Rome and it was snowing. Snow was a rare occurrence here but he was ready for it. He had kept his eyes on the weather reports for the past ten days. It was always best to be prepared.

The name on his American passport was Hannu Hancock, born of a Finnish mother and an American father in Madison, Wisconsin, where his father taught at the university and his mother ran a Finnish craft store. Hancock was forty-six, had attended East High School, followed by a bachelor's and then a master's in agronomy at the University of Wisconsin–Madison. His present job was as a soil-conservation biologist and traveling soil-conservation consultant with the U.S. Department of Agriculture. Hancock had been married for three years to a young woman named Janit Ferguson, who died of lung cancer. He was childless and had not remarried.

Not a word of this was true. Not even the people who hired him knew who he really was. He traveled under a number of passports, each with a different name and fully detailed biography to go along with it. The passports, along with a great deal of money, were kept in a safe-deposit box at Banque Bauer in Geneva.

As alternates he kept several more passports and a secondary nest egg tucked away in a bank in Nassau, Bahamas, where he also owned a relatively small house in Lyford Cay – Sir Sean Connery was his closest neighbor – as well as a self-storage locker on Carmichael Road on the way to the airport. The Bahamas house was his usual destination after doing a job. It would be his eventual destination again, but he'd been told to remain available for another assignment in Rome sometime within the next six days.

Not for a minute did he consider failing, nor did he think about the enormity of the initial act he'd been hired to complete. He never failed; he never made mistakes. Remorse was an emotion unknown to him. Some people would have called him a sociopath, but they would be wrong. He was simply a man with a singular talent and he practiced it with enormous efficiency. He left the motive and morality of his task entirely in the hands of his employers. In his own mind he was nothing more than a technician, a facilitator for the needs of the people who hired him.

Hancock made his way down the Corso Vittorio Emanuele II in the lightly falling snow. He glanced at his watch. It was six thirty in the morning and it was still dark. Sunrise would be in an hour and four minutes. He still had plenty of time. He was wearing a white ski jacket purchased in Geneva, blue jeans from a vintage clothing store in New York and high-top running shoes from a store in Paddington, London. He had a pale gray backpack slung over his shoulder and tucked under his arm was a long, Christmas-wrapped box of the kind usually used for long-stemmed roses. On his head, covering his dark hair, he wore a white balaclava ski hat rolled up into a watch cap.

He'd seen virtually no one on his walk except for a few taxi drivers, and the steel shutters were pulled down over the entrances to the cafés, bars and small pizzerias along the way. Partly it was the unfamiliar snow on the ground and part of it was the day. Most people would be at home with loved ones, and the more pious would be preparing breakfast before heading out to Saint Peter's Square for the apostolic blessing by the Pope, scheduled for noon.

Hancock reached the Via dei Filippini and turned into the narrow alley. Cars were angle-parked along the right-hand side, and the only spaces available were for the large nineteenth-century apartment block on the left. Hancock's own little DR5 rental was where he'd left it the night before. He continued down the alley until he reached an anonymous black door on the right. Using the old-fashioned key he'd been provided with, he unlocked the door and stepped inside.

He found himself in a small, dark foyer with a winding iron staircase directly in front of him. He began to climb, ignoring several landings, and finally reached the top. A stone corridor led to the right and Hancock followed it. The passage took several turns and ended at one of the choir lofts.

He looked down into the central part of the church eighty or ninety feet below. As expected, it was empty. Most churches in Rome, big and small, would be vacant this morning. Every worshipper in the city was hurrying to Saint Peter's in time to get one of the good spots close to the main loggia of the church, where the Pope made his most important proclamations.

There was a narrow door at the left side of the choir loft. Opening it, Hancock was faced with a steep wooden staircase with a scrolled banister. He climbed the steps steadily until he reached the head of the stairs and the small chamber at the top. The floor of the chamber was made of thick Sardinian oak planks, black with age, and the walls were a complex mass of curving struts and beams of the same wood, much like the skeletal framework of a ship from the Spanish Armada; not surprising, since the framework was built by the best Italian shipwrights from Liguria in the late sixteenth century.

The framework supported the heavy outer masonry dome and allowed the much lighter inner dome to be significantly taller than what had been built on churches at that time. A simple wooden staircase with banisters on both sides soared upward, following the dome's curve and ending at the foot of a small round tower steeple that capped the dome.

Hancock climbed again, reaching the top of the dome, and then went up a narrow spiral staircase into the tower. He checked his watch. Still forty minutes until the sun began to rise. He dropped the heavy parcel and shrugged off the backpack. The trip from the outer door on Via dei Filippini to the tower had taken him eleven minutes. By his calculations the return journey would take no more than seven minutes, since he would be going down rather than up and he'd no longer be carrying the extra weight.

Before doing anything else Hancock took out a pair of surgical gloves and snapped them on. He opened the flap on the backpack and took out a wax paper-wrapped fried egg sandwich and ate quickly, methodically making sure that no crumbs fell on to the stone floor at his feet. As he ate he looked out over the city. The snow was coming down heavier now, easily enough to cover his tracks down the alley to the access door but not so heavily as to obscure vision. He finished the sandwich, carefully folded the wax paper and slipped it into the pocket of his ski jacket.

He set the alarm on his watch for eleven thirty, pulled the masklike balaclava over his face to conserve heat and slid down to the floor. Within three minutes he fell into a light, dreamless sleep.

The alarm beeped him awake at exactly eleven thirty. Before standing up he opened the backpack again and took out a loose-fitting white Tyvek suit that covered him from chin to ankles. It took him only a few moments to slip it on. The snow was still falling lightly, and in the suit and the white balaclava he would be invisible against the dull blur of the Christmas sky.

Hancock crouched over the backpack and removed a

device that looked very much like a digital video camera. He stood up and with the viewfinder to his eye he scanned the northwestern skyline on the far side of the Tiber River. The range was still exactly 1,311.64 yards, but he'd wanted to check the windage. He'd guessed from the straight fall of the snow that there was virtually no breeze, but the Leupold rangefinder was sophisticated enough to account for hidden air currents as well as plot a ballistic line that computed the differential in height between him and the target. This was important, since the Chiesa Nuova and its tower steeple were more than three hundred feet higher than the target, which lay across the river from the Plain of Mars.

Hancock bent down and returned the rangefinder to the backpack. He then began to undo the Christmas wrapping, carefully folding the red-and-gold paper and sliding it into the backpack. He lifted the top of the box, revealing the basic components of an American CheyTac Intervention .408-caliber sniper rifle – to Hancock's mind the greatest weapon of its kind ever made. He screwed on the stainless steel muzzle brake and suppressor, slipped the U.S. Optics telescopic sight on to its rails and slid the integral shoulder rest out of the stock. Finally he fitted the seven-round box magazine into its slot in the forestock.

The rifle was immense by most standards – fifty-four inches when assembled, or almost five feet long. The weapon had a built-in bipod toward the front of the rifle and a telescopic monopod at the rifle's point of balance.

Hancock chose neither. Instead he took a custom-made, sand-filled rest from the backpack and placed it on the capstones of the chest-high wall of the tower.

By kneeling on one leg he could bring the target to bear almost exactly. He looked at his watch. Five minutes to twelve. It would be soon now. He took his handheld Pioneer Inno satellite radio out of the backpack and plugged in the earbuds. The radio was tuned to CNN, which was carrying the apostolic blessing live, something the network did every year on Christmas Day.

According to the commentator more than sixty thousand people were gathered in Saint Peter's Square to hear their sins forgiven. Based on the last four *urbi et orbi* blessings, Hancock knew that he had no more than a minute and ten seconds to find the target and take the shot. At two minutes to twelve a huge cheer went up in the square. Hancock tossed the radio into the backpack and rose to his firing position, placing the barrel just behind the suppressor on the sand pillow. He turned the knob on the telescopic sight two clicks and the target area jumped into view: the central loggia, or balcony, of St Peter's Basilica.

There were eight other people on the long balcony with His Holiness: two bishops in white vestments and miters; two priests in white cassocks with red collars; a sound man with a boom microphone; a cameraman; the official Vatican photographer, Dario Biondi; and a senior cardinal who held the large white-and-gold folder containing the blessing.

In the middle of it all was the Pope himself. He sat on a red-and-gold throne with a golden crosier, or shepherd's crook, held in his left hand. He was dressed in white and gold vestments and a matching white-and-gold silk miter. Behind the throne, barely visible in the shadows of the doorway, Hancock could see several dark-suited members of the Vigilanza, the Vatican City security force.

At last, through the sight he saw the Pontiff's lips begin to move as he started the short blessing: *'Sancti Apostoli Petrus et Paulus: de quorum potestate et auctoritate confidimus ipsi intercedant pro nobis ad Dominum.'*

A papal banner draped over the balcony lifted slightly in a light wind and Hancock adjusted the sight minutely. Below the balcony, unseen and unheard, the enormous crowd gave the obligatory response in unison: 'Amen.'

Fifteen seconds gone.

Hancock wrapped his latex-gloved finger around the trigger as the Pope began the second line: *'Precibus et meritis beatæ Mariae semper Virginis, beati Michaelis Arch-angeli, beati Ioannis Baptistæ, et sanctorum Apostolorum Petri et Pauli et omnium Sanctorum misereatur vestri omnipotens Deus; et dimissis omnibus peccatis vestris, perducat vos Iesus Christus ad vitam æternam.'*

Twenty-five seconds gone.

The field of vision clear, a three-quarters profile; not the best angle for the job but good enough.

The crowd responded once again: 'Amen.'

Thirty seconds gone. Through the telescopic sight

Hancock saw the Pope visibly take a breath before beginning the third line of the blessing. His last breath.

Hancock fired.

The two-and-three-quarter-inch, missile-shaped, sharp-nose round traveled the distance between Hancock and the target at a muzzle velocity of 3,350 feet per second, reaching the Pope in just a fraction more than one and a half seconds.

Hancock waited until he saw the impact, striking the Pontiff in center mass, ripping through the chest wall and tipping the throne backward into the doorway of the balcony. Sure of his primary kill, Hancock then emptied the six-round magazine in an arc across the balcony, his object to create mayhem and as much confusion as possible. He succeeded.

With the task completed, he took down the rifle and laid it on the stone floor of the tower. He took a few moments to collect each brass casing and strip off the Tyvek suit. He put the shell casings into the pocket of his ski jacket, stuffed the Tyvek suit into his backpack and then took a small, clear plastic bag from his pants pocket.

The plastic bag and its contents had been sent to him by his employer, along with instructions regarding their use. He pulled open the zipper-top bag and tipped the contents on to the stone floor. The solid gold coin gleamed in the bitter winter light.

After he received it, Hancock had copied the image of the coin and taken it to a specialist in ancient coins. It was authentic, dated 1191. The name of the seated figure in the center of the piece was scrolled around it: *al-Malik an-Nasir Yusuf Ayyub*, a Kurdish soldier born in what was now Tikrit, Iraq, and known to the Western world as Saladin, the man who took back Jerusalem from the Crusaders and defeated Richard the Lionheart. With the coin in place he shrugged the backpack over his shoulders and headed downward from the tower, leaving the rifle behind.

He had overestimated the time it would take for the return journey. Five minutes after beginning the downward trip he reached the alley, locking the anonymous black door behind him. At six minutes, ahead of schedule, he climbed into his rental car and headed for the Roma Termini, the main railway station.

As he drove he heard siren after siren heading for the Vatican, but no one paid him the slightest attention. He arrived at the train station eleven minutes after the assassination, caught one of the frequent Leonardo Express trains to Fiumincino Airport, where he caught a prebooked flight to Geneva on the oddly named Baboo, a short-haul company that used Bombardier Dash 8 turboprops.

The elapsed time from kill to takeoff was fifty-four minutes. By that time neither the Vatican police nor the State Police had even established the direction the onslaught had come from, let alone any clue as to the identity of the assassin.

The job was done. The Pope was dead.

Crusader had begun.

2

'I should be there,' grumbled Peggy Blackstock, curled up in a cracked leather club chair in the very male study of a Georgetown row house, watching a plasma TV mounted above the tiny fireplace. The assassination of the Pope, as well as the deaths of two bishops, a cardinal, the Vatican's official photographer and a member of the Vigilanza, was still very much in the news cycle as CNN commentators analysed every second of the Pontiff's blessing, running the same gruesome footage of the bullet hit over and over.

Every news network had their correspondents reporting about every minimal forward motion of the investigation, no matter how insignificant, and the questions about the lax security around the Pope were flying in all directions. It was a tragedy of global proportions for a billion Catholics, but meat and potatoes for the media.

'You should rest,' said Doc Holliday, Peggy's quasi-uncle. Holliday was seated at the big old wooden desk at the far end of the room, marking a stack of term essays from his students. He was covering for a fellow medievalist who was on a year's sabbatical from his position at Georgetown University, and the newly renovated nineteenth-century, classic row house was part of the deal. When Holliday had been offered the job, he jumped at it. The thought of a year spent in the quiet groves of academe sounded like the perfect answer to the summer of hell and violence he'd just endured. When Peggy's husband, Rafi, had to leave Jerusalem for an extended archaeological expedition, Holliday had immediately offered her safe refuge in the Georgetown house to recuperate from her recent miscarriage.

'Phooey,' snorted Peggy. 'Much more rest and I'll die of boredom. Besides, I knew Dario Biondi; he was a good friend.'

'Biondi was the Vatican photographer?' Holliday asked.

'Ever since Mari hung up his Nikon.'

'What could you do that's not already being done?'

'I've got access at the Vatican. Favors I can call in. To my knowledge there's never been a behind-the-scenes photo story about the funeral preparations for a Pope. Besides, by Friday of next week every world leader will be in the pews at St Peter's.'

'Why Friday?'

'A Pope has to be interred within six days of his death. I checked,' she said, and then smiled ghoulishly. 'Did you know that on his death the Pope's name is called out three times and they whack him on the head three times with a silver hammer to make sure he's actually gone?'

'No, Peg, I didn't know that. I'll file it for future

reference,' Holliday replied dryly. He was less interested in the particulars of a papal funeral than he was in the motive for such an assassination. Watching the tape again and again, one thing was clear: this was no Lee Harvey Oswald amateur taking a shot of opportunity; this was the work of a trained killer, and that meant that somewhere along the line, politics were involved. But who except someone else in the Vatican could benefit politically from the Pope's death?

'It's true. First they whack him with a hammer, then they smash his signet ring with another hammer and finally they steal his shoes.'

'I beg your pardon?'

'They take his street shoes and replace them with red slippers.'

'You seem to know a lot about it,' said Holliday.

Peggy shrugged. 'I've been surfing the Net.' She sighed. 'I really *should* be there, you know,' she said again. Then she put a serious frown on her face. 'It would sort of be like a tribute to Dario.'

'Horse puckie,' said Holliday, laughing. 'You just want to get in on the action.'

'Yeah, well, there's that, too,' grumped Peggy.

Holliday threw down his red pencil and pushed away from the desk. 'Come on,' he said. 'It's St Stephen's Day, and it's a nice, brisk, sunny day out there. Let's bundle up and find an expensive restaurant on M Street to celebrate.'

'St Stephen's Day?'

'The second of the twelve days of Christmas. Second Night. Boxing Day.'

'Oh,' said Peggy brightly. 'You mean Go out and Buy Batteries for the Kids' Toys Day.'

'That's the one.'

They both climbed into boots and ski jackets and left the house. The weather was crisp and the low gray sky promised snow, although so far it had been a totally green Christmas. They turned off Prospect on to Thirty-third and walked the one block down to M Street. From there they turned again and walked along M for half a dozen long blocks, looking for a decent restaurant that was open.

They passed a few options, but Peggy didn't want pizza and Holliday didn't want Mexican. Eventually they crossed Wisconsin Avenue and finally reached Mie N Yu, which, unsurprisingly, was open and doing a roaring trade. The cutely named restaurant may have been expensive, but it had something for everyone. Supposedly serving 'Silk Road cuisine' from Turkey to Hong Kong in half a dozen, long, narrow, themed rooms, it served everything from chorizo-stuffed dates and banana pesto hummus to Bombay peanut salad and Cuban jerk pork sandwiches. All of this was overseen by a distinctly non-Asian executive chef named Elliot.

They settled on the Tibetan Tent Room, which was just that – the entire room was enclosed in a huge tent and furnished with plush couches and big leather ottomans. They found a reasonably quiet table and checked out the menu. Peggy chose the pupu mixed grill, because she thought the name was funny, as well as steak and egg fried rice, because it sounded impossibly odd. Holliday chose Virginia littleneck clams and the twelve-dollar Silk Road burger.

Both ordered watermelon beer just for the fun of it. It also sounded disgusting, which it turned out to be. The food, on the other hand, although a little strange, was uniformly excellent. At the end of the meal Peggy ordered a pecan and chocolate croustade, a puff-pastry concoction, and coffee, and Holliday, a bit of an ice-cream addict, had coffee and the homemade lime gelato. The only thing missing was Holliday's after-dinner Marlboro, but having quit more than ten years ago he barely noticed.

'I really think you should stay away from Rome,' he said. He flagged down a waiter and ordered a coffee refill for both of them. 'It's going to be a zoo until they run down the killer.'

'Look, Doc, I'm not some frail Victorian maiden. While you were in Afghanistan, I was in China, uncovering baby farms with a lot of Chi-com thugs looking for me. While you were in Mogadishu, I was cutting my teeth in the photojournalism business, doing stories about the Cuban mafia in Miami. You're my cousin, not my father, Doc. I thought you were my friend. I *need* to do something right now, not sit around and mourn a child that never happened and probably wasn't meant to be.'

'I am your friend, Peg, but I worry about you.' He shrugged. 'It's natural.'

'It's overprotective. And it's silly. I'm not the same little kid you taught to swim in the river behind Grandpa Henry's house in Fredonia.'

'What if I came with you? Held your camera bag or your lenses – whatever it is photo assistants do.'

Peggy gave him a long, shrewd look across the table, enlightenment dawning. Suddenly she broke into a huge grin.

'That sneaky little devil! Rafi put you up to this, didn't he?'

'Of course not,' answered Holliday unconvincingly.

'Liar.'

'He told me to watch out for you while he was away, that's all. And not to let you do anything foolish. Going to Rome immediately following the very public assassination of the Pope constitutes foolishness.'

'I didn't think you and the Vatican were on very good terms,' said Peggy. 'It's not like you haven't had a few run-ins over the last little while.'

'The same goes for you,' replied Holliday. 'As I recall, your last contact with that esteemed organization involved your being kidnapped and held for ransom in a fishing shack on the banks of the Tiber.'

'Nevertheless, Dario was my friend and someone murdered him indiscriminately. He was nothing but collateral damage. Everybody's concentrating on the

Pope – nobody cares about the little Italian guy with the big camera.'

'They're one and the same, Peg.'

'No, they're not,' she answered hotly. 'It's all about the killing of His Holiness. Dario is doomed to be a footnote in history. Nobody's investigating for him.'

'I see what you're getting at,' Holliday said with a nod, 'even though it's pretty subtle. It's like Lee Harvey Oswald killing J. D. Tippit. They were so busy focusing on J.F.K.'

'Tippit was the cop Oswald shot for no particular reason, right?'

'That's right,' said Holliday. 'Nobody ever bothered to find out why.'

'Just like Dario.'

'I'm afraid so,' Holliday said unhappily. On his tours of duty as a soldier he'd seen collateral damage from entire villages bombed out of existence in Vietnam to children with their hands and feet lopped off by machetes in Rwanda and the hellhole of the Congo. Enough for a lifetime of bad dreams and horror-filled memories.

'So I've proved my point,' said Peggy.

'Sure,' said Holliday. 'Maybe Dario was the intended victim all along; the Pope was just collateral damage.'

'You're making fun of me.'

'It wouldn't be the first time one crime was used to cover another one. Like Shakespeare said: "There are more things on heaven and earth. . . ."'

'I'm not a baby and I'm not an egg that's about to crack. I can take care of myself, Doc.'

'I know that.' Holliday shrugged. 'I just worry about your safety, that's all. Strangers poking around in the Italian State Police's investigations aren't going to be welcome. I guarantee it.'

'Let's get out of here,' said Peggy suddenly. 'I need some fresh air.'

Holliday paid the bill; then they slipped into their coats and headed home. It was finally snowing and the traffic on M Street had already begun to snarl. They made the walk back down M to Thirty-third in silence, both lost in their own thoughts, the whirling snowflakes settling everywhere. They finally reached Prospect and turned the corner.

Sitting on the top step of the old, wrought-iron stairs was a middle-aged man dressed in a plain black suit and a priest's collar. He was smoking a cigarette and he looked like he was freezing. There was spilled ash all down the front of his jacket, which was buttoned to the neck against the snow and the cold.

'My old Irish bones aren't used to this bloody arctic weather,' he said in a heavy, almost theatrical brogue. 'Maybe you could invite me in for a cup of tea in the hand or something a little stronger, Colonel Holliday?' Like most Irishmen, he made every statement a question.

'As I live and breathe,' said Doc, staring up at the priest. 'If it isn't Father Thomas Brennan.' Holliday paused, thinking about the hell this man, the head of the Vatican Secret Police, had put both him and Peggy through not so long ago. Then his curiosity got the better of him. 'Much as I'd like to put a bullet between your scheming, beady little eyes, hospitality prevents me. You're welcome to a cup of cheer and a seat by the fire while you tell us what brought you here.'

'Ah, it's a grand fellow you are, Colonel,' said the priest, standing up, his arms wrapped around himself, the stub of the cigarette dangling from his mouth. 'And how are you, Ms Blackstock?'

'Nauseated, since I saw you,' answered Peggy.

'Now, isn't that a shame and all?' said Father Brennan.

The front living room of the house on the corner of Prospect and Thirty-third had probably been called a parlor by its original owners. It was a pleasant room, and since it was on the corner it had windows on two sides, making it very bright. There was a gas fireplace on the interior wall, and like every other room in the professor's house it was lined with bookcases all stuffed with volumes on every subject imaginable. The furniture was mostly leather dating back to the eighties, the rugs Ikea sisal and the art on the walls a mix of quite nice nineteenth-century landscapes and a serious collection of horses in battle, mostly from the Napoleonic Wars.

Holliday seated the priest on a couch in front of the fire and fetched him a good-sized glass of Irish whiskey, making sure it was the Catholic Jameson rather than Protestant Bushmills. He then settled into a chair on the priest's right, while Peggy took the one on the left. Brennan stared into the bluish flames of the fire and sipped daintily at the whiskey, holding it cupped in both hands.

'It's a myth, you know,' said the priest at last. 'Jameson was made by a Prod and so was Bushmills. Everyone thinks Bushmills is Prod because it's made in the north and Jameson is Catholic because it's made in Cork, down south. It's all mother's milk to me, mind.'

'Get to the point, Brennan. My Christmas hospitality goes only so far.'

'Ah, Colonel, brusque and right to the point as usual.'

'So get to it.'

'You are aware of the recent tragedy in the Holy See, I suppose?'

'Of course,' said Holliday.

'Are you aware of the rituals surrounding the death of a Pope?'

'Among other things, he has to be interred within six days of Cardinal Camerlengo declaring his death,' answered Peggy.

'Quite so, Ms Blackstock. Four days from now, to be exact. Friday.'

'I'm sorry for the loss of your boss,' said Holliday, 'but what does any of this have to do with us?'

'We've heard things,' said Brennan.

'Don't be coy,' said Holliday, his tone sharp. 'What things?'

'We have a number of informants, one of whom is peripherally involved with the CIA.'

'So?'

'Our informant tells us that the assassination was the work of a new terrorist group. Fringe Jihadists. Copycat Al-Qaeda.'

'Do you believe it?'

'I think it's possible.'

'Is it plausible?'

'Is blowing up a subway in Moscow plausible? The only motive for such things is madness.'

'So why are you here on my doorstep?'

'Because I think the Pope is only the beginning.'

3

'What makes you think that?' Holliday asked calmly. Every intelligence officer he'd ever dealt with had something of the paranoiac in him. James Jesus Angelton, counterintelligence head of the CIA at one time – whom Holliday had worked for briefly – was one of the worst, conducting a search for a mole within the CIA for twenty years and never finding one, and tearing the very fabric of the agency to shreds in the process. Holliday doubted Brennan was any different.

'Our source is a priest,' said Brennan. He stared down into his empty glass. Holliday took the hint, stood up and fetched the bottle of Jameson. He poured a generous amount into the glass and set the bottle down on the priest's side of the coffee table. Brennan took another hefty swallow.

'Who is he?'

'Father John Leeson.'

'This is like pulling teeth, Brennan. Who is Father John Leeson?'

'He was a visiting priest at St John's Church in MacLean, Virginia. Old Dominion Drive. Father Connelly was off taking care of his ailing mother; Father

Leeson was filling in. He normally worked at the office of the bishop.'

'Okay, we've got the domestic background. Let's get to the assassination.'

'Father Leeson was doing confessions after late Mass.'

'And?'

'It makes me a little uncomfortable discussing matters of the confessional,' muttered Brennan.

'Bull,' answered Holliday. 'I was born and raised in the faith, Brennan. The confessional is only sacrosanct to people who aren't priests. It's one of the best control and intelligence mechanisms the Church has. Subtle blackmail on an enormous scale. We know all your secrets but you don't know any of ours, including which of your children we're sodomizing.'

'That's not fair, Colonel. The Church has done enough great works in its time to mitigate its foibles.'

'The only group who have started more wars and killed more people in the name of their god was Genghis Khan's armies. Now, what about this confession your priest heard?'

'A parishioner entered the confessional but Father Leeson didn't recognize his voice. But why would he? He'd only been there a few days.' Brennan hesitated.

'Go on,' urged Holliday.

'According to Father Leeson the man was either drunk or on drugs. He was babbling about killing "our father" and then the "poor doomed bastard in the

White House," and there was nothing anyone could do about it now that the Crusader was in play. Then he said something very odd. He said the killing of the Holy Father was nothing but the thimblerig. For the entire project.'

'What did this Father Leeson say to him?'

'He gave him absolution, of course. What else could he do? He thought the poor man was hallucinating. Whatever the case, he was terribly anguished.' Brennan took another sip of his drink. 'And then John telephoned me.'

'In Rome?'

'Yes.'

'Why would he do that?'

'We were old friends. We used to know each other. He knew what I did for the Church. He trusted me.'

Holliday thought for a moment and then it dawned on him.

'He was one of yours, wasn't he? Once in, never out – isn't that it?'

'What are you talking about?' Brennan said.

'You were a mole in the IRA. You were working for Rome even then. What – the eighties, the seventies, even earlier?'

Brennan was silent for a long time, looking out at the falling snow, remembering. He poured more of the Irish whiskey into his glass, then sighed and finally spoke.

'I was already in before I was ordained,' he said. 'I was

just a stupid boy with rocks in my pockets and in my head, as well. When you live on Dairy Street just off Falls Road all you can think about is getting a job in America, and failing that, climbing the ladder in the IRA. I had no one to go to in America, so I joined the Republicans and that was that.'

'And then you became a priest?' Peggy asked.

'They asked me to. There were a lot of squeals in the Belfast priesthood in those days. Patriots, as well. They wanted me to find out who was who.'

'Instead the priests turned you,' Holliday said.

'They offered me a way out. I took it.'

'And Leeson works for you?'

'We were at St Malachy's together. Then we transferred to the college in Rome. We were both ordained in St Peter's. There are a lot like him in America and around the world. In the Mossad he would be called a "sayan," a volunteer helper.'

'All right, so he phones you, tells you about the weird confession. When was this?' Holliday asked.

'Three days before the assassination.'

'*Before*? And you didn't say anything?'

'Hindsight is a wonderful thing, Colonel Holliday, but what was I supposed to say and to whom? He was a drunk parishioner four thousand miles away in a Virginia suburb, babbling about killing His Holiness. It made no sense.'

'But now you think it had something to do with the killing of the Pope?' Peggy asked.

'A thimblerig is the old-fashioned name for the shell game, three-card monte,' said Holliday. '"Crusader" sounds like some sort of code name. And that suburb in Virginia is where the CIA has its headquarters.'

'It gets worse, I'm afraid,' murmured Brennan.

'How's that?' Holliday asked.

'Father Leeson was murdered Christmas Day.'

'Murdered?'

'Two bodies were found in a car in the ditch on the Dolly Madison Parkway, late on the night of the twenty-fifth. The one in the passenger's seat was unidentified. Father Leeson was behind the wheel. The unidentified body had been shot in the face. There was a .45 automatic in Father John's lap. He'd been shot in the right temple. There was a note on the dashboard that said, "Apart in Life; joined in Death." They're calling it a gay murder-suicide.'

'Maybe that's exactly what it was,' suggested Peggy.

'Except that John wasn't gay.'

'You're sure about that?' Holliday asked skeptically.

'Perfectly,' nodded Brennan.

'How?' Peggy asked.

'Because *I'm* gay, God damn you!' said Brennan, his face flushed from the drink. 'I'd have known.'

'How did you find out about all this?' Holliday asked.

'The FBI called me very late last night. They said I was the last number he'd called on his cell phone. My name was in his address book.'

'What did you tell them?'

'Nothing. I said he'd just phoned up to ask about old times. I said he sounded a bit maudlin. Depressed. I played right into their preconceptions.'

'Why didn't you tell them the truth?' Peggy asked.

'By then the Holy Father was dead. I'd figured out that the man confessing meant the Holy Father when he was talking about "our" father. Anyone who can organize the assassination of the Pope is certainly capable of tapping John's phone and mine. I had to speak to you face-to-face. I took the red-eye to Washington from Rome. I got in two hours ago.'

'Why me, and why now?' Holliday said.

'A lot of your background is in intelligence,' answered Brennan. 'You have contacts that I don't. And you know something about crusaders, certainly.'

The priest downed the last of his drink and stared across the coffee table at Holliday. 'While the attention of the world is focused on Rome and the events taking place there, this Crusader organization will be planning their next attack somewhere else, and we've only got five days to find out exactly where and what that attack will be.'

'I still don't understand why you came to me. There are lots of other medieval historians in the phone book.'

'I think Crusader is nothing more than a front for something else. Something much more sinister.'

Holliday sighed. 'Get to the point.'

'The supposedly unidentified man in the car with Father Leeson was someone named Carter Stewart.'

'This is getting a little Byzantine,' commented Peggy.

'Who is, or was, Carter Stewart?' Holliday asked.

'He was one of ours,' said Brennan.

'Vatican Secret Service?'

'Yes. A lay operative. Like the Israeli Mossad's sayanim.'

'And why is this important?'

'Because he'd managed to infiltrate the office of an American senator.'

'Which one?'

'Richard Pierce Sinclair, Kate Sinclair's son. I think Crusader is actually Rex Deus.'

4

'Sinclair's son is hard to miss these days with all that crowing he does about the imminent threat of another 9/11 in the Senate, but you don't hear much from his mother,' said Holliday.

'She's retired,' said Brennan. 'On the surface it would appear that Rex Deus is in ruins, but I'm not so sure.'

'Is she still at that Hickory Hill place or whatever it was called?'

'Poplar Hill,' corrected Brennan. 'No,' he said, shaking his head. 'She's got a private island in the Bahamas, a country place called Edinburgh House in Scotland, a huge spread in Colorado and some sort of estate in Switzerland. She's usually in one place or the other.'

'But why would she want to assassinate the Pope?' Peggy asked. 'What does she get out of it?' She shook her head.

'Forget about motive for the moment,' said Holliday thoughtfully. 'And forget her delusions of grandeur about her blowhard son. Let's look at some basic facts.' He turned to Brennan. 'Have the cops in Rome figured out *anything*?'

'They've narrowed the search for the sniper's position to somewhere on the Capitoline Hill. It's the closest area that has the elevation for a clear line of sight to St Peter's.'

'What's the range?' Holliday asked.

'At least nine hundred meters – a thousand American yards. Possibly more.'

'Then he's a pro, just like I thought,' said Holliday emphatically. 'Military or private. You can pretty much guarantee he was military at one time or another; it's really the only way to get that kind of training. I'm also willing to bet that he's under forty. Much past that and the eyes and the hands start to go. You don't have the reflexes anymore. Carlos Hathcock did all his best work in his mid-twenties.'

'Who is Carlos Hathcock and what was his work?' Peggy asked.

'He was a sniper in Vietnam. He killed people,' answered Holliday. 'I met him once, years later.'

'Nice friends you've got, Doc.'

Holliday ignored the comment. 'The longest successful shot in modern times was by a Canadian at a mile and a half, but our guy is probably an American, Russian or a Brit. There's probably no more than twenty or thirty men in the world who could have shot the Pope from that distance and been sure of success. Whoever hired him would have gone for the best. He shouldn't be hard to track down.'

'Then why haven't the Italian cops already found him?' Peggy asked.

'Because they don't believe such a shot is possible,'

answered Brennan. 'Their ballistics experts tell them a thousand yards, but they think the shots came from much closer. Initially the medical examiner assumed the round had been a line-of-sight shot from straight ahead, so they concentrated their search to the east, assuming that the assassin had fired from some high ground like Castel Sant'Angelo. The bullet disintegrated on impact so the wound was a mess, but the examiner eventually found a concentration of fragments behind the left scapula – the shoulder blade.'

'Which means the shot hit at an angle from right to left. Southwest, not east at all,' said Holliday.

'Which means the range *was* a thousand yards,' sighed Brennan. 'The Italians love to complicate things.'

Across the coffee table Holliday could see Brennan's eyes begin to flutter. The priest was fighting jet lag and a six-hour time difference. It seemed he'd collapse where he sat any minute.

'There's a guest room on the second floor,' offered Holliday. 'Turn left at the top of the stairs; it's the last door at the back.'

'No, no, I couldn't impose,' said Brennan. 'I'll just find a little hotel for the night.'

'I insist,' said Holliday, thinking about the strangeness of bringing an old enemy into the house. 'It's bad luck to kick a priest out of your home on St Stephen's Day.' He smiled. 'Besides, a "little hotel" on M Street will cost you close to five hundred bucks a night.'

'Good Lord,' said Brennan. He stifled a yawn and

got to his feet. 'All right, Colonel, I'll accept your kind offer. No more than a few hours, mind; we're running out of time.'

Holliday was on the telephone in the study when a bleary-eyed Brennan appeared in the doorway at ten thirty the following morning.

'Sweet Jesus, man, why did you let me sleep so long?' the priest said.

'Because you would have been useless otherwise,' said Holliday. He scribbled something on a yellow pad. From the rear of the town house came the smell of fresh-brewed coffee. A few moments later Peggy appeared with a tray in her hands. Brennan flopped down on to one of the old, worn club chairs.

'Anything new?' Brennan asked.

'I've been on the phone since eight,' said Holliday. Peggy poured everyone coffee and sat down in one of the other chairs, tucking her legs under her like only women seem able to do. 'I'm calling in markers and favors from old friends. We've got some names.'

'Bad guys?' Peggy asked.

'The worst,' said Holliday, glancing down at the pad in front of him. 'It's like a top-ten list. Four of them stand out because they specialize in very-long-range targets.' He paused. 'Dimitri Mikhailovich Travkin, GRU Spetsnaz in Afghanistan and Chechnya. He'd be in his early forties, but no one has seen him in years. There's a rumor that he retired when he first showed the early symptoms of Parkinson's disease, which would rule him out. The second name is a Frenchman, Gabir Francois Bertrand, part Algerian, worked with the French Parachute Regiment, which is the equivalent of our Delta Force. Bertrand was involved in some sort of sex scandal involving a superior officer's wife and they turfed him. He's supposedly living in Switzerland and taking contract work, mostly mercenary jobs in Africa.'

'The third name?' Brennan asked, gratefully sipping his coffee and looking a little more alert.

'Edward Adler Fox, the top sniper in the British SAS. He was cashiered for insubordination, refusing to leave the front lines in Afghanistan. He wanted to stay with his men. Lives in a remote corner of England like some sort of hermit. Word is he's a little wacky in the head. No indication that he's active in any way.'

'And the last?' Peggy asked.

'The only American. William Tritt. A good old boy from West Virginia. Shot squirrels as a kid because that's all they had to eat. Wound up in the SEALs and got an education – chemical engineering, and then a second degree in mechanical engineering. Apparently a whiz with any kind of machinery. He's also a dead shot. He won the Wimbledon Cup at Camp Perry three years running.'

'Where is he now?' Brennan asked, helping himself to more coffee.

'He's a "consultant" to both the CIA and the National Counterterrorism Center. They find the terrorists; Tritt gets rid of them. They learned their lesson at Guantánamo; it's more cost-effective to kill terrorists than it is to capture them.'

'You're saying that one of these men is responsible for killing the Holy Father?' Brennan asked.

'I'd bet on it,' replied Holliday. 'My sources are pretty sure of it, too.'

'Then why aren't they looking for them?' Brennan asked.

'Maybe they are but no one seems to want to talk beyond the hypothetical. Something's scaring them off.'

'What could scare such people off?' Brennan said. 'You'd think finding the killer of the Pope would be a coup for everyone.'

Peggy spoke up. 'If nothing else, it's the politics of necessity,' she said. 'The Pope has been murdered. We in this room know there are four possible assassins – a Russian, a Frenchman, a Brit and an American. The last thing the governments of any of those countries want is to be associated with the assassin. The diplomatic damage would be enormous. Even the Italians are probably shying away from it. An Italian assassin killing the Pope? Absolute heresy. It would bring down the government.' She took a sip of her coffee.

Brennan lit a cigarette, his first of the day, and gave a great, racking cough. 'You mean no one is looking for this madman?' he asked finally.

'No more than they ever looked very hard for Kennedy's killer,' agreed Holliday. 'They had a convenient patsy in Oswald, who was just as conveniently murdered less than forty-eight hours later. Case closed and a potentially lethal diplomatic incident between the U.S. and the Russians was averted.'

'So any investigation is nothing more than a dog and pony show?' Brennan asked.

'Until they find out who did the "wet work" and who hired him,' said Holliday. 'You seem to think Kate Sinclair is involved. Among other things Kate Sinclair's father was a war hero who hit the beaches at Normandy, a senator himself and a deputy director of Central Intelligence during the Eisenhower years. He finished up his career as an ambassador. You're screwing around with the daughter of a true-blue American hero. Neither the present administration nor the CIA would like that particular piece of dirty laundry to be revealed, I can assure you. It's much tidier to simply say this is the work of jihad extremists and go with that.'

'So what do we do?' Brennan asked. 'It's David and Goliath.'

'We gather irrefutable evidence,' said Holliday.

'And how, pray, are we to do that?' Brennan said.

Holliday smiled. 'We go to McDonald's for a Big Mac and fries and we ask the right questions.'

The McDonald's in question was on a barren triangle of asphalt at the intersection of Old Dominion Drive and the Dolly Madison Parkway. Unlike the J. Gilbert's Wood-Fired Steaks and Seafood next door, McDonald's was unlicensed, which ruled out Martini lunches, and it also had the advantage of three or four picnic tables for alfresco dining in the emission fog of the highways bordering the restaurant on all three sides of the triangle it occupied.

From an intelligence officer's perspective, it was the perfect place to avoid surveillance – except for the chilly weather, which didn't seem to bother Holliday's companion at all. Unless you were in the parking lot you couldn't be seen from the street, and the constant drone of passing traffic only a few feet away beyond the sickly screen of trees would befuddle even the most sensitive parabolic microphones. The fast-food joint was almost exactly a mile away from the National Counterterrorism Center main entrance at the Dolly Madison Parkway and the Lewisville Road.

'I've only got about half an hour,' said Pat Philpot. Philpot was a senior domestic analyst at NCTC, which meant he tracked smaller fish that had slipped through the nets and traps set up by Homeland Security, covered the Mexican and Canadian borders, and kept his eyes and electronic ears out for a few potential Timothy McVeighs lurking in the backwoods of the continental United States.

He opened up the first of two Quarter Pounders with Cheese and began to eat, alternating bites of the dripping burgers with slurps from his large strawberry shake. Pat was a walking commercial for a heart attack, and it was hard for Holliday to remember that the man across the picnic table from him had once commanded a first-strike combat team for the Rangers.

'So, what do you know about the Pope?' Holliday asked. He sipped his coffee and waited for Philpot to swallow an enormous wad of cheeseburger.

'He wears a funny hat and he speaks Latin,' the big man answered.

'I don't need your bad jokes, Potsy. You wanted to talk to me here, not at the center, so that means you know something. Spill.'

'I'm not even supposed to talk to you, let alone divulge state secrets. You haven't had clearance for years.'

'How's Loretta?' Holliday asked, smiling. Loretta was Philpot's wife. A jealous wife. Like a lot of women Holliday knew, she didn't much care for her husband's old friends, especially those who knew him when.

'What does she have to do with this?'

'It's like John Lennon said – everyone's got something to hide.'

'This is about that thing in Panama, isn't it?' Philpot asked darkly.

'I'm just saying . . .'

'You're blackmailing me?'

'Reminding you what friends are for,' answered Holliday blandly.

There was a long silence punctuated by Philpot dragging on his shake. 'We put traces on them all. The only one we couldn't finger was Tritt,' he said finally.

'You're positive?'

'The others all alibied out. Travkin is in Mariinsky Hospital in St Petersburg with lung cancer and has been for the last three months; Edward Fox, the Brit, is doing something nasty in the Sudan at the moment; and Bertrand, the Frenchman, is in Fresnes Prison.'

'What's the last sighting of Tritt?'

'Geneva passport control. There's no record of him having left Switzerland but that doesn't mean much.' He finished off the first cheeseburger, wiped his mouth and his tie with a napkin, and started on the second burger. His body language told Holiday the man was suffering from a bad case of nerves.

'You worried about something, Potsy?'

'I don't like being used,' said the heavyset man. He shook his head. 'This is worse than it looks, Doc. Stay out of it.'

'That's it?'

'Talking to you is what worries me. You've gotta understand, Doc – I work for the organization that invented the word "paranoia."' He looked around the parking lot furtively. 'Other places, they give random drug tests. At NCTC they put you under random surveillance *and* give you pee tests. It's a brutal environment to work in.'

Something suddenly occurred to Holliday and he asked the relevant question. 'Where was Tritt flying into Geneva from?'

'Rome,' said Philpot. 'November sixth. We're assuming he was doing research for the shot.'

'Before Rome?'

'Glasgow International, Scotland.'

'Before that?'

'Orlando on Virgin Atlantic.'

'Before that?'

'Nassau, Bahamas. He has a little place there, a house on Lyford Cay. All under his own name.'

'You don't find that a strange itinerary?'

'We get everything except Glasgow,' said Philpot. 'What the hell does a man like Tritt find to do in a place like that for three days?'

'Checks in with his employer,' replied Holliday.

'You actually know who hired him to make the hit? Want to share? I've been doing all the talking so far.'

'How about Katherine Pierce Sinclair?' Holliday said. 'She owns a country estate called Edinburgh House within driving distance of Glasgow and a place in the Bahamas as well.'

'So does Sean Connery. So what?' Philpot asked. 'I would have thought you'd have had enough of Sinclair since your run-in over the summer.' Philpot shook his head. 'You should have seen them dancing around, trying to clean up that mess. We called in the Israeli ambassador, who's from Queens, by the way, and tough as nails, but he just stonewalled us.' Philpot took a last bite from the second burger and sucked on the straw in his milkshake.

'I'm going to need a few files,' said Holliday as Philpot drained the last of the bright pink concoction. There was so much exhaust from passing cars and trucks that Holliday was getting a headache. 'Quickly.'

'Don't push it, Doc. I am absolutely, positively not giving you official files and that's final.'

'Tritt, Kate Sinclair and whatever you've got on the senator.'

'You're crazy. They could lock me away forever in one of those secret jails they've got in Colorado. You're talking treason.'

'You owe me, Potsy.'

Philpot picked up his garbage, lumbered over to the refuse bin and dumped the paper and plastic into it. He turned and walked back to the picnic table.

'You ever been to Rock Creek Park?'

'Sure.'

'You know where Ross Drive is?'

'I can find it.'

'Half a mile in off the Ridge Road there's a dry culvert and a bridge. Three steel pipes and concrete abutments. On the west abutment some kid has sprayed his tag with black paint. If it's safe there'll be a bright red strip sprayed under the tag. What you need will be rolled up in the middle pipe closest to the spray-painted abutment.'

'You're a peach, Potsy.'

'You know where you can put your peach, Holliday. Consider my debt repaid.' He turned on his heel and went back into the McDonald's. A minute or so later he reappeared, biting savagely into an apple turnover.

'One more thing,' said Potsy, his mouth full.

'Shoot.'

'Bad choice of words,' said the pudgy intelligence officer.

'Sorry.'

'Our people found the kill site in Rome.'

'Before the Italian cops?'

'Uh-huh,' said Potsy. 'It wasn't all that hard.'

'And?'

'We found something,' said Potsy. He finished off the turnover and brushed the crumbs from his hands.

'Don't be coy.'

'It was a solid gold coin from the time of the Crusades. A dinar, I think it's called. It had Saladin's name on it in Arabic.'

'And?'

'NSA has been hearing from all sorts of Al-Qaeda cell phone and e-mail chatter about a group calling itself Jihad al-Salibiyya. They've secretly been taking responsibility for whacking the man in the big hat.'

'And you've been keeping it quiet?'

'We don't want to start up another shit storm like bin Laden and his pals. At least until we know more about them.' He looked at Holliday carefully. 'The name ring a bell?'

'No,' lied Holliday. 'Not even a faint one.'

'Well, that's it, then,' said Potsy. 'Rock Creek Park.'

'I'll be there.'

Potsy got back into his car and drove off.

Half an hour later, Holliday was back at the house on Prospect Street, the faint chemical scent of the hamburgers clinging to him like a fog. Brennan and Peggy were in the kitchen, drinking more coffee and reading the *Washington Post*.

The picture above the fold on the front page was probably the last photograph of the living Pope taken by Dario Bondi, the official Vatican photographer and Peggy's friend. Brennan and Peggy both put down their sections of the newspaper as Holliday appeared in the kitchen doorway.

'So, how did that go?' Peggy asked. 'Pick up any juicy rumors?'

'It was a setup,' answered Holliday. 'We're being played like a violin.'

'Why do you say that?' Brennan asked.

'A group calling itself Jihad al-Salibiyya is taking responsibility for the Pope's assassination.'

'Fundamentalists?'

'Yeah, but not the Muslim kind. Al-Salibiyya was the name for the Templar Knights who defected to the infidel side. The sworn enemies of the true Templars. It literally means "Enemies of the Cross."'

'Crusaders,' said Peggy.

'Kate Sinclair,' said Brennan.

5

'Philpot's a lot of things but he's no actor,' said Holliday tensely, passing on yet another cup of coffee and sitting down at the kitchen table. 'He just tried too damned hard. He was looking around like one of the villains in a Pink Panther movie. What he *didn't* try very hard to do was to keep back information. I barely put any pressure on him. He confirmed William Tritt as the most likely suspect and had his most recent travel itinerary memorized. Five will get you ten he was wearing a wire or we were being watched from the parking lot.' Holliday sighed and shook his head. 'The whole thing was far too easy. I asked him for some background files and he even had a dead drop organized and ready to go.'

'Sounds like the lads are trying to distance themselves from this Tritt fellow,' commented Brennan.

'And awfully eager to put it on the Muslims,' said Holliday.

'We Americans always think of our enemies storming the gates,' said Peggy thoughtfully. 'It's easy to worry about someone named Ali Sayyid Muhamed Mustafa al-Bakri, but worrying about someone named Bill Tritt, who sounds like a guy who works in the plumbing section of Home Depot, is a lot harder to swallow.'

'An American assassin; good Christ, that'll put the cat among the pigeons,' said Brennan.

Holliday stared blindly up at the ceiling. Something Philpot had said that didn't quite fit. The more he tried to remember, the vaguer the memory got. He looked at Brennan. 'I think you were right. There's a whole other level to this thing.'

'So what do we do about it?' Peggy asked.

'Follow the trail of breadcrumbs that Potsy left for us,' said Holliday. 'We have no other choice and not much time.'

Giving in to the freedom of a fresh divorce, the successful navigation of a midlife crisis and a secret yen to be James Bond after seeing *Goldfinger* as a young boy at the Neuadd Dwyfor cinema in his hometown of Holyhead, Wales, the professor whom Holliday was replacing for a year had purchased a silver Aston Martin DB9 for his fiftieth birthday. He'd given Holliday free reign to drive the car while he was away, as long as he took it in for monthly tune-ups, paid for its maintenance and took out his own insurance.

The magnificent twelve-cylinder brute of a car drank gasoline like a man dying of thirst in the desert, but it was worth every drop; Holliday had never had such fun driving a vehicle in his entire life. Both Brennan and Peggy wanted to go along with him to the dead drop in Rock Creek Park, but the car was only a two-seater.

Peggy cited her superior driving skills while Brennan

simply stated that it was a man's job and 'no task for a slip of a girl, begging your pardon.' In the end Peggy won out after Brennan admitted that it would be extremely difficult for him to last that long without a cigarette, and the one thing stressed by the Aston Martin's owner was a no-smoking rule.

Before they set out for the park Brennan told Holliday to wait for a moment and went upstairs to the guest room. He returned with a flat-black, short-barreled Beretta Storm semi-automatic, small enough to fit in a jacket pocket, and an extra clip. The bullets were .40-caliber hollow points, fifteen to a clip. A police load.

'How on earth did you get that through customs?' Holliday said, astounded that the priest had brought a pistol with him in his luggage.

Brennan gave a very Italian shrug. 'I travel on a Vatican diplomatic passport.' He smiled sourly. 'Anyway, people suspect all priests are pedophiles, not gunrunners.'

'You really think we're going to need that?' Peggy asked.

'Weapons are like the Garda,' said Brennan, referring to the Irish police force. 'When you really need them, they're never there.'

Holliday took the pistol, gave it a quick once-over to familiarize himself with it, then tucked it away.

It was only four in the afternoon when they left Prospect Street for Rock Creek, but it was already almost dark. In an hour or so the park police would be out in force, looking for kids tearing at each other's clothing in the backseats of their parents' cars.

Peggy drove and Holliday rode shotgun, giving her directions. If there was any trouble, Holliday had given her explicit orders to get the hell away as quickly as she could; if it came down to a chase, there wasn't a cop car outside of Germany that could catch an Aston Martin.

It was still snowing as Peggy drove the powerful sports car north toward Ridge Road and their destination, the wipers keeping up a steady metronome beat as night fell and the snow turned to slush under their wheels. It was getting warmer and the snowflakes were getting big and soft. If they had another cold snap the streets would be skating rinks and there'd be hell to pay on the morning commute.

'What good is a dead drop or whatever you call it? Just seems like a lot of trouble to me,' said Peggy.

'Dead drops are used so the parties involved don't have to meet, but in this case I think it's only window dressing to make Potsy's story a little more credible. There's probably nothing to worry about; they *want* us to have this material.'

'So, how do we do this?' Peggy asked. 'I'm not up on my spy-craft techniques.'

'Tradecraft,' corrected Holliday. 'We just do exactly what Potsy said. Coming in from the north puts the passenger's side closest to the abutment and the pipes that make up the bridge. I get out, with the car blocking the view from the other side of the road. I retrieve the files, get back in the car and off we go.'

Holliday guided Peggy north up Nebraska Avenue to Military Road, then east into the park. The pines and cedars were postcard perfect with their heavy mantles of snow, and as night came a peculiar, muffled quiet settled on the park as though the land was holding its breath just before shimmering out of the present day like some illusion, reverting to the empty, lonely place it had been ten thousand years ago.

Peggy turned the powerful car due south down Ridge Road. The snow was pristine, almost phosphorescent in the utter darkness, a gleaming white pathway between the dense stands of trees. No one had traveled here in quite a while; not surprising since the average Washingtonian had little experience driving in snow.

'Spooky,' said Peggy.

'Nervous?' Holliday asked. 'I can take the wheel if you want.'

'I'm fine,' said Peggy defensively.

'Just go slow and easy,' suggested Holliday. 'Put it into the lowest gear you can.'

Peggy blew Holliday an expressive raspberry. 'Sure, Granddad. Then you can tell me how you used to walk five miles to school.' She dropped the shift lever into the lowest of the six gears and headed even deeper into the park.

The snow was developing a light crust and the big

tires crunched over it, making the silence even more profound. For most of the way the road followed the course of an ancient streambed. The trees here were mostly birch and hickory, their leafless branches stark and skeletal as the Aston Martin's halogen headlights swept across the forest with each turn in the twisting road. Holliday watched the odometer. At half a mile, just as Philpot had said, they rounded a corner and the headlights found the three-pipe bridge. The ground sloped away on both sides and the trees were thinly spread. The crunching sound under the tires was louder now; the temperature was rising. If it fell again before morning the roads here would be a skating rink.

'There it is,' said Holliday.

'I see it, Doc,' said Peggy.

She slowed the sports car to a crawl and eased over the culvert bridge to the far abutment. There was a graffiti tag that looked as though it said *Bad Idea*. Below it was a single spray of red. Peggy stopped.

'Kill the lights,' said Holliday. Peggy did so, the only remaining light coming from the faint blue glow of the instrument panel. Holliday eased open the door and kept low as he approached the abutment and the capped ends of the pipes. The middle one unscrewed easily. He'd been expecting a rolled-up bundle of paper, perhaps in a plastic sleeve. What he got was an ordinary mailing-room address tag attached to a USB flash drive.

He grabbed the tag, pulled out the miniature hard drive, then recapped the pipe. The way the snow was falling his footprints and even the Aston Martin's tire tracks would disappear in the next few minutes. He slipped back into the car.

'Mission accomplished,' Holliday said.

'Famous last words,' warned Peggy.

The other vehicle came over the hill in a rush, blinding headlights blazing. Even from the inside of the Aston Martin, both Peggy and Holliday could hear the heavy clatter of tire chains.

Peggy flipped on the Aston's headlights, briefly illuminating the monster bearing down on them. 'Oh, crap,' she said. It was a behemoth of an F150 truck with a gleaming, lethal-looking snowplow attached to the front, half raised. If it hit them head-on, the huge pickup truck would either ride up the Aston Martin and crush them or the snowplow blade would slice through the windshield and the roof. Either way they'd be dead.

Peggy shifted the car into reverse and dropped her foot down on the gas in a long, smooth motion. The Aston Martin raced backward as the F150 came at them, gaining with each second. Peggy suddenly twitched the wheel to the right and simultaneously dragged up on the emergency brake to the left of the driver's seat.

The big car went into a sliding, perfectly executed bootlegger's turn and stopped. Peggy released the hand brake with one hand and pushed the shift lever into second gear. They were now facing back the way they'd come. She hit the gas again and the car gathered speed until they seemed to be skating over the snow, the rear end of the car fishtailing as they went around every turn. The only things that kept it from plunging off the road and into the woods were its weight and its low center of gravity. Throughout the whole operation neither Peggy nor Holliday said a word, Peggy completely focused on her driving and Holliday doing some quick computations in his head.

No matter how he figured it, the truck was almost sure to catch up with them before they reached the relative safety of Military Road. The chains on the tires gave the truck better traction, and it had four-wheel drive, sticking it to the snow-covered road like superglue. What was it one of his instructors at Ranger School had told him? 'Fight or flight. If you can't take flight, then turn and fight.'

Holliday looked behind them. The F150 was less than a hundred yards away and closing fast. 'That turn, can you do it again?' he yelled.

'Say when!' Peggy answered. Holliday took the Beretta out of his pocket, jacked a round into the chamber and then used his right hand to pull open the door latch.

'Now!'

Again Peggy went through the moves for a bootlegger's turn, ending up facing the oncoming truck. Holliday threw open the door and flung himself out on to the snow-covered road. He gripped the gun in both hands, leveled the pistol at the upper sill and began to fire, aiming for the windshield, adjusting his aim from left to right.

At twenty yards the big truck suddenly swerved, tried to climb the incline to the left, then dropped backward in a spin that took it over the drop on the right, eventually stopping as it struck a stand of three oak trees broadside to the road above. Never one for taking half measures, Holliday dropped out the empty clip into the snow, fumbled around in his pocket for the second clip and rammed it into the butt of the pistol.

He began firing, squeezing the trigger again and again, trying to concentrate his fire on the driver's-side window. Halfway through the second clip there was a brief flash of sparks from a ricochet toward the center of the chassis. A split second later there was a flash and then a thunderous explosion as the thirty-gallon gas tank exploded, the concussion throwing the truck over on its side and igniting the trees all around it.

Holliday stuffed the Beretta back into his jacket pocket and climbed into the Aston Martin again, slamming the door behind him. Peggy stared at the blazing truck and the trees turned into torches, her eyes wide and horrified.

'There were people in that thing,' said Peggy, a ghastly look on her face made even more grotesque by the play of the shadows from the flickering flames.

'Better them than us,' said Holliday, his voice cold. 'Drive.'

She dropped the Aston Martin into gear, then eased

the car into a narrow turn and headed north toward Military Drive. Behind them the fiery truck faded into darkness. In the far distance they could hear the first sounds of approaching sirens. Holliday reached into the inside pocket of his jacket and took out his cell phone. He punched in the number for the Prospect Street house. On the sixth ring Brennan answered hesitantly.

'Yes?'

'It's Holliday. Get out of there now; the house has been compromised. No packing, no nothing – just go.' He paused for a second. 'On second thought, bring my laptop. It's in a case in the study. Make it fast. You probably don't have more than a few minutes. Don't wear your collar, nothing that identifies you as a priest. Walk down to M Street and get a cab. Tell the driver to get to the Capital Hilton on Sixteenth. It's a couple of blocks from the White House. We'll be registered under the name of Dr Henry Granger.'

'I don't understand . . .' began Brennan.

'I'll explain later. Go. Now.' He snapped the phone closed. For the rest of the drive into the city they traveled in silence, lost in their own thoughts.

6

'Why here?' Peggy asked as they crossed the discreet and dignified lobby of the Capital Hilton. The lobby was all low lighting and mahogany. It looked like the reception area of a high-priced law firm. Quiet was the order of the day.

'The valet parks the Aston Martin in a garage somewhere nearby, which gets it off the street for the moment, and we have a place where we can lay our weary heads while we figure out what to do next.'

'Why did you tell Brennan the Prospect Street house had been compromised?'

'Because it almost certainly has been,' said Holliday. 'We know it wasn't Potsy's people who came after us, ergo it has to be someone who knows what he knows, and which also means they almost surely know where we live. It's got to be Sinclair's people.'

'Why couldn't it have been this Potsy friend of yours?'

'Why go to all the trouble?' Holliday said. 'Why put a memory stick in the pipe if the dead drop was just bait? Why go through the charade at McDonald's?' He shook his head. 'It wasn't Potsy's people, so it probably wasn't one of the other alphabet agencies either: CIA, NSA,

DIA. Someone who wants to put us down because we know too much about the assassination that they want to keep to themselves. If the killer really was this William Tritt guy and he's on Sinclair's payroll, then she'd go to any lengths to keep it quiet. Rex Deus would be haunted by it for decades. They have to keep up this terrorist front.'

They reached the long reservation counter and a pleasant lady with a brass-colored plastic name tag that read ANNE V. booked them into a suite on the sixth floor and then handed Holliday a note. It was from Brennan: *In the lounge*. It was signed with the scrawled letter *B*. Anne pointed out a curtained area at the far end of the lobby, and they found Brennan in one of the orange-curtained alcoves across from the bar. He was sipping from a fat glass filled with a rust-colored drink that was too dark for Irish whiskey and too light to be Bourbon.

'I must admit a certain fondness for Canadian rye,' said the priest as Holliday and Peggy sat down. 'It's somehow a little bit uncivilized, like something you'd make in a bathtub.' Brennan looked forlorn without the white-notched collar of his profession. His usual ash-flecked black shirt was covered with a ratty green, ash-flecked sweater that had seen better days. 'I always imagine grizzled farmers in Saskatchewan wearing bib overalls and sweating over a hot poteen still hidden in their barns.'

A waitress appeared and took their orders. Holliday

asked for a Beck's beer and Peggy settled on a Jäger Bomb – an Australian monstrosity that consisted of a shot glass of Jägermeister German 'digestif' tipped into a larger glass of Red Bull energy drink. The waitress went away to fetch their orders, and they got down to business.

Holliday filled Brennan in about the snowplow attack as the priest worked his way through a second Crown Royal on the rocks.

'I didn't know you were such a driver,' commented Brennan.

'Me neither.' Holliday laughed. 'I was hanging on for dear life.'

'I took the photos for an executive protection article for the *New York Times Magazine* a few years back, so while I was there I took the whole course. That's the first time I ever used what I learned.'

'Well,' said Brennan, 'we should give thanks that you could use it when you needed it.' He lifted his nearly empty glass. '*Slainte*,' he said, pronouncing the ancient Irish toast as 'slancha.' He put his glass down on the table. 'So, now what, Colonel?'

'We see if there's anything on that memory stick,' answered Holliday. 'Did you bring the laptop?'

'Right here,' said Brennan, patting the seat beside him.

'Then let's go.'

The suite was standard upscale Hilton: two generic prints above the beds in each of the bedrooms and everything in muted shades of rust and pink and beige. Tasteful and inoffensive. There was a Wi-Fi connection, a sitting room between the bedrooms and big screen TVs everywhere except the bathrooms. Holliday set up the computer on the little desk in the room and booted it up. He plugged the USB drive into the appropriate port and waited a few seconds for the menu window to open. There were three files on the memory stick: 'Tritt,' 'Sinclair' and 'Itinerary.'

All three files were CIA reports from what had clearly been a much larger file under the project name Crusader. From what Holliday could tell, Crusader was a classic arm's-length Delaware company like Evergreen International Airlines and In-Q-Tel, a high-technology dummy corporation whose main function was to monitor traffic carried on telecommunication satellites. According to the file numbers, Crusader had been in operation, although inactive, for two years.

'If Crusader involves Kate Sinclair, how come it pre-dates that whole episode during the summer – Sable Island and buried relics and all that?' Peggy asked.

'Sinclair's main objective was to put her son in the White House,' said Holliday. 'Those phony relics were just a means to an end. I think Crusader might well be her version of Plan B.'

'How does assassinating the Pope accomplish that?' Peggy asked.

'That's what we have to find out,' said Holliday.

He went back to Tritt's resumé.

A graduate of the U.S. Army Sniper School at Fort Benning, Georgia, William Spenser Tritt spent the early part of his career in Afghanistan 'advising' the mujahideen rebels, then moved on to Bush Senior's war in Iraq. After mustering out of the army with an honorable discharge he immediately found employment with the DEA and their Condor Group assassination squads operating in Cambodia, Thailand and Central and South America. From there it was a simple step to the CIA. Sometime during his sojourn with Central Intelligence he was offered a great deal of money by one of the Colombian cartels to assassinate one of his rivals. From that point on he freelanced, working for anyone who could meet his exorbitant price. He took assignments from Mexican drug lords, the Russian *mafiya*, African despots and even his old friends at the CIA. He was the perfect candidate to murder the Pope, but there was no clue to the benefit his death would have for anyone, with the possible exception of a cardinal who desperately wanted to be Pope himself, which seemed unlikely. There were lots of intrigues and jealousies at the Vatican, but to Brennan, at least, none that would justify murder.

The Sinclair file was filled with details of the family's high-profile life, including their long association with Rex Deus, but that rumor was in the public domain for most people and fodder for Internet conspiracy theorists. Like the Bush family's membership in Skull and Bones, the Sinclairs' membership had just about as much effect on their image: none. If anything it gave them a certain cachet. Once again there was no perceived threat. Senator Sinclair was mentioned, as were his extreme conservative philosophies, but he certainly wasn't the only one in the senate who had the same views.

Like John McCain before him, Senator Sinclair was a 'maverick,' voting whichever way the wind was blowing, and whichever way suited the aggrandizement of his own career. There had been a number of articles over the years about his mother's influence over his voting, but none that had ever done him serious damage.

The 'Itinerary' file was just as Philpot had described it, but with more detail, including flight numbers, airlines and an annex that turned out to be security camera video clips that showed Tritt leaving one place and arriving in another. The only ones of these not in the file were the clips showing the assassin's arrival and departure from Rome.

'There's nothing here that implicates Tritt as the Pope's killer,' said Holliday. He shrugged. 'All we have is the name Crusader and its association with the Sinclairs, and that could just as easily be coincidence.'

'That truck with the snowplow was no coincidence. Whoever was driving it was trying to squash us like a bug,' said Peggy.

The vague doubts he'd had about Philpot at the McDonald's scuttled across his mind again. What was it he'd said? Something that didn't fit. The thought began to sink into his subconscious again. Then he had it.

'Philpot,' he said.

'What about him?' Peggy asked.

'He said, "This is worse than it looks, Doc. Stay out of it."'

'What did he mean, d'ya think?' Brennan asked.

'He was playing me, but Potsy's not one to betray his old friends. It was as close as he could get to warning me off.'

'But *what* is worse than it looks?' Peggy asked. 'And why is counterintelligence playing you?'

'Potsy's under orders,' said Holliday. 'And I don't think it's the NCTC, either. The National Counterintelligence Center is joined at the hip with the CIA. It's really nothing but an excuse for the Agency to do business domestically.'

'You think the CIA conspired to hire Tritt to kill the Holy Father?' Brennan said. 'Why on God's green earth would they want to do that? The risks would be enormous.'

'Like I said before, forget about motive. The facts all add up. The man who confessed to Father Leeson was CIA, Tritt was CIA and so was Philpot. There's been talk of a rogue CIA faction since the Kennedy assassination. Why not a CIA faction involving Rex Deus? Why couldn't Sinclair's people have a foothold in the Agency?'

'I don't believe it,' said Peggy. 'Now you really are talking like some loony Internet conspiracy theorist.'

'Look,' said Holliday grimly. 'I sat around a conference table in Kate Sinclair's house with a televangelist, a member of the Joint Chiefs, two congressmen, one congresswoman, and I think a presidential national security adviser from the previous administration. There were half a dozen others present. Why couldn't one of them have been CIA?' He shook his head. 'Sometimes there really are conspiracies out there.'

'Do you have any proof that one of them *was* CIA?' Peggy asked, still playing devil's advocate.

'There's no proof that one of them *wasn't* with the Agency, either,' answered Holliday. 'It's a theory that fits the information we have.'

'Actually it's a hypothesis. A theory has to be proven,' said Peggy, her voice prim. 'And we're just going around in circles now.'

Holliday gave her a withering look but Peggy just smiled.

'I'm still not entirely sure why your friend Philpot or the organization he works for want you involved,' said Brennan.

'Like I said before,' stated Holliday, 'they want to distance themselves from Tritt. I can't prove that, either, but they could sure as hell prove that I've got a history with Kate Sinclair. If there is a rogue group within the Agency they'll almost certainly warn their pet assassin.

I think Philpot's people are using us as a Judas goat to bring him out in the open and then take him out with the minimum of fuss.'

'We're bait?'

'Something like that,' Holliday said with a nod.

'I still don't see it, Colonel. Much as you'd like to ignore it we need to address the question of motive. *Cui bono*, as the solicitors and the detectives in crime novels say. Who gains – Kate Sinclair in particular?'

'The only thing she truly cared about was installing her son as both the head of Rex Deus and President of the United States,' said Holliday. 'And she failed.'

'There's nothing to stop her from trying again,' suggested Peggy. 'Like you said, Plan B.'

Holliday stared at the computer screen for a long moment, as though it could somehow give him the answer.

'What was it the man in the confessional said to Leeson? Something about the White House,' said Holliday.

'He talked about killing Our Father, about it all being a "thimblerig" and the "poor, doomed bastard in the White House,"' answered Brennan.

'Who were the last three Popes?' Holliday asked suddenly.

'If you don't include John Paul I, who died after only a month, there were Paul VI, John Paul II and Benedict XVI.'

'Who was invited to the funeral?'

'Every head of state in the world.'

'The president?'

'Of course.'

'He was in attendance for all three?'

'Yes.'

'Then that's got to be it,' said Holliday.

'That's got to be what?' Peggy asked, frustrated.

'Dear God,' whispered Brennan, seeing where Holliday was going. 'They're going to kill the President of the United States.'

7

'I don't get it,' said Peggy. 'How is killing the president going to help the Sinclair woman?'

'You were barely a toddler when Watergate happened, but even before that Nixon already had a scandal,' said Holliday. 'His vice president, Spiro Agnew, was charged with accepting bribes when he was governor of Maryland. Agnew resigned and Nixon appointed Gerald Ford out of Congress. Then Nixon resigned and Ford became president. Ford in turn appointed Nelson Rockefeller, who had been governor of New York State. That meant that neither the president nor the vice president were elected. They were both appointed.'

'If the president is assassinated the vice president automatically takes over and then appoints his choice for VP,' said Brennan.

'And you can bet that Kate Sinclair's got that all locked up. It'll be her son the senator, Richard Pierce Sinclair, one of those "Pry my gun from my cold, dead hands" types.'

'How does she manage that?' Peggy asked.

Holliday lifted his shoulders. 'Lots of ways. Blackmail for some past sin, favors owed, contributions. It's a lame-duck administration. The VP will have a shot at the nomination.'

'I don't think so,' said Brennan. He plucked an errant fleck of tobacco off his lower lip. 'I just don't think that Sinclair would expend the amount of money she has or take the risk just for a shot at the nomination. She strikes me as the kind of person who bets only on a sure thing.' The priest shook his head. 'At least she'd want better odds. As it stands now she'd have to make sure everything went exactly according to plan. I think we're missing something.'

'Well,' said Holliday, 'as our Scots friend Robbie Burns once said, "The best-laid schemes o' mice an' men/Gang aft agley." '

'What does that mean?' Peggy asked.

'It means we follow in William Tritt's footsteps and look for mistakes.'

'Shouldn't we warn someone?' Peggy insisted.

'Who'd believe us?' Holliday replied. 'When you get right down to it we *do* sound like Internet wackos. And who's to say we're not telling someone with a direct pipeline back to Kate Sinclair? Think about it. I talk to Potsy at McDonald's and a few hours later a giant truck tries to run us down.'

'Your rogue CIA unit?'

'Or Kate Sinclair.'

'Or they're one and the same,' offered Peggy.

Holliday turned back to the laptop and booted up Expedia.com.

'There's a US Airway red-eye to Nassau in the Bahamas leaving from Ronald Reagan in an hour. If we hurry we can just make it.'

The three-hour flight got them into Nassau's Lynden Pindling airport just after midnight. They picked up a cab outside the main and only terminal and booked themselves into the old Royal Bahamian on West Bay Street. After renting a car for the next morning they all retired to their rooms and tried to sleep, slowly acclimatizing themselves to the hot, humid weather.

They met up at breakfast on one of the sea-view terraces. Biting into a freshly baked scone and sipping her excellent Jamaican coffee Peggy looked out over the turquoise ocean.

'I could get used to this,' she said, eyes hidden behind a pair of Ray-Bans. Lloyd, their white-jacketed waiter, appeared just as the first sterling silver pot was running out and replaced it with a fresh one. From somewhere farther into town there was the massive booming of an air horn. Peggy could have sworn the tune it was playing was the first four bars from 'When You Wish upon a Star.'

'What the hell is *that*?'

Holliday laughed.

'That, madam,' said Lloyd the waiter, 'is the *Disney Magic*.'

'Which is?'

'A ship, madam. A rather large one,' replied Lloyd. 'It warns us of its arrival by sounding its wretched horn that way. You can hear it on the other side of New Providence. Its passengers rarely come here.'

'I thought ships were always feminine,' said Holliday.

'There are exceptions, sir,' intoned Lloyd. He made a little shivering gesture. 'The *Disney Magic* is most certainly one of them. They have their own private island where Captain Hook takes you on tours in full costume.'

'It sound awful,' said Peggy.

'It is well past awful, madam. "Appalling" is a somewhat better word, I think.' Lloyd went off to find more scones.

'Where exactly is this place, Lyford Cay?' Peggy asked.

'The western tip of the island.'

'On the plane you said it was a gated community,' said Peggy. 'We don't even know which house is his, let alone how to get past security.'

'We'll cross that bridge when we come to it,' said Holliday.

'In other words, you don't have the faintest idea,' said Peggy.

'That about sums it up,' said Holliday.

Mary Breau Luxury Real Estate was located on the floor above the Bank of Nova Scotia at 404 West Bay Street, deep in the heart of Nassau, roughly equidistant from both the harbor and Government House. People often remarked that most of the banking in the Bahamas seemed to be divided between the three major Canadian banks: Nova Scotia, Royal and the Canadian Imperial Bank of Commerce.

There was no mystery about this. During prohibition the majority of bootleggers and smugglers, including the legendary rum runner Bill McCoy, purchased much of their product from Canadian distilleries, ferried it from Nassau to Bimini and then across the narrow fifty-mile strait to Florida. At one point there was so much cash stored in the fortresslike Royal Bank just down the street that people began to worry about the structural integrity of the building.

Mary Breau herself ran a one-woman show, and hers was the only real estate ad in the local yellow pages that had the gall to say that she specialized in Lyford Cay houses. She was coal black, spoke with a faintly British accent, wore floral-print dresses and had enormous breasts that dominated her physical presence almost as much as her charming, broad smile.

'What can I do for you nice people?' Mary asked, looking at them, one to the other. Holliday could see that she didn't know how Brennan fit into the structure of their relationship, but instead of being suspicious she was curious. A smart woman and a shrewd judge of character. They had to watch their step with this one.

'We're looking for a place at Lyford Cay,' Holliday replied, after making the introductions.

'Rent or buy?' Mary asked crisply.

Holliday gave her the answer he knew she wanted.

'Buy,' he said. The real estate agent brightened visibly, her eyes shining with the prospect of a fat commission. Holliday threw in the kicker. 'Bill Tritt recommended you.'

'You know Mr Tritt?' Mary Breau asked, her voice softening.

'Sure, known him for years. We've visited him a few times and we all love the place.'

'Any reason you're buying now?' Mary asked, jotting the information down on a yellow pad.

Holliday nodded in Brennan's direction. 'Uncle Thomas has decided to step down from his chairmanship at the bank and put things into the hands of someone a little younger. Me.' Holliday beamed proudly.

'Bank?' Mary asked.

'Texas Oilman's Trust,' said Holliday without a pause. 'Mainly we finance wells and invest the profits.'

'Well,' said Mary, her chest heaving a little with excitement. 'I'm sure we can find something to suit your needs.'

'A pool,' said Brennan. 'We'll want a pool, and perhaps some grounds. We'll be giving some garden parties, I expect.'

'And a dock,' put in Peggy.

'Yes, a dock,' said Brennan. 'We have a boat, you see.'

'How big?' Mary asked, jotting away on her pad.

'Sixty-two feet,' said Holliday.

'Nice,' said Mary, nodding approvingly.

'Maybe you could take us by Bill's place. I'd like to drop in and tell him we're going to be neighbors,' said Holliday.

'Is he there?' Mary asked. 'He's often gone on business.'

'I'm not sure,' said Holliday, shrugging as off-handedly as he could manage.

'Why don't we call him?' Mary beamed. She pulled out a bulging Rolodex and began skimming through it.

'Let's make it a surprise,' said Holliday. 'We're probably the last people he'd expect to drop in out of the blue.' True enough, he thought.

'All right.' She smiled. The cardinal rule of real estate: please the buyer when you're with the buyer and the seller when you're with the seller. 'Your car or mine?'

'We left our rental back at the hotel and walked,' said Peggy, playing her part in the little script. 'Your office is only a few blocks from the Royal Bahamian.'

'Nothing's very far from anything in Nassau,' Mary said with a laugh. She turned up the wattage on her smile even more. 'I've got the Land Rover parked in the back. Why don't you meet me out front?'

The Land Rover looked brand-new, silver paint gleaming. It projected confidence, success and good taste, and hinted at adventure and imagination. A surgeon driving a Mercedes usually elicited thoughts of greed and gouging, but a vehicle like Mary's was a mark of her success.

The real estate agent wheeled the big car around, narrowly missing one of the little, privately owned jitney buses and headed west down Bay Street. At the corner of Charlotte Street they stopped for a horde of adults and children wearing Mickey Mouse ears and led by a tall, young, black man dressed as Captain Hook and looking terribly embarrassed about it.

The Mickey cluster was taking digital snapshots of everything they could see and clogging up the sidewalks. Nobody seemed to mind, which wasn't surprising, since according to Mary a single cruise ship in harbor for twenty-four hours could leave behind as much as half a million dollars, not including docking fees.

They drove down Bay Street past the low, yellow building that housed the U.S. Embassy, then turned sharply and passed by the Royal Bahamian. After the big hotel the town quickly disappeared, replaced by dense, lush foliage on one side and the ocean on the other, the inshore water an impossible translucent green.

They continued past fish-fry shacks and scattered stucco residences, past low-rise condominiums, corner stores, gas stations and liquor outlets, Saunders Beach, one of the few public beaches for native Bahamians and finally reaching the 'golden mile' of the major hotels on Cable Beach, just past Goodman's Bay.

In the middle distance, standing on one heavy leg in the shallow water like a stork, was a building that looked as though it came right off *The Jetsons* cartoon show. According to Mary it was a defunct tourist attraction meant be an underwater fish observatory.

Past the hotel, restaurants, clubs and open-air native markets they went around the long, sweeping curve that took them toward the south or 'hurricane' side of the island. The farther along Bay Street they went the more the landscape changed. The houses grew larger, were set back farther from the road and had more junglelike foliage and coconut palm groves between them.

Just as the street curved again, they turned left off Bay Street and headed for the coast along Clifton Bay Drive to a long, narrow peninsula with the ocean visible on both sides. There had been a security booth at the Clifton Bay Drive entrance to the community, but Mary had barely paused as the man in the bright white uniform with the old-fashioned, white English bobby's helmet had waved them through with a smile as wide as Mary's own.

Mary Breau turned the Land Rover to the left and they followed the road toward the end of the peninsula. The houses here were much smaller than the others, more like the kind of neat cottagelike structures you found in suburban Dublin or Galway.

'E. P. Taylor Drive,' said Mary. 'Taylor was a Canadian billionaire who originated the idea of the gated community. At one time he owned and developed all of Lyford Cay. Just for fun he bred racehorses. Northern Dancer, the greatest sire in the history of thoroughbred racing, was his.'

'You sound like a fan,' said Brennan.

'I get over to Hialeah every chance I get.' She smiled. 'My not-so-secret vice.' They pulled up in front of a neat, yellow stucco bungalow with a short, crushed-stone drive. Through the palms they could see the open ocean and a small stretch of private beach. 'Here we are,' said Mary.

Holliday, Peggy and Brennan climbed down from the Land Rover and made a show of knocking on the glass-paned double doors. Holliday cupped his hands and peered through the glass. No telltale blinking red light of a security system visible, but that didn't mean much. The alarm panel could just as easily be in the closet to the left of the door. He turned back to Mary, who was waiting patiently in the Rover.

'Maybe he's round the back,' he called out. Mary nodded.

They all trooped around the side of the house to the back lawn and the patch of white sand beach. He checked the back door. It was much like the front except here it was a single door, not a double. It would be a snap to open. There was a small lanai with lawn chairs and a round table, a furled umbrella rising out of the center of it.

'You better have some sort of plan, Doc,' warned Peggy. 'Or we're in big trouble. That security guard isn't going to have a big smile for us the way he did for Mary.'

Holliday looked from the open ocean, then back to the house. No more than 150 feet from the house on the left of the beach with a pile of old paving stones that might have been a breakwater or a private pier once upon a time.

'No problem,' said Holliday. 'I've got a perfect plan.'

'Famous last words again,' answered Peggy.

8

'Are you sure you really know how to drive one of these?' Peggy asked, obviously nervous and clutching the nylon rope handholds on either side of the inflatable. The boat was a twenty-one-foot Zodiac powered by a fifty-horsepower Evinrude outboard engine, and it was skipping easily over the calm waters offshore from Cable Beach, sending up a salt-tanged burst of spray every few seconds.

To their left the long line of hotels and an unbroken strip of pure white sand stretched into the distance along the curve of Delaport Bay. It was getting close to sunset and the western horizon was on fire in a spectacular pyrotechnic display of yellow, red and orange.

Driving out of Nassau past the fish-fry shacks with Mary Breau, Holliday had seen a sign that read ARAWAK CAY BOAT RENTALS with an arrow pointing down a packed-earth road, but at the time he'd thought nothing of it. After spending a couple of hours with the real estate agent for the sake of appearances, they had her drop them off at the hotel. A few minutes later they were in their rental driving back along West Bay Street to the dirt road.

The road led to a roughly made combination seawall

and causeway, which led on to Arawak Cay, a messy, industrial wasteland with the Conch fleet of fishing boats in the protected, shallow harbor of the inner bay and larger ships, including the barges shipping the big casks of bottled water from the mainland, since Nassau had no fresh water of its own. Conch, the familiar, large pink shellfish, was protected in most parts of the world, but here the stony beaches of Arawak Cay were littered with literally thousands of them, tossed aside after their meat had been removed. Conch – pronounced 'konk' by the natives – was used for almost everything: conch salad, conch chowder, deep-fried conch, breaded conch, grilled conch, conch burgers, barbecued conch, even smoked conch. There weren't many restaurants along the Cable Beach strip that didn't have it on the menu somewhere. One of the more successful conch fishermen, a big Sumo wrestler type who went by the nickname Big Bambu, had branched out into renting Zodiacs and selling conch burgers as well as Kalik and Red Stripe beer to people who wanted to have a picnic and explore.

No experience was necessary to pilot the boat, just the name of your hotel and your passport left behind for security. After listening to Big Bambu giving Holliday firm instructions about bringing the inflatable back before dark they set out for Lyford Cay, this time approaching from the sea. The only equipment they carried with them was the jack from their rental.

'Yes,' said Holliday, 'I really know how to drive this thing.'

Peggy didn't look convinced, but Brennan was thoroughly enjoying himself, sitting happily in the bow, the spray hitting him squarely in the face, and reveling in the sensation. Holliday suddenly had a brief, compassionate vision of a young, unhappy Irish boy with very little childhood, raised by stern Jesuit priests who frowned on simple pleasures like boat rides.

'How about in the dark?' Peggy asked sourly. 'Because no matter what you told that Big Bambu character, there's no way were getting back before nightfall.'

Holliday smiled. 'I've had a little experience in Zodiacs at night,' he said, remembering making landfall on the wide beaches of Mogadishu in Somalia for a little surgical payback after the Black Hawk Down incident. Twenty-two miles from the carrier USS *Abraham Lincoln* to landfall, and all done in darkness as black as tar.

By the time they reached the old breakwater marking Tritt's unpretentious little house, the sun had almost disappeared, leaving nothing but a streak of crimson bleeding over the glimmering sea. Holliday cut the engine to a soft putter and scanned the area. The neighboring cottages were hidden by jungle foliage, and what could be seen was much closer to the road than Tritt's. Somehow Holliday got the feeling they were used more as vacation homes than as full-time residences.

As the sun set completely Holliday guided the Zodiac

to shore, keeping his course straight, aiming for the almost luminescent strip of beach at the foot of the assassin's property. The boat slid up on to the beach, sand grinding under the hull, and Brennan jumped out, mooring rope in hand. He held the rope while the other two got out of the Zodiac, and all three of them dragged the inflatable well up the beach. Holliday carried the jack.

He checked his watch. 'Fifteen minutes, in and out,' he said. 'That's probably the response time for the cops. It's a pretty small force.'

They went up the slightly sloping lawn to the back door. Holliday took the jack, positioned it across the doorframe horizontally and began to crank. After a few moments the ends of the jack were tight against the wood. He kept cranking. Slowly but surely the wood of the doorframe began to bow out left and right; then finally the bolt on the lock mechanism popped and the door came open.

'I'm impressed,' said Brennan, lifting an eyebrow. 'A scholar with the skills of a burglar.'

'Fifteen minutes,' reminded Holliday.

They ducked under the jack and stepped into the cottage. They found themselves in a kitchen-dining area simply furnished with a teak dining table, four chairs and a buffet containing silverware and table linens. The furniture was neither new nor antique and had probably been sold to Tritt along with the rest of the house.

There were two small bedrooms at the end of a short hallway as well as two bathrooms, one a powder room or WC and the other a full en suite bathroom leading to the third and largest of the bedrooms. The master bedroom was as anonymous as the kitchen-dining area. There was a queen-sized bed, end tables, a chest of drawers and a walk-in closet full of folded shirts, a variety of sportswear and shoes, plus a row of suits still in dry cleaning bags. The bags read *New Oriental Laundry and Cleaners Ltd: Looking Good Is Our Pride and Joy.* The suits were all expensive, mainly Brioni and Zegna. There was a single painting on the bedroom wall above the bed, depicting a pot of flowers on a windowsill with palm trees and a Caribbean beach done in shades of blue and white and pink. Without a word, Peggy and Brennan split up and began searching the spare bedrooms and the bathrooms. Holliday went down the hallway to a pair of pocket doors and slid them back.

The front room of the cottage was a living room, though it was outfitted as an office rather than a place to relax at the end of a busy day. There was a desk in front of a brick-lined fireplace that looked as though it hadn't been used for a very long time. The floors were hardwood, possibly cherry, and looked freshly waxed and polished. There wasn't a spot of dust anywhere.

On one corner of the desk was a black, high-intensity Tensor lamp; in the other corner a complicated-looking desk phone. There was a Wi-Fi box connected to a cable outlet, but no computer visible. Tritt was no fool when it came to security. The reason there was no alarm system was there was nothing to hide and no incriminating evidence of any kind.

Facing the desk on the opposite wall was a flat-screen TV. There was a high-backed leather swivel chair behind the desk and an upholstered chair with a pole lamp beside it next to the front window. Holliday crossed the room in the gloomy half-light of dusk and pulled the drapes closed. He went back to the desk and switched on the Tensor light.

The desk was utilitarian and made of dark blond oak. It was a pedestal style, probably bought a long time ago as government surplus. There were three drawers in each pedestal and one drawer in the middle. There was nothing in any of the drawers except the center one, which contained some loose drawing paper, a few Rapidograph drafting pens, a CD-ROM in a clear plastic case with no label and a neat stack of bills held together by a big paper clip.

Without even pausing Holliday slipped the CD case into his pocket, took out the bills and removed the paper clip. There was nothing very interesting. A Cable Bahamas receipt for both his Internet and television service, another receipt from Vonage but no actual bill listing calls, and a receipt for home delivery of Chelsea's Choice drinking water.

He rechecked the other drawers and again found nothing inside. Why have a desk with six useless drawers? Was it simply that the desk had been here when he bought the house, or was there another reason the drawers were empty? He thought about it for a moment. The desk hadn't been in this room when he bought it – it wasn't the kind of furniture you wanted in your living room, which meant Tritt had placed it here, either bringing it from another room or perhaps even farther afield.

But why lug a big desk around when all you really needed was a simple, modern desk from somewhere like Ikea? It wasn't logical, and if there was one thing he knew about Tritt and the place he lived in, it was that plain, clear logic prevailed. He started taking the empty drawers out and examining their outer surfaces, sides, backs and bottoms. He found what he was looking for on the back of the second drawer down on the right. Three phone numbers, the top two in faded pencil and the bottom one inked neatly with one of the Rapidograph pens, the sevens crossed in the European manner.

He sat up straight in the chair, the drawer upright in his lap. He let out a shrill whistle, then took one of the pens and a sheet of paper from the middle drawer. A moment later, Peggy and Father Brennan appeared in the doorway.

'It's rude to whistle, even if you're Lauren Bacall,' said Peggy, referring to the old Bogart movie based on a Hemingway book.

'What country code is four-one?' Holliday asked.

'No idea,' said Peggy.

'Switzerland,' said Brennan.

'You're sure?' Holliday said.

'Positive.'

'What city code is two-two?'

'Geneva,' answered Brennan.

'I found three phone numbers on the back of one of the drawers,' said Holliday. 'One of them has the Geneva city code, one is in France, I think, and the last one is in Switzerland, too.' He looked at Brennan. 'Any ideas?'

'Call the last one,' said the priest.

'It's two in the morning over there,' warned Peggy.

'Maybe you'll get a message.' Brennan shrugged.

Holliday reached for the phone.

Peggy stopped him. 'Wait,' she said abruptly. She crossed to the desk. 'This phone has a redial function.' She hit the speaker button, pressed REDIAL and watched as the numbers scrolled out on to the caller ID screen. Geneva again. The phone double buzzed for four rings before a sleepy voice came over the little speaker, rising and falling in the particular way associated with satellite calls.

'Mandarin Oriental, Jean-Pierre speaking.'

'You're a hotel?'

'And have been for quite some time, monsieur. I am the night manager. Would you like a reservation?'

Holliday gently cradled the phone receiver.

'There's a Delta flight to New York via Atlanta in an hour and a half. . . . If we hurry we can just catch it.'

*

By the time they reached New York it was all over the news. Senator Richard Pierce Sinclair stood on the broad steps of the Capitol and made his announcement.

'It has come to my attention that the various intelligence agencies in this great country of ours have been withholding information that is fundamental to the safety of our citizens, and those citizens have a right to know where the danger lurks, believe you me.' Here the senator paused and gave the cameras one of his patented scowls.

'According to my sources the people responsible for the assassination of the Holy Father in Rome are yet another organization of fundamentalist fanatics hell-bent on destroying the very fabric of our democratic society and the moral standards set by the founding fathers. The name of this group is Jihad al-Salibiyya, the "Enemies of the Cross," and I have it on good authority that this group of madmen intends to strike here, at the heart of America – and soon.'

'Cat's out of the bag,' said Holliday, staring at the monitor in the Avion Airport bar. 'We don't have much time.'

9

General Angus Scott Matoon sat across from Kate Sinclair in the baronial living room of her immense vineyard estate at Chateau Royale des Pins just outside the town of Aigle, Switzerland. Instead of the red wine bottled at the vineyard, the general sipped from his favorite Woodford Reserve Bourbon, a case of which the elder Sinclair always kept on hand especially for him. Matoon was supposedly attending a NATO conference in Brussels, but Belgium was less than an hour away by private jet and Chateau Royale des Pins had its own landing strip. He could have his meeting with the crazy old bitch and be back in Brussels before the evening session began.

The general wasn't at all sure that Kate Sinclair's harebrained scheme was going to work, but both her connections and her money were good, and he would need them in the near future. The defense industry was going down the toilet with the present wishy-washy administration in power, and there weren't many prime jobs left for an aging and not particularly noteworthy member of the Joint Chiefs. Sinclair had already paid him well for his cooperation and promised him a top security job if things went as planned.

'The name of the terrorist group has been leaked, just as you requested,' said the general.

'Excellent,' said Sinclair. 'The stage is set; now the public has an identifiable bogeyman.'

'You really think Holliday will come out of the woodwork?'

'Certainly,' said Sinclair. 'Despite the foolishness in Washington, at the very least the name al-Salibiyya will let him know the Templars are involved.'

The general took a healthy belt of the smoke-and-honey-flavored Bourbon and put the glass down on the coffee table between them. 'Look, I don't like this guy any more than you do,' said Matoon. 'But isn't it sort of like poking a rattlesnake with a stick? Maybe it'd be smarter for us just to whack the guy before he can cause us more trouble.'

Sinclair's eyes narrowed. 'He was responsible for my daughter's death,' the old woman said, her voice full of barely contained fury. 'Because of him she felt she'd failed our sacred cause. Because of him our plans for the future were shattered. I do this for her as much as I do it for our great country. Holliday must be found and brought to me before this ends.'

The general nodded. He'd heard this rant before. He'd also met Sinclair's daughter, the late Sister Margaret Emily. The redheaded nun had always seemed a few bricks short of a load, and she'd had that faraway look in her eyes he'd seen on guys who'd spent *way* too much time in a combat zone. The fiasco at the Rex Deus conclave had put her over the edge. He wasn't surprised when she drank herself into a stupor and drove one of the family cars into a brick wall.

'There is also the question of the notebook,' said Kate Sinclair, her fury tightly controlled now. The general smiled. Trust Kate Sinclair to reel it in and get back to the practical side of things – namely money.

'The one the monk supposedly gave him?'

'The monk's name was Brother Helder Rodrigues, and the notebook is not *supposed*, it is very real; that much is fact. It holds the ancient secret of the Templar Knights, the key to their fortune, a fortune that rightfully belongs to the inheritors of the true bloodline of Christ, to Rex Deus, not some half-baked history teacher who stumbled on the secret.'

'Your security people found this out?'

'They tracked down a man Holliday talked to in France.'

'And?' General Matoon asked, already knowing the answer.

'Let's just say that enhanced interrogation techniques only begin with waterboarding.'

'And you think Holliday has it?'

'Or at least knows where it is.' The old woman leaned closer. Matoon could see the madness boiling in her eyes. Not for the first time he found himself having second thoughts about his decision to ally himself with the Sinclair cause. It was starting to look like he'd made a deal with the devil, and the devil, it seemed, was right out of her mind.

'So what are you going to do about it?' asked Matoon.

'Breau, our contact in the Bahamas, said they're on their way. They've been through Tritt's place. I think they may be expecting to beard the lion in its den.'

'What are you talking about?' General Matoon said warily.

'I have no doubt they'll wind up on our doorstep sooner or later.'

'You'll hit them here?'

'Don't be silly, General. As my father always told me, don't piss where you eat.' The old woman shook her head, eyes glinting wildly. 'I have other plans for our little school teacher.'

10

After ten hours in the air and plane changes in three different airports, they arrived at the newly renovated Geneva International. Through the dubious magic of time zones they lost most of a day traveling, and by the time they arrived in the Swiss capital it was sunset again. In only three days Tritt would strike again, and somehow they had to stop him.

'I don't think we can pull this off,' said Peggy as they rode the airport shuttle into the city, only a few miles away. Snow was a blanket, piled in drifts beside the airport road. The windows of the bus were crazed with curlicues of frost. 'There just isn't time.'

'So what do you think we should do?' Holliday asked. 'Give up?'

'Tell someone,' answered Peggy. 'The authorities.'

'What authorities would those be, dearie?' Brennan said. 'The rogue CIA group that's probably running this whole operation? The FBI, which has no jurisdiction outside the United States?'

'The president,' grumbled Peggy. 'He's the one Tritt's gunning for, after all.'

Holliday shook his head. 'We don't have any real

proof of that. Even if we had a way of getting to him, what would we bring to the Secret Service to convince them? They'd laugh us off the front porch at the White House. And who's to say that Mama Sinclair doesn't have a mole in the presidential detail, anyway?'

'What about the stuff we found at Tritt's place last night? Is that a bust, as well? Did we waste our time going out there?'

Holliday sighed. 'We found three phone numbers in Europe and a CD-ROM full of information about some corn-fed town in Kansas that no one's ever heard of; Tom's Hill or something. Nothing that means anything to anybody.' He shook his head. 'We're it, Peg. Either we get some hard facts about an assassination conspiracy or the president is a dead man.'

The rest of the trip into Geneva was completed in silence. The bus took them to La Gare de Cornavin, the city's main railway station. From there they took a taxi to the Mandarin Oriental, a modern, upscale hotel on the banks of the Rhône River. They booked themselves a trio of adjoining rooms, then reconvened in Rasoi, the Indian restaurant on the main floor.

The entire hotel, restaurant included, was a shrine to the ultramodern, everything black granite, shining chrome and mirrors everywhere. The restaurant itself had the theatrical look of a modern *Phantom of the Opera* set, full of dark shadows and brilliant pools of light. It was a place to be seen and to see others. The food was supposed to be 'revolutionary,' but it was hard for everyone to get their heads around the idea that they were eating tandoori chicken and tikka for breakfast.

'I called all three of the numbers we found,' said Holliday. 'The first one, and the oldest by the looks of it, was for the Gamma Bank on the Quai du Seujet.'

'Tritt's ill-gotten gains, presumably,' said Brennan.

'Presumably.' Holliday nodded.

'The others?' Peggy asked.

'Another is for a vineyard in Aigle, and the last one is a private garage in a town called Thonon-les-Bains. Wherever that is.'

'A bank, a vineyard and a garage. What's that all about?' Peggy mused. 'It doesn't make any sense.'

'I don't know about the vineyard and the bank, but the garage is easy enough to figure out.'

'Do tell,' said Peggy.

'Switzerland is just about the only country in Western Europe that's not a member of the EU. Once he's in Thonon-les-Bains, he never has to go through customs again.'

'Thonon-les-Bains,' said Brennan. 'Sounds like a spa town. Lots of them on the French side of Lake Geneva, places like Evian. From there it's just a skip and a jump to Rome.'

'A staging base?' Peggy asked.

'Could be,' said Holliday. 'It's the only number written in ink. It's not a place he's used very often.'

'What about the vineyard?' Brennan asked. 'Where does that fit in the great scheme of things?'

'The only way to find out is to go there and see,' said Holliday.

'I still think it's a waste of time,' said Peggy. 'As far as I can see none of this has anything to do with your friend Kate Sinclair. The only connection we have is between the CIA and Tritt, and even that's pretty thin. When you get right down to it we have nothing. We're not even sure about Tritt. All we have is the opinion of your friend Philpot.'

'All the more reason to check out the only leads we have, which are those phone numbers.'

'Maybe he has a rotten memory,' Peggy said.

'Then why hide the numbers on the back side of a drawer?' Holliday said. 'If he's got nothing to hide, why did he hide them?'

'Time is running out,' said Peggy. 'I still think we should tell someone.'

'So do I,' said Holliday. 'Once we have something to tell them.'

Peter Van Loan had been on the Presidential Protective Detail for eleven years and a Secret Service agent for twenty. This was the third president he'd worked for, and as presidents go, he was a bit of a wimp. Of course, his job was not to reason why; it was but to do or die and all that. But sometimes the Man was worth taking a bullet for, and for others you'd hesitate just a tad, perhaps.

Eleven years was a long time to be on any detail within the Secret Service, but Van Loan was well-liked, always willing to accept even the boring assignments, like taking the kids to school or standing forever on post for interminable meetings. At fifty-four he was getting a little long in the tooth for the wear and tear on the nerves and of being constantly on the alert, not to mention the fact that his knees were starting to give out, his blood pressure was too high and his bank account was too low for someone as close to retirement as he was. He had a few more years left to cash in by working in private security and he was seriously thinking about taking the early retirement option.

Tab Hartmann, head of the detail and senior agent, was empathetic enough to throw Van Loan the occasional bone, such as being on the advance squad that vetted locations the Man was about to visit. Today it was Rome. This time Hartmann wasn't taking any chances. He'd doubled the size of the advance team from six to twelve. The assassination of the Pope less than a week ago had everyone on edge.

Not that Van Loan was unduly worried. Presidential security was always tight, but for this trip there'd be enough security to protect God himself. The president of Russia's Federal Protective Service was already prowling around the Eternal City, as were Canada's RCMP Protective Services Section, the United Kingdom's MI6 and France's GSPR (the Groupe de sécurité de la présidence de la République, or the Security Group of the Presidency of the Republic) and the German Bundespolizei.

On top of that there were smaller contingents from thirty other countries and the personal bodyguards for more than three dozen celebrities and bigwigs from Bill Gates and Arnold Schwarzenegger to George Clooney and the Archbishop of Canterbury. Van Loan had been on dozens of junkets like this, including one for the death of the previous Pope, and he knew he could do the whole thing with his eyes closed.

This is how it would go. Sometime just before midnight tomorrow two U.S. Air Force C-17 Globemaster III transports would arrive at Pratica di Mare Air Force Base, just south of Rome. The first would carry two identical presidential limousines while the second would be carrying six heavily armored Cadillac Escalades for use by the Secret Service.

The main vehicles would be followed by White House staff and support personnel traveling in locally rented Chevrolet Suburbans and the whole procession would be headed and tailed by a dozen motorcycle police on their customized blue and white BMWs.

Long before the arrival of Air Force One the following morning, Van Loan, as chief of the advance team and acting with the advice of the State Police, would have chosen the fastest and most discreet routes both to and from the Vatican, as well as two primary escape routes and one alternate in case of emergencies. Manhole covers would be temporarily spot welded shut and all refuse bins, newspaper boxes and mailboxes along the chosen route would be removed.

An Italian State Police AugustaWestland AW109 helicopter would act as aerial surveillance; it was also fitted out as a medevac unit. Trauma rooms at three local hospitals had also been reserved for the president. Nothing was too good for the Man and nothing was too mundane for his chief gofer.

Procedures at the Vatican itself were relatively easy to deal with. All guests, regardless of their VIP status, would be funneled through metal detectors and sniffer units programmed to detect any explosive residue. Women's purses would be checked for concealed weapons. As the requiem Mass began, the heads of state and other dignitaries would be asked to leave St Peter's and wait on the steps. Eventually the Pope's plain cedar coffin would be brought out and carried to the center of Saint Peter's Square for the final funeral rites and the liturgy. With that completed, the coffin would be taken to the grottoes beneath the immense basilica and laid to rest with his predecessors.

For Van Loan and the other Secret Service agents, the period when the president was waiting on the steps of St Peter's was critical. The crowd gathered in the square would be processed through several security checkpoints, but for almost an hour the Man would be vulnerable. Whoever had assassinated the Pope the previous week had done so at a great distance. This time there were armed Italian Special Forces teams in every tower and on the roofs of tall buildings for a mile and a half around the basilica.

It was this measure that led to the discovery of the sniper's nest in the bell tower of the Chiesa Nuova on the Via dei Filippini, an incredible thirteen hundred yards away. The fact that the nest, the weapon and the Arabic coin had been discovered by accident only the day before didn't do much for Van Loan's already low expectations of Italian security measures.

He'd rented a limousine from a local agency and made the trip from the air base to the Vatican twice, instructing the driver to proceed at a steady sixty miles per hour while Van Loan carefully processed each likely ambush spot along the way, seeing nothing that really looked like a weak spot. A sniper taking out a seated figure like the Pope was one thing; hitting an armored limousine traveling at sixty miles per hour was something else again. The moving target was the one thing that had always bothered him about the Kennedy assassination. Shooting downward at such an extreme angle was difficult, but hitting a perfect head shot while the moving target negotiated a curve was virtually impossible for anyone except a very experienced and talented sniper. By the end of the day, Van Loan was satisfied that all the bases had been covered. He went back to his hotel for a well-earned drink and a decent meal.

The man who called himself Hannu Hancock, back in Rome after his meeting with his employer in Switzerland, stood atop the air-conditioning unit on the roof of the condominium building on the Viale America.

Through a pair of binoculars he looked out over the reflecting pool to the Piazzale dello Sport, searching for a marker on the Via Cristoforo Colombo. He finally settled on a set of wide marble stairs leading up to the stadium parking lot.

The point of entry into Rome had been well chosen by the Secret Service. The four-lane roadway was split around the stadium, the nearer side stretching south, the farther side heading north into the city. Dividing the one-way strips was a deep, heavily treed berm of earth to cut traffic noise.

By his estimation, the range was about eight hundred meters, or a thousand yards, well within the weapon's eight-thousand-meter range, but he didn't need any accurate reading since the weapon ranged and sighted itself automatically.

His own escape plan was relatively straightforward. A well-dressed man in an Armani suit and driving a black Audi A8 luxury sedan certainly didn't fit most people's profile of a terrorist assassin. Just in case, he packed the trunk of the automobile with a large sample case of upscale Swiss jewelry findings, and of course he carried the proper ID to back up the façade. By his estimation it would take the police the better part of forty minutes to establish roadblocks around the city; by then he'd be long gone. At an average highway speed of seventy miles per hour he could easily be back in Switzerland by the late evening and out of the country on the red-eye to New York by midnight.

Standing on the rooftop and staring out over the prospective killing ground, he went over the plan of attack in his mind one more time. He saw no serious flaws. All he needed now was for his employer's people to provide him with the final detail and the small piece of equipment necessary to making the whole thing work. Satisfied, he dropped down from the top of the air-conditioning unit, then went down the utility stairway to the elevators on the top floor.

11

The President of the United States nodded to Mattie, his secretary, and quietly walked down the carpeted hallway to his chief of staff's office. He passed a mirror and noted once again the gray at his temples. It had happened to every president before him, but when he had entered office he thought he was going to escape it because of his youth. The First Lady said it made him look distinguished, but she was biased. It wasn't six and a half years of being the leader of the free world that aged you – it was having all those people who hated you.

An ordinary guy in his fifties had a few good friends, a bunch of acquaintances and maybe a few vague enemies. The President of the United States rarely had friends who didn't want something from him, no acquaintances at all and all sorts of enemies, from wacko heads of state with unpronounceable names to members of his own senate and congress, to half the population of the country that didn't vote for him.

He'd never once been hung in effigy while he was teaching law at Yale, but now it happened somewhere at least once a week. It was a very pissed-off world out there, and a lot of people, rightly or wrongly, thought it was all his fault.

He turned into his chief of staff's office at the end of the hall. He liked it better than the Oval Office. Morrie Adler kept it messy, with papers piled everywhere and the whole place stinking of cigar smoke. Morrie also got to put his feet up on his desk – a luxury not allowed to presidents, at least not without criticism. Morrie had a fishbowl full of miniature Mars bars, which he occasionally sent down to the kitchens to be deep fried in batter – a habit from his days at Oxford as a Rhodes scholar. It was funny how things worked out. Morrie'd gone to Oxford right after their time at the Abbey School in Winter Falls, while he'd gone on a backpacking tour of Nepal, but he was the one who wound up being President of the United States. He smiled. He'd long ago learned that life and politics were a crapshoot; you never knew how it was all going to turn out.

The president gave a little knock on the doorframe and stepped into the room, closing the door behind him. Morrie was reading the *New York Times* op-ed section. The president dropped down into the only other chair in the room, a Barcalounger that Morrie'd had back in their days rooming together and taking One L.

'Do I have to go to the Pope's funeral?'

'One of the Castros will be there. You want to be shown up by a graybeard commie commandant in his eighties?'

'I'm serious,' said the president.

'So am I,' said Morrie, putting down the paper. 'Yes, you have to go. If for no other reason than protocol and tradition. The Prime Minister of Israel will be there. Muslims will be there. Even Tonto's going.' Tonto was the Secret Service code name for the vice president. The president himself was the Lone Ranger. Morrie's nickname was Bullet, the Lone Ranger's faithful German shepherd, which was appropriate enough; they'd been best friends since high school.

'Speaking of Tonto . . .'

'I know,' said Morrie. 'I heard. The party isn't going to back his nomination. He's too old and he's too tired, among other things.'

'He's also too stupid,' said the president. 'I mean, he's a nice guy and all, but if we hadn't needed Chicago so badly, he never would have been on the ticket.'

'True enough,' said Morrie.

'Any ideas who they'll pick?'

'Rumor says our esteemed secretary of state. A woman, maybe – there's that California senator. And then, of course, there's Senator Sinclair.'

'You've go to be kidding,' said the president. 'Put that trigger-happy lunatic within a heartbeat of the big chair? Sarah Palin was a pussycat in comparison.'

'Sarah Palin couldn't find Canada on a map of North America,' Morrie said, laughing. 'Choosing her was the last act of a desperate old man. Besides, Sarah Palin didn't have any money. William Sinclair does. Lots of it. And he's also got his mother.'

'He's got to know I won't endorse him. He's the kind of knee-jerk, "Take my assault rifle from my cold, dead hands" kind of idiot who gave us the hillbilly reputation that's been keeping us back for the past few years. He's a Glenn Beck, weep-for-joy wet dream. He's got to be weeded out.'

'Kate Sinclair doesn't care and neither does the party. The other guys are putting together a slate of hard-nosers and gun-toters, and that means we've got to do the same. In eighteen months you're old news as far as they're concerned.'

'Where does that put you?'

'On to the lecture circuit with a seven-figure book deal, kemo sabe. That's where it puts me.'

They both laughed for a moment. The president leaned dangerously far back in his chair, a habit they used to take bets on back at Yale Law. Finally, almost sadly, the president spoke.

'Can you imagine him in the Oval Office?'

'No, but that's not the point. Nominate him for vice president and it gives us a bit of breathing room to find a real candidate come election day. A candidate who'll reflect your legacy.'

The president stared out of Morrie's window. The view was pretty much the same as the one from the Oval Office, but here it wasn't obscured by drapery and thick, bulletproof glass. 'You know what I really hate?' the president said finally.

'Bad Chinese food? Those creepy vampire books the First Lady reads?'

'Funerals. They depress the hell out of me.'

'Get drunk on the trip home,' suggested Morrie.

'You know I'm not much of a drinker.'

'Sorry, kemo sabe, this one you can't cut. It's not like Tank Gemmil's Latin class back at the Abbey.' There was another silence. The president folded his hands behind his head and closed his eyes. Morrie found himself thinking about the bottle of Glenlivet in his desk drawer. Was it half empty or half full? An alcoholic's philosophical conundrum. One way or another the problem was always solved the same way and the bottle was eventually completely empty.

'It's the fortieth reunion in a few weeks,' murmured the president.

'It's been that long?' Morrie said. The fact was enough to make him take the bottle and its accompanying shot glass from his drawer and pour himself a wee dram.

'I'll go to the funeral if you'll come with me to the game,' said the president, opening his eyes.

'The game?' Morrie said. And then he remembered. 'Not the Abbey School–Winter Falls High game?' The chief of staff groaned.

'Glory days,' the president said with a grin.

'For you, maybe,' said the chief of staff. He snorted. 'You were the star, the captain of the team. I was a third-string goalie because I had weak ankles.'

'It'll be fun,' said the president.

'Shannon O'Doyle,' said Morrie. He poured himself another shot.

'Shannon O'Doyle.' The president nodded, remembering the Winter Falls Snow Queen as though it was yesterday. All that long blond hair and the whisper of her panty hose when she crossed her legs.

'You sure you want to remind the electorate you went to a fancy prep school?'

'What have I got to lose?' the president said.

12

They woke early, asked for a car to be delivered from Hertz, had a quick breakfast and were on the road to Aigle by nine. They took Highway 1 out of Geneva and headed north, staying close to the shoreline of the long, silt-colored lake. They were almost halfway to Aigle before anyone spoke.

'Remind me why we're going to this place,' said Peggy.

'Aigle is the area code on that number on the back of Tritt's desk. When I called the number it was for a vineyard called Chateau Royale des Pins. I did some checking on the computer; it's about two miles outside the town. Apparently they make a nice Chablis.'

'Never cared much for white wine,' said Brennan from the backseat.

'It sounds like a bit of a wild-goose chase,' said Peggy. 'If there's anything to find it will be at that private garage on the French side.' She shook her head and stared out the window at the passing landscape. There was a dusting of snow on the ground and a cold wind was blowing in gusts, pushing a flotilla of sailboats around the lake. 'We should be in Rome,' she grumbled softly. 'That's where the action's going to be.'

'That would be your veritable needle in a haystack.' Brennan laughed. 'There's two and a half million people in Rome. How do you propose we track him down?'

'You got a picture of him in that file from your friend in counterintelligence, didn't you?' Peggy said.

'Tritt must know there's a CIA file on him at the very least,' said Holliday. 'It's easily a decade old. He'll have changed his look since then.' The photograph in the computer file showed a handsome, narrow-faced man with aristocratic features and neatly parted honey blond hair. If he was an actor he could have played the part of an Oxford student or the ne'er-do-well son of an English lord.

'Still, it's a photograph of the bastard; it's something to go on.'

Holliday couldn't fault Peggy's enthusiasm, but after half a lifetime in intelligence he'd learned that enthusiasm, intuition and hunches had little to do with it. Finding and identifying Tritt would be a matter of hard, slogging work, assembling small pieces of information like a jigsaw puzzle until the whole picture took shape. Privately he gave them one-in-a-million odds on finding the assassin before the president arrived. They simply didn't have enough time.

Even though traffic was fairly light, it took them the better part of two hours to make the fifty-mile trip around the lake to Aigle at the head of the Rhône valley. The town was a quaint little Alpine village of eight thousand, named for the eagles that circled on the upward air currents of the valley below, looking for rabbits taking shelter under the camouflaging grapevines in the summer months and foxes in the winter.

Aigle had been the seat of government for the canton since the eleventh century. Still the seat of municipal government for the district, now the town relied heavily on tourism and the vineyards in the area. They stopped at the Place de la Gare in the center of town to ask for directions and were told to follow the Chemin du Fahey to its end two and a half miles east of the town.

Fifteen minutes and two wrong turns later they reached Chateau Royale des Pins. Less a chateau than a full-blown castle, it sat at the summit of a large, flat-topped hill. It was surrounded by pruned grapevines that made it look like a gigantic military cemetery filled with makeshift, gnarled crosses, dark against a recent fall of fresh snow.

They parked in the lot at the bottom of the hill and trudged up the narrow path to the top, snow crunching under their shoes. They reached the old gatehouse at the entrance to the huge stone building. Left and right were turrets and arrow slits in the heavy walls. Here and there Holliday could actually see rusted cannonballs embedded in the walls that probably dated back to Napoleonic times. They went through a pair of imposing oak, iron-strapped doors and stepped into the castle.

They found themselves in a large foyer with La Boutique

de Chateau on one side and the requisite suit of armor on display to the right. The boutique was really nothing more than a souvenir shop selling castle key chains, wine-bottle key chains, bottle-opener key chains, eagle key chains, assorted postcards, a Swiss Post Office first-day cover of a stamp to commemorate the castle and View-Master slide sets that looked as though they'd been on the shelves, untouched, for decades.

Feeling the beady eyes of the concierge staring at him suspiciously, Holliday bought a wine-bottle key chain and gave the woman, a faint mustache distinguishable on her lip, a smile. The woman took his money and didn't smile back.

A bored-looking tour guide who was probably the concierge's husband levered himself up off his stool and started giving them the tour, not bothering to see if they were following. Finally he turned and spoke.

'English?'

'American,' answered Holliday.

The man nodded. 'American. Of course,' as though it should have been obvious to him.

Holliday spent the next hour learning far more about Chablis than he ever wanted to know; it was made from high-altitude Chardonnay grapes that were slightly more acidic than the grapes grown in a warmer, lower valley environment. He also learned that Chateau Royale was a traditional winemaker, storing the wine in oak casks rather than the more modern stainless-steel tanks.

When Holliday asked a simple question about Chateau Royale's ownership he was basically told it was none of his business.

The tour was confined to the main floor, which contained the shop and a viticulture museum, and the old dungeons in the basement, now used as the actual manufacturing, fermentation and storage area. The upper floors of the castle held the private apartments housing the owners, who demanded strict privacy.

Holliday began thinking that Peggy had been right – the whole thing was a waste of time. He didn't see how he was going to find any proof of a connection between whoever owned Chateau Royale and William Tritt, the onetime CIA assassin.

The tour finally ended with a quick run through the museum and a brief history of the Chateau Royale label, carefully skirting the whole matter of ownership. The little group exited the suite of expansive rooms that made up the museum and stepped out into the looming entrance hall with its inlaid marble floor and tapestries on the walls.

As they headed back to the shop, Holliday thought he saw movement out of the corner of his eye and turned slightly. He recognized the man instantly. The last time they'd met Holliday had elbowed him in the throat hard enough to crush his windpipe.

He tried to keep his expression neutral and carefully turned his face away. The man kept on coming down the stairs, then turned and went into the museum. Five minutes later the trio were back out in the cold again, heading down the steep path to the parking lot.

'Well, that was a bust,' said Peggy.

'I thought it was quite educational myself,' said Brennan. Peggy shot him a look to make sure she wasn't being mocked.

'I found out exactly what I needed to know,' said Holliday, dropping his little bombshell.

'Which would be?' Brennan said.

'As we were going out in the main hall, did you see the man coming down the stairs?'

'Big man. Jowls, distinguished-looking. Gray tips at the temples. Maybe seventy or so,' answered Peggy.

'That's the one.' Holliday nodded.

'And who would he be to us?' Brennan asked.

'His name is Angus Scott Matoon,' explained Holliday. 'He's one of the Joint Chiefs at the Pentagon. He's also Rex Deus. He was at that meeting where I was supposed to play pet archaeologist. I hit him pretty hard when I made my unceremonious exit from Sinclair House.'

'Did he see you?' Brennan asked.

'I don't think so,' said Holliday, shaking his head. 'And if he did, he didn't recognize me.'

'You'd better hope not,' said Brennan. Holliday got behind the wheel.

'Where to now?' the priest asked.

'France,' answered Holliday. 'Thonon-les-Bains.'

*

Kate Sinclair sat in the baronial hall that passed as a living room in the castle's private apartments, drinking coffee and staring out through the three churchlike arched windows at the panorama of the Alps, rising only a few miles distant to the north. Pacing up and down across the giant Tabriz carpet that covered the cold stone floor, General Angus Scott Matoon sipped from a snifter of Dudognon Heritage Cognac and scowled as though the expensive brandy had gone sour. He looked somehow diminished out of uniform, thought Sinclair.

'Did he see you?' the brittle woman asked.

'I saw him, so I'm assuming he saw me,' answered Matoon.

'Excellent,' said the elderly woman.

'You're sure that leaking Crusader is a good idea? Holliday was only a lieutenant colonel but he's got some very heavy connections in the intelligence business. He could be big trouble.'

'For God's sake, get some spine! You're one of the Joint Chiefs! We're far too wealthy to have big trouble. We simply have problems we have to surmount,' said Sinclair. She let out a smoker's coughing laugh and lit another cigarette. 'Quit worrying about Holliday. It'll be taken care of.' She paused for a moment. 'When they left, which way were they going?'

'North,' answered the general. 'I had Jean-Pierre follow him for a while like you asked. He says they turned west, heading for the border on the coast road.'

'France,' murmured Sinclair. She took a deep drag on her cigarette, then let the smoke dribble out through her aristocratic nostrils. 'They're going to Thonon-les-Bains.'

'What's there?' Matoon asked.

'Bad news for the colonel and his friends, I'm afraid.'

13

Thonon-les-Bains is a town of eighty thousand, about halfway down Lake Geneva on the French side. The old Roman baths have long since lost their cachet and the town now relies on tourism for the better part of its income. It didn't take them long to find the self-service garage used by William Tritt. There were only two in the city: Auto Express, which was a too upscale and open concept for Tritt by a long shot. The second was more his speed – a run-down, narrow, tin-roofed warehouse at the end of a narrow street, its twenty or so cubicles roughly divided by rotting canvas curtains hung on thin steel frames. There was a pneumatic lift, a workbench, an assortment of tools and a canvas flap over the rear of the cubicle that afforded some privacy. The place was called Paulie's Garage and it was Paulie himself who oversaw the place, seated on a creaking, old wooden office chair behind an invoice-piled desk. Paulie was immensely fat. He sweated profusely even with a fan blowing directly over him. He wore bib overalls with the bib section dropped around his waist. Underneath he wore only a sagging, stained wife-beater undershirt. His English was fluent.

Holliday took out the photocopy of the picture Potts had given him. 'You ever seen him?'

'Maybe yes; maybe no.'

Holliday put a hundred-euro note on Paulie's desk. 'Seen him?'

'Maybe yes; maybe no.'

Holliday added another hundred euros.

'Seen him?'

'Yes.'

'Where?'

'He has a booth here.'

'Which one?'

'Nineteen, down at the end, *à main gauche*. The left side.'

'Mind if we look around?'

'I feel bad letting you go through another man's things.'

Holliday laid another hundred on the pile. 'Feel better?'

'Much better, monsieur.' The big man scooped up the money and stuffed it into his overalls. 'My conscience is clearing as we speak.'

'What kind of car does he drive?'

'Audi A8. Black. Brand-new.'

'Nice car,' said Holliday appreciatively.

'At a hundred and fifty thousand euros, it better be nice,' said Paulie, laughing like a large barnyard animal clearing its throat.

'What kind of thing was he doing to a brand-new car? You'd have thought it would still be under warranty.'

'One would think so, *oui,* m'seiur.'

'So why did he need to rent a cubicle from you?'

Paulie just shrugged his big, fleshy shoulders.

'You don't know or you're just not talking?'

'I am having, how you say, moral doubts.'

'Losing the doubts?' Holiday asked, laying another hundred-euro bill on the desk.

'They are completely gone, as quick as magic,' said Paulie, sweeping up the bill and slipping it into his pocket with the others.

'So, what was he fixing?'

'It had something to do with the exhaust system.'

'How could you tell that?'

'Because he came in here two days ago with a complete left-hand side, after-market set of mufflers and pipes. That would leave me to assume that he was working on the exhaust system, *n'est-ce pas?*'

'When did he leave?'

'Very late that same night.'

'You're sure of that?'

'One in the morning. I have rooms in the back.'

'And did the car sound quieter?'

'If anything it sounded louder.' Paulie shrugged.

'Show us his cubicle.'

'That wasn't the bargain you made.'

'Which would you rather have?' Holliday bluffed.

'Your guts turned into tails for your best tuxedo or a nice hot cup of battery acid?'

'I don't have a tuxedo,' whined Paulie.

'Try to imagine it,' said Holliday. 'Just like the John Lennon song.'

'And if you can't imagine that, imagine us stuffing your private parts down your mother's throat,' offered Brennan mildly. 'A revelatory vision, I am sure, my son.' He took the little Beretta Storm out of his black clerical jacket and aimed it at the big man's sweaty forehead. 'As is this,' Brennan added with a smile.

'*Viens m'enculer,*' said the garage owner, eyes widening, horrified by the sight of a parish priest with a gun in his hand.

'The man, which booth did he work in again?' asked Holliday. 'Show us.'

Paulie stumped down the center aisle of cubicles to the last one in the row. The fat man pushed open the grimy canvas curtain. Inside, the cubicle was as neat as a pin. It looked as though every surface had been washed down with some ammonia solution, which it probably had. Set out on a workbench were a series of what appeared to be brand-new baffles for a muffler. Holliday spotted a small slip of paper caught behind the bench and grabbed it. It was a receipt for something incomprehensible from a place called Activite Audi on the Chemin Margentel.

'Where is this place?' Peggy asked.

'Three blocks from here.'

'Who owns it?' Holliday asked.

'An *encul* from Marseille. He runs – *comment* . . . how do you say it? – a chop shop. Sometimes he will steal a car to order for you. His name is Marcel.'

'Call him. Tell him you have three customers who want to see him.'

'He'll tear my face off if he finds out I set him up.'

Brennan brought an old-fashioned switchblade out of his jacket pocket, flicked it open and held it to Paulie's neck.

'And I'll slit your throat if you don't call him.'

Paulie called. He spoke for a moment, then hung up the phone.

'He's expecting you.'

Brennan used the switchblade to slice through the line of the rotary telephone on Paulie's desk.

'Warn him and I'll come back and slit more than your throat,' said the priest.

Paulie nodded mutely.

It took them less than five minutes to walk the three short blocks. The district was full of places like Paulie's and a scattering of small, anonymous warehouses, small windows painted over on big sliding doors, and hasps hung with sturdy locks.

There was a plain sign made of stick-on, fake bronze letters on the narrow door that read ACTIVITE AUDI. Beside the narrow door was a big, windowless roll-up. From behind it they could hear the faint echoing sounds of cutting torches, hammers and drills.

Holliday hammered his fist on the small door. It looked as though it had about fifty coats of paint on it, each color some pastel variation of yellow, blue, red or green. There was no response, and he knocked a second time, even harder. Eventually the door opened a few inches revealing a tall, skinny man in a blue boiler suit and a leather workman's apron. He appeared to be in his fifties. He had a heavy wrench in his right hand.

'*Qu'est-ce que tu veux?*' asked the man. Holliday noticed a long, thin scar that ran from the man's eye socket down to his chin, pale against the stubble on his cheek. Once upon a time someone had opened up his face with a very sharp knife or a razor.

'We're here to see Marcel. Paulie sent us.'

'Paulie is a pig. Why do you want to see Marcel?'

'To ask him about a car he worked on.'

'Who are your friends?' He nodded toward Brennan and Peggy.

'Colleagues.'

'You a real penguin?' the man asked Brennan, nodding toward his collar.

'Yes,' said the priest.

'What car are we talking about?'

'A black Audi A8. Owned by an American.'

'Sure, I know it.'

'You're Marcel?'

'Yes.' He stepped out on to the narrow, crumbling sidewalk, closing the old door behind him.

'What did you do for him?' Holliday asked.

'What's it worth for you to know?'

'Five hundred euros,' Holliday said.

'A thousand.'

'Six hundred,' said Holliday.

'Seven fifty,' said Marcel.

'Done,' said Holliday.

'Cash,' Marcel demanded.

Holliday took out his wallet and counted out the money. 'Talk.'

'He wanted to know if it was possible for me to bypass one set of headers on the exhaust system and run them through a single pipe.'

'Plain language, please,' asked Holliday.

'The A8 has twin pipes. He wanted one of them to be a dummy.'

'Why would someone want that?'

'He also told me he wanted the baffles removed. He wanted a stash.'

'How big?'

Marcel held his hands about a yard apart. 'A meter, maybe a little more.'

'How wide?'

'Twenty-five, maybe thirty centimeters.'

'Ten inches.'

'Enough for half a dozen kilos of heroin.' Marcel smiled.

'He told you he was smuggling heroin?'

'He was pretty clear about it,' Marcel said. 'He knew the right names, anyway.'

'When did you do the job?'

'Four days ago. He picked up the car yesterday. Paid extra for the rush.'

Holliday couldn't think of anything else. He thanked Marcel for the information.

'Anytime. Bring money.' The man in the leather apron grinned and slipped back into his shop.

They walked back to the rental car, then found a place to stop for lunch in Thonon-les-Bains.

'Why would he be smuggling heroin?' Peggy asked.

'He wouldn't,' said Holliday.

'Then the false muffler was for something else?' Brennan asked.

'Presumably.' Holliday nodded.

'Then it's a riddle,' said Peggy, using her chopsticks to sort through the small delicacies in the bento box she'd ordered. 'What's a yard long and ten inches in diameter?'

'Some sort of weapon, perhaps?' Brennan said.

Something tickled the edge of Holliday's memory. Something about America's first foray into the impossible country called Afghanistan.

'It's your town,' said Holliday to Brennan. 'What airport would Air Force One use?'

'Pratica di Mare Air Force Base, southwest of the city. It's a little bit out of the way but it can be absolutely secured. The Holy Father uses it.'

'So that's how all the foreign heads of state would arrive?'

'Almost certainly.'

'What route would they use to get into the city?'

'The Pope uses the Via Cristoforo Colombo. A high-speed auto route where you can control access and there are no tall buildings until you get into the city proper. Even for our assassin it would be an impossible target. Kennedy's limousine was traveling at something like eleven or twelve miles per hour when Oswald shot him. The Holy Father's limousine generally travels at a hundred and twenty kilometers an hour – roughly seventy miles per hour. No assassin in the world could make a shot like that.'

'He could if he had the right weapon,' murmured Holliday. He poked thoughtfully at the tiny salad on his plate.

'What's that supposed to mean?' Peggy asked.

'He knows security around the Vatican is going to be fierce. He knows that there will be countersnipers, dogs, dozens – if not hundreds – of highly trained Secret Service types from every major nation in the world. Trying to kill the president in an environment like that would be suicide. Somehow I don't see our man as a martyr to the Rex Deus cause. He's going to do the job efficiently and he's going to get away with it unless we stop him.'

'You said something about the right weapon,' prompted Brennan.

'I once saw a man named Emil, dressed in rags and rubber-tire sandals, destroy a Russian Mil Mi-24 attack helicopter from two miles away.' He turned to Peggy. 'It's the answer to your riddle, Peg. What's a yard long and ten inches in diameter? A portable Stinger missile. Just about the only one-man device capable of opening up the presidential limousine like a tin of sardines.'

14

Driving out of Thonon-les-Bains, they headed west, back toward Geneva. There were trees and small villages scattered along the busy strip of two-lane highway as it meandered along a few miles inland from the lake.

'If you're right about the Stinger, we have to go to the cops; there's no choice anymore,' said Peggy.

'What cops?' Holliday asked grimly. 'The FBI, the Italians, Homeland Security?'

'How about the ones hanging off our back bumper?' Brennan said, looking out through the rear window. A dark blue police cruiser with its light bar flashing had cut in behind them, its two-tone siren suddenly blaring.

'Now what?' Holliday muttered. He pulled the rental off into the first lay-by, which happened to be in front of a Chinese takeout place called l'Asian. He stopped the car and watched as two Gendarmerie Nationale cops climbed out of their cruiser and approached the rental, one on each side of the car.

'Speeding?' Peggy asked.

'On this road, no way,' said Holliday shaking his head. A dark yellow Mercedes Sprinter panel truck with Chinese lettering on the side pulled out from the alley beside the takeout restaurant and stopped.

One of the cops motioned for Holliday to roll down his window. The second cop squatted down and looked through the car on Peggy's side. Holliday rolled down his window.

Why, thought Holliday, do cops all over the world think mirrored sunglasses are so cool?

'*Votre papiers, s'il vous plait*,' the cop said pleasantly.

'Sure,' said Holliday. He leaned over and pushed the button on the glove compartment.

'Hey!' Peggy yelled. There was the sound of breaking glass and then a crackle of electricity.

I've been here before, thought Holliday, as unconsciousness washed over him. Then everything went dark.

Peggy Blackstock had a pretty good idea of where they were, at least in general terms, even though their captors had pushed blinding cloth bags over their heads once they were in the truck. Neither she nor Brennan had been Tasered by the phony cops, although the threat was there if they decided not to cooperate. The truck with the Chinese lettering on the side had driven for about an hour when she heard the sound of airplanes low overhead, which almost certainly meant Geneva airport. After that they definitely were going uphill, the road twisting and turning enough to throw them around in the truck's interior. They were in the mountains outside Geneva, the Haute Savoie – the French Alps. The way the truck slowed, then speeded up, Peggy could tell that they were going through one alpine village after another. Baptieu, Les Contamines–Montjoie, maybe La Chapelle. Wherever they were, it was up one of the long, narrow, glacial valleys: ski country.

Another hour, and then the rich scent of pine. The road was narrower with no traffic at all. They had to be climbing steeply because the truck engine was straining in its lowest gear. They were being taken to some out of the way spot in the mountains. But who was doing the taking? Fake cops, or bribed ones, plus access to private places in the Alps implied that whoever it was had a great deal of money. She'd dealt with everyone from Al-Qaeda to the Taliban to the Lord's Resistance Army in Uganda, and most of their headquarters were in caves, mountain camps or jungle clearings; she'd never done a photo story about Swiss terrorists. Maybe Doc was right, and Jihad al-Salibiyya was an invention of Rex Deus, or – God save America – the Central Intelligence Agency.

Across from her she could hear Brennan muttering under his breath. It was too Byzantine to think that the church was involved, but she'd made that mistake before. Brennan could be up to his neck in the whole thing. The little Irishman was certainly capable of cooking up any number of plots within the church hierarchy. He'd been party to at least a dozen murders that she knew about – he was hardly a trusted ally. The only people she could trust were Doc and Rafi.

She felt a dull ache in the pit of her stomach at the

thought of her archaeologist husband. He'd been so good to her after she'd lost the baby and he was even willing to give up his Africa expedition to stay with her. The ache grew worse, but it wasn't in her stomach; it was in her heart. He'd wanted a child so badly and she hadn't been able to give him one.

'We've got all the time in the world,' he'd soothed, but she knew it wasn't true. Another few years and she'd be in dangerous waters when it came to pregnancy, and she was goddamned if she was going to go through the infertility hell she'd seen some of her friends dealing with. Maybe they could adopt, cliché or not. She laughed briefly at the thought; Rafi had enough love for a dozen children. Maybe they could become the Israeli version of Brangelina.

'You find this amusing?' Brennan asked as they continued to rattle up the mountain road.

'I wasn't thinking about now,' she answered quietly. 'I was thinking about the future.'

'The way things stand right now, I'm not sure the future looks very bright, dearie,' said the priest, a sour note in his voice. 'We're tied up with bits of plastic in the back of a truck. On top of that, your uncle's been spirited off. We'd better start thinking about the immediate present because I'm afraid we're on our own.' Suddenly the truck jerked and stopped. They'd reached their destination. The doors banged open noisily and Peggy felt herself being lifted down out of the truck. There was gravel beneath her feet, and then as she was pushed forward, the gravel changed to something softer. Grass, maybe. The air was fresh and clean and even through the bag she thought she smelled snow. They were definitely in the mountains.

She stumbled up a short flight of wooden steps with Brennan right behind her, if his colorful swearing was any indication. Suddenly her nostrils were filled with the definite smell of cedar. A chalet of some kind. She was brought up short by a hand on her shoulder. Two voices began a heated discussion in Italian and then a third joined in. Finally one of the voices, clearly someone in charge, judging by the tone, commanded quiet. Peggy was pushed forward, and a few seconds later Brennan came stumbling after her. The bag was removed from her head and she caught a brief glimpse of a man's face, and then the door in front of her was slammed shut. A key turned in the lock.

There was absolutely no furniture in the room.

'Fecking hell!' Brennan's voice boomed. 'What in the name of Jesus, Mary and Joseph is going on here?' His hood was still on; presumably Peggy was supposed to remove it, so she did.

'I didn't think priests were allowed to swear or take the Lord's name in vain,' Peggy said with a grin.

'Vanity has nothing to do with Jesus, Mary or Joseph, and the word "feck" isn't swearing in the Republic. Little children say it.'

'Little children say it in America, too, believe me,' said Peggy, laughing.

'I don't find any of this funny at all. I don't,' said Brennan, his Irishness growing with his anxiety. 'You don't speak Italian, now, do you?'

'*Ciao, bella* is about the extent of it,' replied Peggy. 'Why?'

'Our captors were having a discussion just before they threw us in here.'

'I heard,' said Peggy.

'The question of the day was whether they should slit our throats now or later. Thankfully they chose later. We're being held hostage until your uncle tells them what they want to know.'

'Which is?'

'The location of a certain notebook.' Brennan eyed her closely. 'Do you have any idea what notebook they're talking about?'

'Not the slightest,' lied Peggy. She'd seen the blood-stained notebook put into Doc's hands by the dying monk, Helder Rodrigues, on the tiny island of Corvo in the Azores – a notebook that contained the secrets of the immense Templar fortune lost to the world centuries before.

'You're absolutely sure of that, are you?'

'Perfectly,' said Peggy, not liking the sudden, feral look in the old priest's eye. She walked to the high, small leaded window and looked out into the purple light of dusk.

'On top of everything else we don't have the foggiest idea where we are,' muttered Brennan. He tried the door handle, but it was futile. They'd been locked in a room about the size of the average bathroom. It wasn't much bigger than a walk-in closet.

'I know exactly where we are. We're in the French Alps, facing east. We're about nine miles south of Chamonix and about three thousand feet directly above the resort town of Les Contamines,' said Peggy.

'And just how did you arrive at such a detailed conclusion?' Brennan said skeptically. 'You're friends with that MacGyver fellow, are you?'

'That's the west face of Mont Blanc,' said Peggy, looking out at the high, spiny mountain looming above them. 'I actually climbed it doing a photo shoot for *National Geographic Traveler*. A lot easier going up than coming down, believe me. Especially if you're in the middle of a blizzard, which we were.'

'Fascinating, I'm sure. But we're still trussed up like poultry ready for the oven, and these people are going to kill us as soon as they get what they want from your uncle – and they will; believe me.'

'I wouldn't be quite so quick to count Doc out if I were you,' Peggy warned. 'He might surprise you.'

15

He dreamed of blood and war and the death of his wife, Amy, so long ago now. And then surprisingly he dreamed of baseball and the smell of pine tar.

And then he woke up. There was a dull pain dead center in his back where the first Taser had hit him and a second dull ache high on his left shoulder where the other cop had zapped him through Peggy's broken window.

That was no ordinary cop stop, he thought, his senses focusing again. Holliday opened his eyes. It was dark but he could see well enough to know that he was in what looked as though it might have been a cell-like servant's bedroom. At the end of the narrow bed he was on there was a small TV set with rabbit ears on a chest of drawers, and a straight-backed chair next to it. A single small window was covered by chintz curtains with a blue flower pattern. There were no pictures on the walls.

He got to his feet and went over to the window. He pulled back the curtains. Outside it was dusk. Enough pale winter light to see the wall of pine trees twenty feet from the window. He was in the middle of a forest. There was a heavy layer of snow on the ground. The window was eighteen inches square under a deeply overhanging roofline; even if he broke the glass there was no way he was going to squeeze through the opening, and it was a good thirty feet to the ground, anyway.

Holliday turned away from the window and went to the door. Locked. He sat down on the bed and looked around the room. Nothing much in the way of weaponry. The cops had been fake, or bought, at the very least. The question was, Who had kidnapped them and why?

The CIA was a good bet, but it was even more likely that it was Kate Sinclair and her religious fanatic friends. Fanatic, perhaps, but like a lot of zealots, Sinclair also had an animal shrewdness that could be lethal. Her Jihad al-Salibiyya had caught the imagination of the dozen or so men and women who chose what went into the news cycle, and by achieving that she was getting to the basic fears of most Americans.

Sinclair was rattling the Muslim sword and doing it extremely effectively. It was the same pattern of guilt by religious association that Hitler had used against the Jews, but it didn't seem as though the cultural history of the United States went back that far. Heaven help the news pundit who pointed out that little bit of history. Holliday was as patriotic as the next guy and had the battle scars to prove it, but sometimes it seemed to him that his country was blind to its own deeply entrenched, xenophobic madness. Who knew? The CIA had been infiltrated by the Soviets; why not by

Kate Sinclair's people? Maybe there really was an inner CIA cabal of Rex Deus members steering American intelligence into its own, self-serving waters. After seeing Matoon at Sinclair's vineyard estate he was willing to believe just about anything now.

He looked around the room again. Eventually someone was going to come for him and he had to be ready when they did. He'd probably have only a second or two to make his move and he had to make it count. His chance came sooner than he expected. Someone on the lower floor had clearly heard Holliday walking around and knew he'd risen from his electrically induced slumber.

There was the sound of a key being turned in the lock of the bedroom door and a moment later it opened.

'*Vo bist hellwach*,' – you're awake – said the man in the doorway. German Swiss, 260 pounds, six-four and built like a linebacker. He had huge feet encased in sturdy hiking boots. In one ham-sized hand he held a chubby little HK P30 9mm, and in the other the door key. He was smiling, thick lips parted to show a single gold tooth in the corner of his mouth. He had brown eyes with eyelashes a debutante would have killed for.

Holliday didn't hesitate for a second.

He took one lunging step forward as he slid the snapped-off TV rabbit ear he'd hidden up his sleeve into his hand and rammed the broken end as deeply as he could into the big man's left eye. The eye burst like a grape, fluid dripping down the man's cheek like a sudden gush of tears, and he made a brief *whoof* sound as the rough metal end of the stainless steel antenna sliced through his frontal lobe and Broca's area and then slid through the occipital lobe to finally scrape against the back of his skull. There was almost no blood. The man was dead standing up, and Holliday had to act quickly, grunting as he took the full weight of the fresh corpse under the armpits and gently lowered him to the floor. He slid the gun out of the man's hand and checked the magazine. It was fully loaded. He went through the man's pockets. A wallet, a set of car keys, an extra magazine for the HK and an SWR suppressor. He kept the extra magazine and the car keys, and screwed the suppressor on to the barrel of the HK.

Holliday slipped off his shoes and stuffed them into the front of his shirt. As quietly as he could he jacked a round into the chamber of the pistol and opened the door. He found himself in a dark, short hallway. There was a narrow doorway to the left that was either a closet or a bathroom, and a steep flight of stairs.

He went to the head of the stairs and listened. From somewhere he could hear a TV blaring, a news program by the sound of it, and kitchen noises. There was the sudden gassy hiss of a soda can being popped open and then footsteps, the squeak of springs and finally a sonorous belch. The TV channel switched. A game show in French and then a sitcom in German. *Happy*

Days, judging from the music. Somebody was working a remote.

Holliday headed barefoot down the stairs, keeping to the wall, the HK held in two hands at gut level. Eight rounds in the magazine. If he needed more than that he was in serious trouble. He reached the bottom of the stairs and another short hallway. An archway on his left led into a brightly lit kitchen. To the right he could see the jumping shadows of the TV show on the far wall of the living room. He took a step to his right and a floorboard creaked.

'*Heinrich? Ist ihm hellwach sein?*'

'*Ja,*' said Holliday, unable to come up with something more original. He took a turning step into the living room. In front of him was a leather couch. The man seated on the couch half turned his head. At the sight of Holliday with a gun in his hand the man's eyes widened and he struggled to get up and haul his weapon from its shoulder holster. On the big plasma screen, the Fonz was flirting shyly in German with Mrs Cunningham.

Holliday shot him in the right shoulder. The silenced pistol made a sound like somebody bursting a paper bag. The man screamed. Holliday fired again, this time shattering the right elbow, the bullet exiting in a blur of blood and tissue, finally hitting Henry Winkler right in his leather jacket. The plasma-screen image blurred, then dissolved like melting candle wax. A can of Fanta grape soda dropped from the man's hand and he sagged back on to the couch, moaning. No one else appeared. Leaving the wounded man where he was, Holliday checked the kitchen and the dining room. No one. He turned his attention back to the wounded man.

'*Können Sie Englisch?*' Holliday asked.

The bleeding man shook his head, his teeth clenched. 'Only a little.' He was about the same size as poor, dead Heinrich upstairs, but his face was pocked and scarred by the memory of a bad case of adolescent acne.

'There was a young woman and a priest. *Ein Pfarrer.*'

'*Ja.*'

'Where are they?'

The man gave him a hard scowl and sneered.

'*Mach es dir Selber, Mutterficker.*'

That wasn't hard to figure out. He shot the man in the left kneecap.

'*Wo sind Sie?*' Holliday asked a second time. The man was turning pasty white, the blood literally draining out of his face. The man was silent. The holstered gun at his shoulder was an MP5. The man could see it but with his useless arm he couldn't get at it. The little machine pistol could have turned Holliday into hamburger. Holliday shot him in the right ankle. '*Der Pfarrer und der Fraulien. Wo sind sie?*'

'*Die anderen Haus,*' screeched the man on the couch. The other house.

'*Was andere Haus?*'

'*Die Strasse.*'

'*Vas?*'

'*Aussensite! Die Berg Strasse.*' The mountain road outside.

'*Nach oben, oder unten?*'

'*Oben!*' grunted the man. Up the mountain road. Another house.

'*Wie viele Wachen?*' How many guards?

The man said nothing. He stared up at Holliday, sweat beading on his forehead. The man gave his best imitation of a resolute scowl again. A name, rank and serial number type of guy. Holliday didn't believe it for a second. The wounded man was beginning to shake as the pain took over. Another few seconds and he was going to pass out.

'*Wie viele Wachen?*' Holliday repeated. He put the muzzle of the suppressor against the man's left eye and pushed a little.

'*Drei! Drei Wachen!*' Three guards.

Holliday slid the MP5 out of the man's shoulder holster and took a step back. The man was slipping into unconsciousness but there was no telling how long he'd stay there. His eyes rolled up and his head slumped to one side. He clearly needed medical attention and it was obvious he'd be out for a good, long time. On the other hand, he'd seen a soldier with his legs blown off at the knees trying to crawl his bloody way across a rice paddy to an evac chopper.

'I'm sorry,' said Holliday, meaning it. He put the suppressor an inch from the man's ear and pulled the trigger. He jerked a little as the paper bag popped.

Holliday slid the HK into his pants and put on his shoes. He picked up the machine pistol and wondered about the effort involved in taking the shoulder holster from the dead man.

There was a faint, familiar sound behind him. Outside? Feet coming up the steps? He turned as the door opened, the MP5 in his right hand. He thumbed off the safety.

A man in a dark blue ski jacket closed the door behind him, then turned and stood in the foyer, a quizzical expression on his face. 'You're not Heinrich.' His right hand went behind his back.

'You're right, I'm not,' said Holliday. He squeezed the trigger on the machine pistol, center mass. There was a sound like someone ripping a piece of heavy cloth and the man went down. Holliday went to the body, his finger on the trigger just in case, but the man had half a dozen holes in his chest and one in his throat. Holliday teased the man over with the toe of his shoe, then dug around a little.

He found a Para Slim Hawg .45 in a waistband holster and a passport and wallet in the man's buttoned back pocket. The passport was a brand-new diplomatic with the embedded microchip, and it identified the owner as Major John Boyd Hale, assistant military attaché to the embassy in Rome. Holliday had enough military experience to know his name might be John Boyd Hale or it might not be. He might or might not really be a major, as well, and he was or possibly wasn't really an assistant military attaché. Considering Major Hale's appearance at this particular door, it was more likely that he was CIA and his job here was to interrogate Holliday. On the other hand, considering Matoon's presence at the vineyard, the dead man in the foyer could also be Defense Intelligence Agency, or even be tied into Kate Sinclair's oddball construct, the Jihad al-Salibiyya. He shook his head. Since the so-called Jihadists had taken credit for the Pope's assassination no one had made the Templar connection, or if they had, they'd ignored it. As far as the media was concerned, the people's interest ended at the word 'Jihad.' Eventually some scholar would come forward but by then it would be too late. The president would be dead.

Or maybe not. If he could get them out of this there was still a chance. He stepped over the body of Major John Boyd Hale and opened the door. He cautiously moved out on to the wide porch of the chalet. It was fully dark now but he could make out the enormous, deeper blackness of the mountain on his left and the paler line of the road ahead. There was a black, late-model Volkswagen Phaeton and an older-model Mercedes parked in front of the chalet, but he ignored both vehicles; he wasn't about to announce his arrival.

He began to climb.

Brennan had been slouched against the wall facing the door for the last hour and a half, singing the same song over and over in a whispered, grating soprano. It was beginning to get on Peggy's nerves. Apparently it was called 'The Orange and the Green.'

> Oh, it is the biggest mix-up that you have never seen.
> My father, he was orange, and me mother, she was
> green . . .

'Quiet; they're talking again,' said Peggy, her ear to the door. 'Yelling actually.'

Brennan stopped singing and stumbled to his feet, his tied hands making it difficult. He made his way to the door and leaned toward it, pressing his ear against the wood panel.

'What are they talking about?' Peggy said.

'Someone called Heinrich; they've been trying to call him but he doesn't answer. They think something's wrong.'

Peggy smiled. 'I told you so.'

'You think it's your uncle?'

'"Wrong" is his middle name. Heinrich is not in the best of health right now, I guarantee it,' said Peggy. She eased away from the door and let herself slowly slide down the wall.

'You sound pretty sure of yourself,' said Brennan.

'I've been with Doc in situations like this before; I know what I'm talking about.'

'Once a soldier, always a soldier?' Brennan said.

'Put it this way: he's not the kind who simply fades

away.' She listened to the men arguing on the other side of the door. 'I'd get as low as possible,' suggested Peggy. 'There's going to be bullets flying any minute now.'

The priest lowered himself toward the floor.

It wasn't minutes; it was seconds. There was the sound of breaking glass and then a heavy thud. Two voices began screaming in Italian. More glass broke and then there was silence. Peggy could hear the men whispering. 'Get over here,' she hissed at Brennan. The priest crawled across the room on elbows and knees. 'What are they saying?' Peggy demanded.

'One of them was shot and killed. The other two are figuring out what to do.'

'Which is?'

The priest listened and then translated. '"Vittorio, go to the window and see where he is." "Feck you, Mario," or words to that effect. "Go see for yourself."' Brennan paused. There was more panicky conversation.

'Now what?'

'Vittorio wants to kill us and try to get away. Mario is telling him he's an idiot.' There was a pause. 'Mario wants to use us as human shields.'

'I don't much like the sound of that,' said Peggy.

'There's not much we can do about it,' said Brennan.

'We'll see about that. Give me your shoes.'

'I beg your pardon?'

'Your shoes damn it! Hurry!'

Brennan untied his shoes and slipped them off.

They were heavy black brogues that would have suited a cop. Peggy picked one up and threw it at the little window in the back wall. The old glass smashed loudly and the shoe disappeared into the night. Peggy yelled at the top of her lungs.

'Doc! There's two of them! We're in a room at the back!'

Both Peggy and Brennan clearly heard the raised voices outside the door.

'*Mario! Chiuso loro in su!*' Shut them up.

'*Figlio di Puttana!*'

There was the sound of pounding feet.

'He's coming in!'

Which was just what Peggy wanted. As the door opened she launched herself forward at a dead run, hurling herself at the doorway like a charging bull, head-butting the man named Vittorio in the groin and sending him flying backward to collide with Mario, who was standing in the middle of a small living-dining area.

They went down in a tumbled heap of arms and legs, and Mario's weapon went flying across the hardwood floor. Mario managed to throw off Peggy and crab walk his way across the floor toward the weapon while Peggy turned her attention toward Vittorio, who was screaming and holding his ankle, which was now twisted at a grotesque angle.

Peggy went for Vittorio's eyes, hooking her index fingers into his ears and her thumbs into the eye sockets just like Doc had taught her. She pressed hard and the razor-thin edges of her nails punctured both eye-balls, covering Peggy's hands in a rush of warm fluid and changing Vittorio's scream into a screech of terrified agony as he suddenly went blind.

Out of the corner of her eye Peggy saw Mario reach his pistol and turn it toward her. Off to her left the front door opened and Mario swung the weapon toward the new threat. Holding the pistol two-handed he pulled the trigger, but it was too late. Holliday came into the room in a low roll, stitching an entire clip of fifteen 10mm bullets in Mario's direction. Mario's shots had gone high. Holliday's were low, almost cutting the kneeling man in half. Peggy head-butting Mario to the gruesome blinding of Vittorio and Mario's execution had taken no more than thirty seconds. The room was full of the hot-sharp smell of gunfire and Vittorio's screaming. Peggy clambered to her feet.

'Honey, I'm home!' Holliday grinned from the doorway.

Peggy stumbled toward him. 'That's the worst Ricky Ricardo I've ever heard.' She threw herself into his arms, then burst into sobs.

Brennan came out of the back room, frowning. 'Now, which one of you is going to fetch me my other shoe?'

16

Lieutenant John Charles Fremont sat at the communications center in the basement of the Pentagon, scrolling through that day's orders from the Joint Chiefs. The particular bunker he and a dozen other men and women occupied was officially known as a Crisis Control Operations Center, and on this particular midnight-to-eight shift he was the designated communications watch officer. In other words, in Pentagon-speak he was the DCCWO of the JCS CCOC. Unofficially, he was King Rat of the Big Cheese Rat Hole. Sergeant Knox Bellingham, the man seated beside him, was a senior console operator, more simply known as a Big Rat.

'You been noticing a lot of traffic for something called Prairie Fire?' Lieutenant Fremont said.

'Yes, sir,' said Bellingham. 'I've got personnel tickets for a whole bunch of people en route to Colorado Springs, Houston, and Sunnyvale, California.'

'You notice anything weird, Sergeant?'

'Yes, sir,' answered Bellingham, squinting at the screen in front of him. 'They're all O-one to O-six. And they're all SOCOM.'

Fremont sat back in his chair and looked at the screen pulsing in front of him. All of them on duty were officers, from lieutenant to lieutenant colonel, and all were part of the Special Operations Command. Colorado Springs was NORAD and the Consolidated Space Operations Center, Houston was NASA and Sunnyvale was the Air Force Satellite Test Center. Put them together and you had the complete command-and-control capabilities for every military communications satellite in the sky.

'What's the transit coding on the orders?' Fremont asked.

'USTRANSCOM,' Bellingham responded, checking the file on his screen. That made sense, sort of. USTRANSCOM stood for United States Transport Command.

'Subcoding?'

'DCS/AMC.'

That made sense, too – Defense Courier Service, Airborne Military Command, the people who transferred sensitive material from one place to the other.

'What about the unit budget line?' Every individual unit within a larger command had its own designation for defense budgeting purposes. It was where the buck stopped, literally.

'STRATCOMCON.'

'Never heard of it,' Fremont said, frowning. In Pentagon-speak STRATCOMCON probably stood for Strategic Communications Control, and Prairie Fire was probably some kind of operation it was running. Given the number of officers being shifted around, it was going to wind up costing the taxpayers a load of dollars. He made a query note about it in the computer log and then forgot all about it. The weekend was coming up and he was going hiking with his girlfriend in Cunningham Falls State Park in the Catoctin Mountains. One more night of being cooped up in the bunker and he'd be out in the fresh air. He couldn't wait.

'So, what do we do now?' Brennan asked from the backseat of the big VW luxury car. They were heading south just beyond Les Contamines, ninety minutes away from the Geneva airport.

'I'm phoning Pat Philpot in D.C., and you're calling your people at the Vatican and any bigwig antiterrorist cops you know in Rome,' said Holliday from behind the wheel. 'We've got to get to the cops with what we know about Tritt and our so-called Jihadist friends. The funeral is the day after tomorrow.'

'They took our cell phones,' said Peggy.

'Mine, too,' said Holliday. 'They've got satellite phones at the airport. We'll call from there.'

'You have an address book?' asked Brennan. Peggy turned in her seat; the priest had that feral, Gollum-like tone in his voice again.

'I keep some numbers in my head. I know Pat's by heart,' Holliday answered.

'By the time we get to the airport it'll be past midnight in the States,' said Peggy, checking her watch. It was almost five a.m., Geneva time.

'So I'll get his big, fat ass out of bed,' replied Holliday.

When the satellite phone pinged, General Angus Scott Matoon was over the mid-Atlantic aboard one of the army's blandly designated C-37 transports, which was a drab military euphemism for a leather-chaired and whisper-quiet Gulfstream G650. The Pentagon, for whatever reason, had 120 of the forty-seven-million-dollar aircraft.

He unlimbered the receiver from its mount on the bulkhead. 'Yes?'

'Neville, sir.'

His adjutant – a bloodless, lickspittle, brownnoser forced on him by Kate Sinclair, more a spy for her than an assistant to him. As Matoon had long ago discovered, Sinclair had little moles like Neville everywhere, even in the White House, although no one was absolutely sure who *that* was. Sinclair was a firm believer in the adage that good intelligence was the basis of a good offense.

'What is it?' Matoon asked brusquely. The ice was melting in his glass of Bourbon on the table in front of him. The interior of the aircraft was dark except for the pool of light over his comfortable leather swivel chair and the glow of the computer screen in its niche across the aisle.

'We have a situation, General.'

The satellite phone on a jet used by a member of the Joint Chiefs was probably as secure as you could get, but there was always the possibility that the NSA simply monitored and recorded *all* government and military calls as a matter of protocol. It was perhaps far-fetched, but not impossible, and Matoon hadn't gotten to his present position by being sloppy. Discretion, especially with the home office, was the rule.

'What kind of situation?'

'A prairie fire, sir.'

'A bad one?'

'It's spreading slightly.'

Which meant that somebody within the Pentagon had made a nominal query about either Prairie Fire or its big brother, STRATCOMCON. Nominal or not, any leakage at this point could be disastrous.

'Is it likely to get worse?' Matoon asked.

'It's possible.'

'Can you put it out?'

'Yes, of course, General. There might be collateral damage, however. Should I put the fire out completely?'

Which meant that there was a civilian involved. 'Would extinguishing it completely be difficult or hazardous?' Matoon asked.

'Not at all, General.'

'Then do it,' said Matoon. He hung up the phone and picked up his drink. He took a sip, cracking an ice cube with his teeth. Another sacrificial lamb for Kate Sinclair's cause.

'Shit,' said the general. The jet flew on through the night.

17

Early on the morning of the sixth day following the assassination of the Pope, dignitaries of varying status began arriving at Pratica di Mare Air Force Base, lining up in their positions on the overlong single runway like so many preening pheasants. By dawn there were two dozen heads of state and their aircraft on the tarmac, from France's Airbus A330 to Moldova's Yakovlev Yak-40. At precisely seven thirty in the morning United States Air Force One, carrying the president, the secretary of state and half a dozen guests in its distinctive blue-and-white livery, came lumbering down the runway and pulled to a stop. Two big C5 transports had arrived the night before, carrying two presidential limousines and four Cadillac Escalades, all black, all armored and all twice the weight of their civilian counterparts. Other than the Americans only the Russians and the Chinese brought along their own ground transportation; everyone else relied on local embassy vehicles.

There was no movement on the runway, and the only sound was the steady whining of engine start generators. This was a visit of obligation, and as little time as possible would be spent on the niceties of state. The motorcades would move out in protocol order, and within an hour of the conclusion of the funeral almost everyone would be on their way back to the military airfield. By midafternoon all the aircraft would have departed for home.

Peggy, armed with her brand-new Nikon and a long lens, stood with Brennan and Holliday on the domed roof of the PalaLottomatica, the sports complex that stood on the little garden island between the two enclosing arms of the Via Cristoforo Colombo. In their estimation, the PalaLottomatica roof was the most likely place for the assassin to strike from, but when the Vigilanza and the local Rome police had checked, there was no sign of the man, past or present.

On the off chance that Brennan and his friends were right, the Italian police, in cooperation with the Vatican authorities, had established their own lookout point on the roof. After being woken out of a dead sleep Pat Philpot had cleared the way with his people in Rome and expressed his fears of a tangible threat to the Secret Service, although he hadn't mentioned Tritt's name or his onetime affiliation with the Company.

While Peggy took a few shots of the observation post with her Nikon, Holliday paced around the very summit of the clamshell roof and Brennan listened to his police scanner. At ten past ten he looked up and spoke.

'The American motorcade just pulled off airbase property. They'll be here in less than fifteen minutes.'

'This is a waste of time,' said Peggy. 'We should be doing something, not standing around waiting for the sky to fall.'

'We've still got the car,' said Holliday. 'Philpot's team is on the ground, keeping their eyes open for an Audi A8 with Swiss plates. There can't be too many of them in town.'

'We still haven't managed to trace all this back to the old witch, Sinclair,' said Peggy, swinging her camera and its huge telephoto lens around. So far she'd noticed nothing even mildly suspicious.

'First we stop her plan; then we stop her organization.'

'I'm still not sure about what she's doing,' said Brennan, monitoring the scanner. 'It all seems insane to me.'

'Kill the president, who's a little too liberal for her tastes, which installs our esteemed hard-hat vice president. A real "whites of their eyes" type. When the Indian ambassador came over to arrange a state visit the VP asked the man if he was in the Cherokee caste or the Apache. He becomes president and appoints the young Senator Sinclair as his VP. Two terms later he backs our boy for the presidential nomination. She gets what she wants with a bullet, not an election.' Holliday shook his head. 'It is insane, but if you get enough insane people together who're still fighting the Civil War, it changes from insanity to political conspiracy.'

There was a burst of crackling Italian from the scanner.

'What is it?' Holliday asked.

'Masterpiece is eight miles out.'

'Masterpiece?'

'The president's code name. The First Lady is da Vinci.'

'Where did that come from?' Holliday asked.

'They must have liked the book. The secretary of state is called Symbol.'

'How long is eight miles, timewise?'

'Five minutes, maybe six.' The priest shrugged. 'Motorcades can be pretty ponderous even under the best circumstances.'

Presidential motorcades are often made up of up to thirty vehicles, including two identical Cadillac limousines, both armored and with bulletproof glass. These are inevitably followed by several Secret Service Escalades, a communication vehicle and a number of other cars for the press and invited guests. Since the twin presidential limousines are identical, there is no sure way to know which one is occupied by the president at various times. The limousines and the Secret Service vans are known as the secure package and can separate from the rest of the motorcade within seconds.

The radio crackled again. 'Vigilanza Twenty-nine.' One of Brennan's.

'Vigilanza Twenty-nine, *andare*.'

'*Confermato Automobile nero, Audi A8, Targa Svizerri SZ193.*'

'He's got the car!' Brennan hissed.

'Where?' Holliday asked.

'Dove?'

'Viale Europa. Davanti Gioielliere Brusco.'

'Got it,' said Peggy, the big Nikon in her hands. 'One block up, one block over, once you get over the bridge. No action on the roof so far.'

'Give me your gun,' demanded Holliday.

Brennan hesitated for a moment, then handed it over. 'I've never seen that gun in my life,' said the priest. In other words Holliday was on his own if he was caught with it. 'I'll stay with the radio.'

Holliday took the small transmitter-receiver out of his pocket, looping it over his ear like a Bluetooth device. Peggy had slipped the telephoto off and was snapping on a standard lens.

'I'm going with you,' she said. There was no room for argument in her voice and Holliday didn't even try.

'Come on, then,' he said.

They scrambled around the roof to the maintenance stairwell, went to the shipping elevator and rode down to the main floor of the gigantic, empty arena.

'Masterpiece now five miles out. Four minutes,' said Brennan's voice in Holliday's ear. Holliday found their rental car and climbed in, Peggy hard on his heels. He cranked up the little Fiat and, tires spinning, zoomed across the empty parking lot to the exit ramp. Barely slowing, he threw the car into traffic. They tore across the bridge, over the artificial reflecting pool, then hurtled down the Viale America ramp and went into the brief darkness of the underpass. They popped out into the sunlight and headed west.

'Masterpiece at two miles. Ninety seconds, maybe less.'

'Shit,' said Holliday. Dead ahead in the far distance was the dome of the enormous Peter and Paul Basilica.

'There!' Peggy yelled. She'd spotted the jewelry store.

They went through the yellow light and through the striped crosswalk, Holliday blessing his good luck at renting one of those ridiculous smart cars. He slipped into an empty spot across from the jewelry store on the corner and jumped out of the car without bothering to lock it. He ran across the wide street, setting up a symphony of horns and shouts as he dodged through the oncoming traffic, Peggy right beside him.

They reached the sidewalk. To the left of a pair of graffiti-covered recycling bins there were two doors, one leading into Brusco's watch and jewelry store, the other into a miniature lobby with nothing in it but an elevator door. The outer door was locked. Directly in front of the jeweler's was a sleek black Audi A8.

Holliday didn't stop to think about it. He pulled out Brennan's automatic and used the butt as a hammer on the glass next to the lock mechanism. Nothing happened. He hit the glass even harder, aware that someone was screaming for the police. This time the entire bottom half of the glass door disintegrated into thousands of little hexagons. Holliday freed the broken glass with the pistol butt, reached in and turned the latch. The door opened. A woman's shrill voice kept calling for the police. In a few more seconds people would start paying attention.

'We have movement on the roof! Dark-haired man carrying a sports bag, black. Motorcade is in sight. It looks like a big black snake. Mother of Christ, Holliday, hurry!'

Holliday jammed his palm against the single button and thankfully the door slid open immediately. He and Peggy crowded into the little cage and a few seconds later the door hissed shut and the elevator began its long, slow grind upward. It stopped automatically at every floor, and by the time they reached the top floor Holliday's nerves were wire taut.

He racked the slide on the little automatic. 'You stay back, Peg. I'm not kidding. I've got a peashooter. This son of a bitch has a guided missile. Remember that.'

'Yes, Uncle John, Doc, sir,' she mocked, grinning broadly and hefting the camera.

'Rafi would string me up in the Negev if anything happened to you,' said Holliday.

'Yeah, he would, wouldn't he?' Peggy laughed. 'Such a romantic.' The elevator door hissed open on to the top floor. Holliday stepped out into the corridor with Brennan's gun extended. Empty. Three doors on the left, three doors on the right and an exit light at either end beaming out USCIRE. Holliday headed along the corridor toward the exit, the gun steady in his hand.

He stepped into the stairwell, Peggy on the step

behind him, and headed upward. The metal steps were noisy. The earpiece crackled but there was no sound. He was in some kind of audio dead zone. They reached a little vestibule at the top of the stairs. There was a metal door with a panic bar.

'Stay back,' he ordered, pushing down on the panic bar. He stepped out into the near-blinding sunlight that streamed down on to the gravel roof. His earpiece came to life in midsentence.

'. . . not a Stinger. It's a – Dear Lord, he's fired!'

There was a fireball riding the shoulder of the man on the far side of the roof. The fireball expanded with a snapping roar and the figure disappeared in a cloud of yellow-white smoke. Holliday aimed into the center of the smoke screen and fired, again and again. He was vaguely aware of movement, and then an enormous pain blossomed in the middle of his chest and the world went black. Somewhere Peggy screamed his name and then she was gone.

PART TWO
Opus

18

'Fools rush in, Colonel Holliday, and there's no doubt that you're a fool,' said Pat Philpot, overflowing a plain chair beside Doc's hospital bed. A big Starbucks cup and a pastry box full of fat cannoli sat on the night table beside him. The rotund CIA analyst took alternating sips and bites. Powdered sugar from the cannoli dusted his several chins.

It was hard for Doc to remember back when the two of them used to jump out of airplanes into war zones together. Then again, it was hard for him to remember much at all except for the gigantic pain in his chest. It felt like someone had ripped out his heart and lungs and then forgot to put them back again. The anonymous hospital room wasn't much help to his memory; aside from a simple crucifix that hung over the bed, it was the same as every other civilian hospital he'd been in. It was a Catholic hospital, which meant that he was probably still in Italy. But why was Pat Philpot sitting beside him? Where were Peggy and Brennan?

Philpot read his mind. 'We don't know where your niece and her priest friend are. At the moment.' He took a slurp of coffee, eyed a half-eaten cannoli in the box and then thought better of it. 'If it wasn't for the fact that Ms Blackstock almost certainly has a photograph of a known Company operative firing a Russian Igla missile at the presidential limousine, we'd have conveniently put a bullet in your brain and buried you in an olive grove by now.'

Holliday cleared his throat. 'You're telling me that olive groves are the equivalent of the New Jersey Meadowlands here?'

'Quit being a smart-ass, Holliday. You're in a lot of trouble; don't make it any worse.'

'Then tell me what happened, why I'm here.'

'Billy Tritt fired a Soviet Igla "needle" missile at the lead limo in the motorcade and blew it all to hell and gone. He fired a Glock .40 at you, but you were smart enough to be wearing the wop equivalent of a bullet-proof vest.'

'He killed the president?'

'The VP and the secretary of state. It should have been the A car, but the Secret Service flipped at the last second because of the warning.'

'How did Tritt know?'

'Because there was a big X on the roof of the lead car.'

'And nobody noticed?'

'Nobody. The X was some clear coating and UV sensitive. Nobody could see it except for Tritt.'

'You're talking about an inside job, then,' said Holliday.

'I'm talking off the record, just like before. You mention any of this and you really will wind up in an olive grove.'

'Off the record, then.'

'Thank God it was an Igla and not a Stinger. It muddies the water some. On the other hand, some unfriendly colleagues of mine have an unregistered Beretta in their possession with your prints all over it. They also have evidence connecting you to a pair of homicides in Rock Creek Park a week or so ago. They can tie you to a conspiracy to assassinate the president without breaking a sweat. Get the picture?'

'You're telling me there really is a rogue section of the Agency?'

'I'm not speaking to you at all,' said Philpot. He stuffed half a cannoli in his mouth and inhaled the sweet cream at its center, then savored the outer layers of flaky, butter-rich pastry. 'In fact,' he said, methodically licking his fingers, 'this is so off the record that I'm not even here; I'm sitting at my desk in MacLean, picking my toes and wondering who's going to win the Super Bowl.'

'The Giants,' said Holliday.

'Bah, humbug.' Philpot scowled. 'It'll be the Steelers again.'

'So, what are you trying to tell me, Pat, seeing as how you aren't here?'

'I'm telling you to find your pretty Peggy and get out of Dodge, pronto. There are people out there who want you dead and have the ability to make it happen.'

'We're talking about the so-called Jihad al-Salibiyya?'

'We're not talking about anything. I'm not here, remember? Have a cannoli.'

Chief Randy Lockwood, head of the Winter Falls Police force for the last thirty years, strolled down South Main Street bundled up in an official Winter Falls Wolves jacket. The cold weather had creaked and blustered its way down from Canada, putting an even thicker layer of ice on Big Cache Lake. The iceboats were whizzing around, practicing for the races to be held the following month, and he could see half a dozen fishing boats already set up. It was all part of the Falls' somewhat limited attempt at turning itself into a winter wonderland as well as a summer resort.

He reached Gorman's Restaurant, the unofficial divider between South Main Street and North Main Street. He pulled open the steel door with one leather-gloved hand and stepped into the overheated diner. His booth in the back next to the kitchen's swinging doors was empty, a glass of water and a copy of the *Trumpet*, Winter Falls' only newspaper, laid out on the Formica. At eleven in the morning, Gorman's was packed with the inner circle of Winter Falls' gossips and flapjaws, including Sandy Gorman, who was standing behind the counter and wrangling a huge pile of bacon that was being precooked for the all-day breakfasts that were one of the favorites. Beside the bacon was an equally huge pile of hash browns and beside the hash browns was Reggie Waterman, frying and scrambling eggs, turning sausages and even taking care of a few burgers and the French fry baskets.

Randy, Sandy and Reggie had all been stars of the 1964 Winter Falls High School football team and they'd all gone off to serve in Vietnam two years later. Sandy Gorman had come back minus half a leg, and stumped around behind the counter on a prosthetic; Reggie Waterman scrambled eggs with a fork clamped to the hook that had once been his right arm. Randy returned with nothing but a Silver Star and a white streak of hair above his ear where a Vietcong bullet had creased his skull. In the years since, it had gradually earned him the nickname 'Streak.'

Winter Falls, New Hampshire, was a resort town and always had been. It was one of a half dozen towns that stood on the edge of Big Cache about sixty miles west of Portland, Maine, the closest city of any size. In winter the Falls had a population of a little more than six thousand. In summer it blew up to twice that, the number of parking tickets growing exponentially with enough revenue to pay the salaries of the entire sixteen-man, two-woman Winter Falls Police Department. There hadn't been a murder, rape or violent crime since the Hartwell twins' bizarre double suicide twelve years ago, and one missing person back in the mid-nineties that Streak Lockwood figured for a runaway. Pete McGoogan was a mean bastard living in the backwoods around Front Bay with a dull-witted wife and a beautiful sixteen-year-old who could have been a movie star. Her old man always had a strange, proprietary look on his face when he was around her, and if Streak had been in Cindy McGoogan's shoes he would have split for the big city himself.

Whatever it all was it amounted to Winter Falls being voted number one of the top-ten safest towns in America by *Time* magazine for the fourth year in a row. There were about a hundred copies of the issue in Zeke's Smokes and Sundries down the way, but Cyrus Dorchester at the *Trumpet* pretended that no one in town had heard and had a huge headline announcing FALLS #1 AGAIN!!!

The lake was just beyond Gorman's back-door patio and a sudden wind rattled the entire rickety, two-story clapboard building, the freezing air chattering through cracks in the joints and around the heavy double-pane storm windows. If it wasn't for the grill, ovens and fryers being fired up from dawn to dusk, the place would be as cold as the inside of a freezer.

Lockwood dropped down into his booth, his back to the wall under a 1974 Boston Bruins calendar turned to February so it eternally showed the rampaging Phil Esposito grinning with his front teeth out, Sandy Gorman's favorite, even if Esposito was a Canuck.

Reggie Waterman came out from behind the counter and slid on to the bench opposite Lockwood, a plate clamped in his steel claw and a cup of coffee in his good hand. He set the food down in front of his old friend and leaned back against the cracked green vinyl of the booth.

'Poached eggs on dry toast, one slice of bacon, no home fries and a cup of decaf coffee that tastes like brown water. You're letting that woman destroy your golden years, Streak. Booze, broads and bang.'

'Sadly, Reg, those days on Duc Do Street are long gone. We're old men now.'

'Yeah,' snorted Reggie, waggling his bright steel claw in the hair. 'I'm not half the man I used to be.'

'And Maggie Irish is my doctor, not my wife,' answered Randy. 'Booze, broads and bang are harder on your cholesterol than any wife could ever be.' There was an awkward pause. Reggie and Sandy had lost body parts in Vietnam, but Randy's wife, the former cheerleader Dory Cramer, had aborted the baby they'd conceived just before Randy shipped out, and ran off to be a big star in Hollywood. Nobody had ever seen her again. She was a year younger than the rest of them, which meant she was sixty now – probably playing grandmothers in Depends ads if she was doing anything at all. More likely she'd hit the skids and died of an overdose decades in the past. Forever young; forever the thief of his child that was never allowed to be. It had always struck him as odd that he could hate someone so thoroughly who had disappeared from the face of the earth so long ago, and love someone so thoroughly who had never existed. How could you hate a ghost or love a shade?

'So how was Christmas, Streak?' Reggie asked.

'A positive love fest,' said Lockwood, carving a dripping chunk of egg and toast away from the plate and popping it neatly into his mouth.

'Yule logs and chestnuts roasting?' Reggie asked.

'Something like that,' said Lockwood. More like a can of Dinty Moore Beef Stew over the sink and endless reruns of *Home Alone* and *It's a Wonderful Life*. Once upon a time he'd liked the idea of Turner Classic Movies, but now they just made him think about other Christmases he'd rather not reminisce over. He'd tried to ignore the sappy holiday films, but everything else on cable depressed him even more. CNN was a constant stream of first the Pope getting blown out of his miter and then the attempt on the president. Fox News was full of Glenn Beck weeping along with that cracker idiot named Sinclair, who just happened to be the junior senator from New Hampshire, babbling about the 'festering sore of domestic terrorism about to appear like the plague in America if something isn't done quickly.' Yeah, Christmas had been a blast.

'So, you going to run for mayor?' Reggie asked. He waved his claw in the air and one of the harried waitresses brought him a mug of coffee. He sipped it and sighed happily.

'Why?' Lockwood smiled. 'Just because *Time* magazine says I'd be a shoo-in? No, thanks.'

'I'd get to call you Your Honor.' Reggie grinned. 'Better than the Blanchette woman.'

'Snotty' Dotty Blanchette was in her sixties, unmarried and hard as nails. She'd started off as secretary to a town councilor and clawed her way up the municipal ladder. In a Republican town, she was all Democrat.

'Mayors come and mayors go,' said Lockwood. 'Even Dotty Blanchette.' He broke his single strip of crispy bacon in half and popped it into his mouth. 'Besides, nothing ever happens here. All I have to do is sit in my office, rescue cats from trees and eat doughnuts all day. The mayor has the real job.'

There was a howl of freezing wind as the front door opened and shut. Streak Lockwood looked up and saw that it was a stranger. A tall, lean man in a long leather coat. He had longish dark hair and eyes half hidden behind tinted sunglasses. The only really odd thing about him was his out-of-season tan, and it didn't come from Sun-N-Go from up on Porter Street, either. Lockwood took a mental snapshot of the man and then got back to his poached eggs and his conversation with Reggie.

Billy Tritt found a space at the counter and sat down.

19

'He's right, this CIA friend of yours,' said Brennan. A week had passed since the murder of the vice president and the secretary of state, and Holliday was clandestinely staying in Brennan's spacious apartment in the Palazzo del Quirinale, along with Peggy. The enormous insult Holliday's muscles and ribs had taken from Tritt's Glock had healed to a hand-span's livid bruise across his chest. 'Historically you can seek sanctuary within the walls of the Vatican, but the new Holy Father is no friend of mine nor of Cardinal Spada, who will not be Vatican secretary of state much longer, I fear. You will have to leave, and soon. If word gets out that I've been harboring wanted fugitives, excommunication will be the least of it. It'll be like the McCarthy era all over again, or the Salem witch trials. They're on the hunt for any whiff at all of this Jihad al-Salibiyya, or whatever it's called.'

'What will happen to you when the new secretary of state is selected?' Peggy asked.

'At best I'll be given a dreary parish in Sligo, where it rains sideways all day long and all the stray cats are always coughing with tuberculosis. If they find out about your involvement and my doings they'll quietly reach out for one of their *assassini*, who'll see to it that I fall down a flight of stairs or lean too far over a balcony while I'm watering the petunias.'

'How long do we have?'

'Days, maybe a week at best. I'll only have a few hours' warning.'

'So what do you suggest? This rogue group with the Company is probably on watch everywhere.'

'The Vatican's been slipping things in and out of here for a long time, my son. There's a container ship leaving for New Orleans from the harbor at Leghorn in three days. You'll be on it. Her name is *Smeraldo Nero*, the *Black Emerald*.'

'Sounds piratical enough.' Holliday smiled, then grimaced.

'Thank you, Father,' said Peggy, giving him a peck on the cheek. He reddened. Then he grew serious again. 'Remember what my man in Washington said. I don't think Crusader is over yet. I think you're right in the middle of it. So take care, my friends.'

There had been no arrests or even leads on either the murder of the Pope or the attempted murder of the president. Both events had caused everyone's terrorist meters to zoom into the red zone, especially Homeland Security's back home. So far the president had not chosen his second in command, but Kate Sinclair's son, the junior senator from New Hampshire, was stumping around half the nation, calling for action against the upcoming holocaust of domestic terrorism that was going to engulf the nation if some hard choices weren't made and soon.

Brennan left a few moments later to make travel arrangements, leaving Peggy and Holliday alone in the apartment. He looked out across the road to the offices of Vatican Radio, the roof of the building topped by aerials, domes of various sizes and one enormous tower. Less a broadcast station, Holliday knew, than a giant signaling intelligence facility. For that matter, Timothy Brennan was also much more than a simple parish priest.

'I wonder ... ' he said slowly, putting a hundred shards of idle thought and speculation together.

'What do you wonder, Doc?' Peggy asked, lounging on the couch and reading through a copy of the *International Tribune*.

'I was marking term papers and you were watching CNN. We went out for dinner on M Street and then walked back to the house.'

'Okay,' said Peggy, 'so you proved you don't have early onset Alzheimer's. So what?'

'Who was on our doorstep?'

'Brennan.'

'Never a friend of ours by any means, so why choose us? What the hell did we have to do with any of this?'

'What are you getting at?'

'He fed the whole thing to us like feeding pabulum to a baby. His so-called informant who was confessed to by a so-called CIA agent with a dose of conscience.

The murder of both of them. Subtle connections to Rex Deus and the Sinclairs. All of it meant to pique our interest.'

'Pique?' Peggy grinned. 'I've never been piqued in my life.'

'You know what I mean.'

'Sure, you think we were being set up. But for what?'

'He gets me interested enough to call some old colleagues, and leads me by the nose right to William Tritt, lets me think it was all my idea.'

'You really think he's that subtle?'

'He's the head of the Vatican Secret Service,' said Holliday. 'You can't get any more subtle than that. Most people aren't even aware that Sodalitium Pianum even exists.' Holliday shook his head. 'Damn it to hell! He led us right down the garden path, every step of the way. If I hadn't mentioned Pat Philpot he would have worked the name in himself somehow. Philpot leads us to that disaster in Rock Creek Park, and before you know it we're on the run. I knew something was wrong back then but I just thought Philpot was using me to bird-dog Tritt for him, to take the American assassin out of the picture before anyone found out.'

'And now?'

'I think Philpot was telling the truth about the rogue division of the Agency, but now I think he may well be part of it.'

'And Brennan?'

'Him, too. He's part of it, as well.' Holliday paused. 'And then there's the assassination.'

'Which one?'

'The VP and the secretary of state. The X on the roof of the limo.'

'What about it?'

'Tritt's not the kind to make mistakes like that. Maybe the vice president was the target all along. The president's going to have to appoint a replacement soon.'

'Sinclair,' said Peggy, getting it, her eyes widening.

'Sinclair.' Holliday nodded.

'So, what do we do?'

'We sure as hell don't get on the good old SS *Black Emerald*, I can tell you that much.' He paused. 'Pack up anything you need, bring the memory stick with those pictures of Tritt on the roof and let's get out of here.'

'Where are we going?'

'Back to Geneva. Let's begin at the beginning.'

It was close to midnight when the nondescript Mercedes taxi pulled up in front of 16 Via Tunis in Rome and let out its passenger, a tall, elegantly dressed man in a topcoat and carrying an attaché case. The door into the gray, five-story stucco apartment building was covered by an ornate wrought-iron grille. A dozen buzzers and an intercom were set into the doorframe. Mike Harris, deputy director of operations for the CIA, pressed the buzzer for number 6. He glanced to his left; the restaurant next door was already closed and there was no one on the street.

'*Sì? Chi è?*'

'Crusader,' replied Harris, speaking clearly into the intercom grille.

There was a long silence. Then the buzzer sounded and the lock on the wrought-iron gate clicked. Harris pulled open the gate, opened the door and stepped into a dim hallway. Directly ahead of him was a grimy, winding staircase leading upward. He climbed all five flights to the top story. The floor was black-and-white checkerboard tile and there was only a single door. The lighting in the hall was bright and the walls were clean and freshly painted. It was anything but grimy. Discreetly placed above the door on the ceiling was a small eye-in-the-sky camera, a miniature version of the ones they used in Las Vegas casinos. Harris knocked firmly on the door, feeling metal under his knuckles rather than the wood it appeared to be. He smiled and waited.

A few seconds later the door opened. It was Brennan. The two men shook hands and Brennan ushered the CIA director into the apartment.

'Been a long time, Mr Harris.' Brennan said.

'Indeed it has, Father Brennan. Is he in?'

'Of course,' answered the priest. He led Harris down the hallway to a spacious living room that faced the street. There were three large windows, the shutters all firmly closed. Once again the slats of the shutters appeared to be varnished wood, but the CIA man was willing to bet they were steel, just like the door.

The room had a plain, grandmotherly feel to it. There were brass lamps here and there, lots of book-cases everywhere and an old Persian carpet on the floor. There were two short couches, two armchairs, a gas-fed fireplace and an old wooden desk covered with stacks of paper and file folders. Antonio Niccolo, Cardinal Spada, Vatican secretary of state, was seated behind the desk, dressed in a simple black suit with a red collar tab to mark his rank. He had a cigar – Harris assumed it was Cuban – in his hand and there was a heavy-looking glass full of amber liquid in front of him. The photograph behind him on the wallpapered wall was of him and the late Pope in better days. The cigar, at least at the moment, was unlit. Brennan took a seat in one of the armchairs. Harris dropped down on to one of the small upholstered couches.

'Good flight?' Spada asked.

Harris shrugged. 'I took the company Citation. Seven hundred per, without any screaming babies or other people sneezing on me.'

'The benefits of power.' Cardinal Spada smiled.

'Not for long if the present administration has its way,' grumbled Harris. 'The son of a bitch wants me to pool with Homeland Security and the Bureau.' He shook his head. 'What does the Bureau need with a plane that can fly seven hundred miles an hour? They couldn't find the key to the executive bathroom.'

'A sad state of affairs,' commiserated Spada.

'Every president's the same. They're going to shake things up, get things done, pull the country up by its bootstraps. They don't seem to understand we're the ones who really run things and we always have, and that's never going to change.'

'Certainly not if you can help it,' said the cardinal dryly.

'Damn right,' snorted Harris. 'Speaking of which, how's your new boss doing?'

'Coming along,' smiled Spada. 'As Cardinal Urbana he was desperate for the job, although the scales were tipping toward Washington. Imagine that! An American Pope, and black, as well. Foley almost made it last time. Everyone was becoming nervous. I called in a few favors, rattled a few old bones in their hiding places and made sure we had an Italian in the chair. Too many outsiders recently – Poles, Germans. Urbana knows I put him in power and knows that I can keep him there; he won't be choosing any new secretary of state until I tell him to.'

'Want the big job yourself?' Harris laughed. 'You're young enough to keep it for a while.'

For the first time Brennan realized that the CIA man must have been drinking heavily on the flight to Rome.

'Good Lord, no! The Vatican is much like your country, Mr Harris. It is controlled and operated by the bureaucrats like you and me, not the figureheads. Being the Pope requires far more Latin than I ever learned.

Not to mention the fact that I like my favorite restaurants too much to give them up. The Pope has little in the way of privacy.'

'What about Holliday and the Blackstock woman?' Harris asked, turning toward Brennan.

'As of nine o'clock tonight they slipped out of the museum entrance into a taxi, rented a car in Fumicino and are headed back to Geneva, presumably on the trail of our Mr Tritt.'

'You have the pictures Ms Blackstock took?'

Brennan dug into the pocket of his plain black jacket and took out a USB memory stick.

'Right here.' He smiled. 'Downloaded them from her camera while they were sleeping. We've got everything. It's proof positive of Holliday's involvement with the attempt on the president.' Harris reached for the plastic memory device but Brennan pulled it out of his reach. 'Not yet, Mr Harris. There are a few quid pro quos to be dealt with.'

'How did you get them out of your hair and on their own?' Harris asked. 'The senator's mother will want to know.'

'Holliday is smart. He's like an old trout thinking about taking the hook; he has to convince himself that taking it was his idea. I had to play him for a long time, but you could see him putting it together piece by piece. It was too convenient and everything came back to me in the end. Too much coincidence for a man like that to swallow.'

The older priest smiled and made a vague attempt to brush ash off his lapels before going on. 'The pièce de résistance was telling him Cardinal Spada was due for the chopping block and I was about to be exiled to the bog country of my youth. It was one thing to have me around when I could get him some access, but he had to know I'd be useless from now on.'

'Excellent.' Harris nodded.

'What about the fingerprints from the Tritt house in the Bahamas?' Brennan asked.

'Safe and sound.' Harris nodded benignly.

'And Tritt himself?' Spada asked.

'In place,' Harris said.

'He has what he needs?' Spada asked. 'He's been given the information?'

'Yes. Nothing will connect him to us. It's quite ingenious, if I do say so myself.'

'Holliday's next jigsaw piece?'

'Done.'

'Matoon?'

'Firing on all cylinders.'

'Your Jihadist?' Spada asked.

'Ready and waiting. We're primed. Crusader is good to go.'

20

The Maine Mall is a 1,200,000 square foot sprawling shopping complex in the southern part of the city of Portland and is anchored by JCPenney, Sears, Best Buy, Macy's and Sports Authority. It contains another 140 shops and services, including a food court and several sit-down family restaurants. It is the largest shopping mall in Maine, and more major drug deals are completed here than in any other place in the state, mostly in the food court, particularly the McDonald's section. The food court is located on the main level at the western, or JCPenney, end of the mall.

Today the blank-faced Chinese group was at Arby's and the Vietnamese were chowing down on Big Macs. There were four of each, but the principals were obvious. One Vietnamese, a short man in his early twenties, was eating nothing and neither was his Chinese alter ego in the seating section next door. The noise level was deafening, like a Niagara Falls of chatter. Most people avoided sitting near the young Asian men in their black leather jackets, slicked oily hair and opaque or reflective sunglasses. Their privacy was guaranteed.

At an unseen signal the Chinese leader got up from his place, accompanied by one bodyguard. He slipped into the booth occupied by the Vietnamese man. He, too, had a single bodyguard with him. They spoke for a moment, probably in English, although William Tritt couldn't be sure. He watched from just outside Ben & Jerry's as the meeting came to an end and the two men shook hands. It was the handshake that gave it away, of course. Hand shaking was distinctly non-Asian and rarely practiced by them except with whites. Ergo it had a purpose, and if you were watching as closely as William Tritt was you would have seen it: two sets of car keys being exchanged. It was the perfect pass over and any narcotics agent arresting either group at this point would find no evidence of any sort of drugs on the men. The keys would have no identifying tags and no electronic beepers. Checking all of the thousands of vehicles in the enormous parking lots surrounding the mall on three sides would be impossible.

The Vietnamese were almost invariably the buyers in situations like this, so when the little party broke up Tritt followed the four Chinese, who were probably collecting the cash. Tritt had no interest in the drugs, whatever they were. They headed for the northwest exit.

The parking lot was a crisscross maze of snow piles and narrow, half-cleared paths. It was snowing now, the blustery wind off the nearby ocean cutting visibility as the fat flakes whirled and danced. The only people in the lot were hurrying either to or from their vehicles. The car was a tan Chevy Impala from the last decade.

The leader of the small Chinese group put the key in the trunk lock and opened it. All four men leaned inward to inspect the contents.

A firm believer in simple solutions, Tritt removed the .50-caliber Desert Eagle from the brand-new black nylon sports bag he carried in his left hand, then screwed on the suppressor he took from the pocket of his newly purchased ski jacket from Sears. He had already snapped on surgical gloves as he walked along behind the four Chinese in the mall. From fifteen feet away he shot each of the young men in the base of the spine.

The weapon made a stiff cracking sound like ice breaking underfoot on a frozen pond and the four men dropped to the ground without any other sound. Their heavy jackets soaked up the blood pouring out of the exit wounds in their lower abdomens, so there was very little mess. No one had noticed anything; the piles of snow had acted like sound buffers, stealing away any echo. He dropped the Desert Eagle and the suppressor into the sports bag and zipped it up.

Tritt took one quick look around, then stepped forward. He removed a pair of large, green Samsonite hard-shell suitcases from the trunk, then heaved the bodies of the four dead Chinese into the empty space.

He took the Desert Eagle out of the sports bag a second time and emptied the clip into the bodies, just to make sure. He slammed the trunk closed, took the key out of the lock and put it into his pocket. He slung the sports bag over his left shoulder, picked up a suit-case in each hand and walked back to his rental.

In this weather it would be a while before the bodies in the trunk began to emit an odor, but somewhere along the line the missing money and the absent men would surely be missed. Almost certainly the Chinese murders and the disappearance of the cash would be blamed on the Vietnamese. Maybe the whole episode would turn into a gang war and he'd be instrumental in lowering Portland's crime rate.

His rental was a black F150 truck equipped with out-sized snow tires, quite a common vehicle in Maine at this time of year. The same people who'd provided the Desert Eagle had also given him a complete identity package for a man named Art Barfield, including vari-ous hunting permits, a driver's license in the same name and a letter of introduction to a radical and obscure paramilitary group named Maine's Right Arm.

Maine's Right Arm had a membership of barely twenty active participants. The leader of MRA was Wilmot DeJean and the group was located just outside Arkham, a hamlet in the northwestern part of the state. Arkham was the largest of four villages with a total population of two thousand spread out over forty-one square miles. According to the information Tritt had been given, Wilmot DeJean was a onetime high school teacher offered early retirement for psychiatric reasons.

DeJean apparently had delusions of grandeur of an

extreme nature. He used an eagle clutching a swastika as both the symbol of the organization and the tattoo on his right bicep, and he had once been investigated by the Secret Service for writing a threatening letter to the current president. This event was thought to have precipitated his early retirement. The group had been infiltrated by Homeland Security and was deemed to be a minor threat, if a threat at all. The files on both DeJean and the MRA were still open with both Homeland Security and the Secret Service, however.

'We could always just bail on the whole thing,' suggested Peggy as they neared Geneva. It was almost dawn and there was a light snow falling. Both Peggy and Holliday were exhausted after their long drive, and Holliday's nerves were near the breaking point. 'You go back to the university and I'll go back to Israel. Forget any of it happened.' She lifted her shoulders. 'You were right. None of this was our business in the first place.'

'It's too late for that now,' said Holliday, seated behind the wheel. 'We're the patsies for whatever they have in mind.'

'Which is?' Peggy asked.

'I don't have the faintest idea,' said Holliday. 'I don't even really know who "they" are. The Vatican? The CIA? Rex Deus and that bitch Sinclair?'

'Maybe all three,' said Peggy. 'The Pope gets assassinated because he's some kind of threat to Brennan and his organization, this rogue element in the CIA is trying to alter the balance of power by getting rid of an administration that's been trying to marginalize it, and Kate Sinclair gets a shot at putting her son into the White House, or near it.'

'Sounds a little complicated. Don't you think?' Holliday asked.

'Conspiracies usually are,' answered Peggy. Holliday laughed. He swung the rental down the ramp at the first Geneva exit off the auto route.

'Conspiracies usually don't exist at all,' he said. 'They're just a lot of Internet fantasies.'

'Tell that to Julius Caesar, or what's-his-name, the guy with the eye patch like yours, the Nazi Tom Cruise played. He and his buddies tried to blow up Hitler.'

'Von Stauffenberg,' said Holliday.

'A conspiracy only exists when it's discovered. If it succeeds no one knows it was ever there.'

'Who knows?' Holliday shrugged. 'Maybe you're right.'

'And maybe Tritt left something behind to give us some clue.'

Brennan had run Tritt's Geneva phone number and the plates on Tritt's vehicle several days before the rocket attempt on the president, and discovered that the car was registered to a man named Emil Langarotti. Langarotti's address was given as 1 Rue Henri Frederich Amiel, Apartment 5B. Holliday and Peggy booked themselves back into a suite at the Mandarin Oriental Hotel, slept until noon, then headed to Tritt's pied-à-terre.

The address turned out to be a five-story, peach-colored stucco building just off the Rue des Delices, half a mile or so from their hotel. It was a quiet neighborhood around the corner from a busy thoroughfare and seemed made up almost entirely of buildings like Tritt's, done in varying pastel shades of stucco.

There was a wide, arched front door, the glass protected by ornamental ironwork. Above the door there was a large, black ONE. From a quick study it looked as though there were six apartments on each floor. Presumably Tritt's apartment was on the top one. They pulled open the big door and stepped into the building's lobby. There was a concierge's cubicle on the right but it was empty. On the left was a brass-doored elevator with a little porthole window. Directly ahead was a narrow flight of winding stairs. They took the coffin-sized elevator that creaked and groaned its way to the top floor. The elevator door opened on to an X-shaped intersection of four short corridors, badly lit by old-fashioned wall sconces. The floors were covered in green institutional carpeting that was stained and worn.

Tritt's apartment was at the end of the left-hand corridor. The door was brown-painted wood and the lock was a dead bolt.

'How are we supposed to get in?' said Peggy, a slightly sour tone in her voice. 'You bring your handy-dandy lock picks with you, by any chance?'

'As a matter of fact I did,' said Holliday. He reached under his jacket and pulled out the tire iron from the rental. The dead bolt was new, but the doorframe was as old as the building. He inserted the chisel end of the tire iron into the frame just above the lock and heaved. There was a sharp cracking sound as the frame around the lock set splintered. The door was open.

'You could patent that,' whispered Peggy. 'You could call it E-Z Key.'

Holliday pushed open the door. The apartment was small, a one-bedroom. Two windows looked out on to Rue des Delices but the shutters on both were closed, letting in only slivers of daylight. The main room was anonymous, an Ikea ideal without a hint about the kind of person who lived there. Peggy crossed the old, dark hardwood floor and flipped open the louvers on the shutters. The room brightened. Couch, two bucket armchairs, all red Ikea, a glass-and-steel coffee table with a big glass ashtray. Beside it there was a remote control. A pole lamp in the corner and a small, high-intensity lamp on an end table to the right of the couch. Between the two windows was a modern desk made of some sort of maple veneer and the docking station for a laptop. A giant plasma TV had been installed above the old gas fireplace. To the left of the fireplace was an expensive, sleek Bang & Olufsen media center with a stereo and digital video recorder. Beneath the system was a large, fully filled cabinet of CDs and DVDs.

'Nothing here,' said Holliday. He went down a short hall, heading for the bedroom. Peggy stayed in the main room and crouched down, investigating Tritt's taste in movies and music. Holliday returned a few minutes later, a sour expression on his face. 'Not a thing,' he said. 'The man's a ghost. It's even more sterile than the place in Lyford Cay.'

'Strauss, Wagner, Mozart, Verdi, Beethoven, Vivaldi, Susan Boyle.' Peggy was still kneeling in front of the rack of CDs and DVDs.

'I beg your pardon?'

'It's almost all classical except for the Susan Boyle.'

'Who in hell is Susan Boyle?' Holliday asked.

'You're kidding, right?' Peggy stood up. She opened the plastic case and put in the Susan Boyle disc.

'Never heard of her,' said Holliday.

'You've really got to get out more, Doc,' Peggy said with a grin, shaking her head. She crossed the room to the coffee table, picked up the remote and pressed the power button. Nothing happened for a second and then the huge TV over the fireplace flickered into life. A grainy image appeared of a man standing in what appeared to be some sort of derelict summer camp, an AK-47 cradled in his arms. The image was saturated with color almost to the point of being garish, and Holliday instantly thought of old home movies shot on Super 8 film. An amateurish title appeared over the figure of the man with the classic Soviet assault rifle:

Below the title was a crude drawing of a screaming eagle clutching a bloodred swastika.

'What the fuck?' said Peggy.

'I'll tell you one thing: it sure as hell isn't Kansas any-more, Toto,' answered Holliday.

21

The Maine's Right Arm Camp had formerly been known as Camp O-Pem-I-Gon, a two-hundred-acre tract on the shores of Lake Watson purchased by the Boy Scouts of America in 1922. That camp ceased operation during the 1960s for a variety of reasons, not the least of which was the fact that any twelve- or thirteen-year-old boy in 1965 wouldn't have been caught dead in a Boy Scout uniform.

In the early seventies a man named Reinhold Hodge tried to develop the entire lake as cottage lots. The Boy Scouts had chosen their wedge of property at the end of Eagle Road, the only property that wasn't swampy, mosquito infested or solid bedrock with no possibility of ever having anything except outdoor privies for sanitation. Hodge began by offering the lots at $2,500 apiece, went bankrupt by the time they were knocked down to $500 and left town when they hit $300 without a single lot sold.

In the end Wilmot DeJean purchased the entire lake, including the old Boy Scout camp, for $10,000 from the bankruptcy trustees in 1989, with the intention of changing the name of the property to the Light of the Lord Boys' Camp. As a result of the nebulous mental health problem that sent him into early retirement in 1991, the boys' camp idea was never brought to fruition.

By the mid-nineties DeJean finally found his niche. With the Russkies and the commies out of the picture, and the hippies all working on Wall Street or running health-food conglomerates and computer corporations, DeJean reinvented the old enemies that America needed so badly.

In his new world order, the ills of society were all caused by those good old standbys: the blacks, the Jews and the fags. On top of that he threw in wetbacks sneaking over the border to steal jobs, and just about anyone who spoke a foreign language. Not surprisingly, it worked like a charm.

There wasn't a single black family in Arkham, nor a Hispanic one. If there were any gays they weren't talking, and the nearest synagogue was three hundred miles away. DeJean's original screed sheet, *The Eagle's Voice,* had secret subscriptions from about a hundred people in the area, and DeJean, no slouch, was an early user of the Internet. His Web site drew in even more subscriptions.

Within a year after 9/11, subscriptions to the renamed *Eagle of Truth* had jumped to more than ten thousand, giving the sixty-six-year-old DeJean a comfortable enough living and enough funds to start bringing the old Boy Scout camp back to life.

By 2003 DeJean was having regular rallies at the old

camp, drawing people from all over Maine. By 2006 he was having three summer sessions a year, with people coming to the camp from all over the country.

By 2008 DeJean had recruited twenty-three full-time 'Patriots,' none over the age of thirty. Several of them were ex-military and had done tours in Iraq and Afghanistan. Four others had done time in various penal facilities, and each and every one of them enthusiastically shared DeJean's hatred of just about every minority you could name.

There had been very little in the news cycle about militia groups for some time, the Oklahoma City bombing having been trumped by the destruction of the World Trade Center. Ruby Ridge was a distant memory, and the Branch Davidians an embarrassing stain on the reputations of both the ATF and the FBI. America had a new enemy now, and Al-Qaeda and the Taliban were stealing DeJean's thunder. As the news media shifted their focus to other stories, subscriptions, income and interest began to drift away.

Senator Sinclair's strident warnings about the enemy within and the potential threat of domestic terrorism helped somewhat, especially with young Muslims sneaking off to Pakistan on spring break to be all that they could be for Osama, and blanket bombs on flights to Detroit, but it wasn't enough. The sudden appearance of Billy Tritt and his two suitcases at the Eagle's Nest, as it was now called, was a godsend.

It was also a bit of an anticlimax. As Tritt approached

the camp entrance along the dusty, aptly named Eagle Road, he saw that DeJean had never bothered to take down the rustic Camp O-Pem-I-Gon wooden archway over the entrance, simply replacing the Boy Scout fleur-de-lis in the center with a red, black and yellow plywood rendition of his screaming eagle and swastika symbol.

Security consisted of an overweight and pimple-faced man in his late twenties dozing on a stump with a cigarette drooping out of the corner of his mouth. He was wearing jeans and a down coat, which bore the screaming eagle logo. He had what appeared to be a Kalashnikov AK-47 across his lap, but as Tritt pulled the truck to a stop and the pimple-faced idiot stood up, he saw that it was a .22-caliber German knockoff. In Pimple Face's big hands it looked like a toy, which was, effectively, what it was.

'Outa the truck,' said Pimple Face, gesturing with the rifle, stepping forward. He was wearing scuffed high-tops. Some uniform. Tritt could see the long lever safety was blocking the breech. It would take the oafish young man a good second to thumb it off and then charge the weapon by pulling back the bolt.

'Put it away,' said Tritt, pulling the big Desert Eagle out from under his Windbreaker.

Pimple Face stared at the gleaming handgun and fumbled with the safety on the baby AK. From the driver's seat, Tritt shot him in the foot, blowing off the front of one of the old, floppy sneakers. The young man screamed, his howl lost in the booming echo of the big automatic as it rumbled around the surrounding cedar-clad hills. Pimple Face dropped to the ground, screaming, blood pumping out of his ruined foot. Tears poured down his fat cheeks. The blood from his foot congealed in the snow like cat crap in a litter box.

'You shooted me!' moaned the fat young man, writhing in the dirt.

'No, I shot you,' said Tritt, staring down at him from the truck. 'And I'll shoot you in the other foot unless you tell me where DeJean is within the next ten seconds.'

'Up to the communications center,' groaned the young man, his teeth gritted with pain. The blood still poured into the snow. He was losing a lot of blood and he was going pale. Tritt recognized the signs of shock.

'Where's that?' Tritt asked.

'Up ta the lodge. By the tennis courts,' grunted Pimple Face. He was looking nauseated now, flop sweat running down his jawline.

'You're going to pass out in a second. You might puke, so make sure you're on your side. Don't worry. I'll send someone down to patch you up when I find DeJean.'

'You bastid, you shooted me,' whispered Pimple Face, snot streaming from his nostrils in two gleaming snail trails. His eyes rolled back and he faded out. He was rolled into a fetal ball, his back against the stump. The blood kept coming. He'd need a hospital soon or he'd lose the foot. Fortunes of war, thought Tritt. He put the big black truck into drive and rolled slowly up the road.

There was an old tumbledown log building on the crest of a low rise on his left and an open field with what looked like a giant plywood tepee in the center of the clearing. The tepee was stained and weathered, tilting slightly to the right, painted Indian symbols almost completely faded away by time and the elements. The field was snow covered, but Tritt could still see the raised wooden tent platforms. He passed an old gravel parking area. There were half a dozen vehicles, mostly trucks, mostly old and all American made, parked.

Standing on its own as though the other vehicles didn't want to chance scratching the paint was a bright red army surplus Humvee. Driving past, Tritt read the license plate on the back of the brutal-looking vehicle: PATRIOT. Not difficult to figure out who owned it. Beyond the parking lot on a ridge overlooking the lake was a large, rough log structure with a snowy roof. There were two flags on the wooden pole in front of the lodge: DeJean's screaming eagle riding above Maine's moose and pine tree.

Tritt parked the big truck in front of the building, putting the Desert Eagle back in the vertical sling holster under his nylon Windbreaker. He walked up a rickety flight of steps on to the wide, covered porch and rapped on the flimsy wooden door. A few seconds later the door was opened by a man wearing civilian clothes and a screaming eagle armband.

His hands were grimy, the nails thickly rimmed with grease, and there were long grease stains on his work pants. He was wearing heavy construction boots. He looked to be in his early twenties. A car mechanic, perhaps, or somebody who worked with machinery.

Behind him half a dozen people sat around a long, ersatz conference table made from two sheets of plywood supported on wooden trestles. The plywood had been covered with dark green oilcloth. There were six men of various sizes and ages standing around the roughly made conference table. Tritt was reminded of von Stauffenberg and the plot to assassinate Adolf Hitler. Hitler was in the room, too, in the form of a large, framed portrait over the mantel of a big fieldstone fireplace at the far end. Unlike any conference room of Hitler's, however, the room was thick with smoke, clouds of it rolling up to the rough-log ceiling beams.

'Who are you?' The man at the door said. 'Whadda you want here? This is private property.' He scowled. 'Why didn't Skinny stop you like he's supposed to?'

'Skinny, wearing one of those screaming eagle coats? Fat, lots of zits?'

'Yeah.'

'He's down at the gate, lying on the ground with half his foot blown off.'

'Shit,' said the man at the door.

'Yeah, maybe that, too,' said Tritt.

Another voice spoke up. This time it came from a short man standing at the head of the table. He was dressed in full desert camo and wearing a Fidel Castro–style green, flattop cap with two stars on it. Like the man at the door he was wearing a screaming eagle arm-band. There was a huge screaming eagle banner on the wall to one side of the table that bore Maine's Right Arm's motto: THE RIGHT ARM IS GOD'S ARM.

'You shot one of my men?' asked the man in the camo gear. Tritt noticed that he was wearing a sidearm. It looked like an old Colt auto.

'That's right.' Tritt nodded. 'And if you don't get someone down there in a hurry he's going to bleed to death. Take him to a hospital and tell the doctors he shot himself in the foot. He looks stupid enough.'

'Daniel?'

The man standing in front of Tritt nodded at the man with the stars on his kepi and hurried past Tritt.

'You must be DeJean.'

The man nodded. 'I am Colonel DeJean, yes.' He stepped out from behind the table, one hand on the butt of his open-holstered automatic. The holster was scarred and battered. War surplus. Tritt saw that he was wearing expensive-looking cowboy boots. The heels gave him at least two extra inches.

'In whose army?' Tritt responded belligerently.

DeJean's hand tightened on the butt of his weapon. 'Mine,' he said finally.

'This bunch? The fat guy at the gate? You must be joking.'

'There are others,' said DeJean. Under the cap, white, fluffy hair extended. 'This is merely a training session for new recruits.'

'Training for what?' Tritt asked. 'The circus?'

'They laughed at Hitler in the beginning,' said DeJean. 'As far as the British were concerned George Washington was a traitor and Benedict Arnold was a great war hero.'

Tritt laughed. 'You're comparing yourself to Hitler and George Washington? Hitler was a madman and Washington was a career soldier from the age of twenty.'

'I prefer to know with whom I am debating,' said DeJean, drawing himself up stiffly.

'My name is Barfield,' said Tritt.

'What exactly is it that you want, Mr Barfield? The Eagle's Nest is a little out of the way for idle conversation.'

'I'm here to make a donation to your cause.'

'We don't take checks, I'm afraid.' DeJean smirked.

'Send one of your boys out to my truck. There are a couple of suitcases on the passenger's seat. Bring them here.'

'Pritchard, Samson, get the suitcases,' DeJean ordered. Two of the men standing at the big plywood table headed for the door. They were back two minutes later, each one carrying a suitcase.

'Put them on the table,' said Tritt. He reached into his pocket and threw a ring of small keys in DeJean's direction. He tried to scoop them out of the air with one hand but they fell at his feet. One of his 'trainees' bent to pick them up and handed them over. The men put the suitcases on the table. DeJean dismissed them.

DeJean gave Tritt a long look, then fitted the keys into the locks of the big green suitcases. He threw back the lids. Each suitcase contained hundreds of pressure-wrapped bricks of used cash. DeJean tried not to look surprised, but Tritt could see his hands shaking slightly as he reached for one of the bricks and pulled it out.

'Uh, this is very generous of you Mr, uh . . . Barfield. Might I ask where it came from?'

'This isn't quite a donation, Colonel DeJean. It's a buyout. Maine's Right Arm is now mine to do with as I want. Your men will now follow my orders and only mine. Understand?'

'You must be crazy. This is a grassroots political movement. This is a cause!'

'Bullshit.'

DeJean looked down at the immense amount of cash.

'There's slightly over two million dollars there, all in untraceable bills.'

'Why are you doing this?' DeJean asked.

'September eleventh was a wakeup call to America,' said Tritt, reciting the carefully written script he'd been given and which he'd memorized. A script written to ease DeJean's conscience and excuse his greed. 'But that was nearly ten years ago, and this great country has fallen into a complacent slumber once more. It's time America was roused from its dangerous sleep. The men of Maine's Right Arm can be the ones to do just that.'

'How?' DeJean said.

'By doing exactly as I tell them,' said Tritt. He

watched as DeJean stared down at the suitcases. He could almost see the wheels turning in the old man's head. Those suitcases were the stuff of pipe dreams and DeJean had been living in a pipe dream world for much of his adult life. He and Maine's Right Arm were the perfect thing for what was to come.

DeJean drew himself to a soldierly attention. 'Mr Barfield, Maine's Right Arm is yours to command. May God bless your endeavors, and may God bless America.'

22

Mike Harris, deputy director of operations for the CIA, sat in the darkened bunker of the Homeland Security Predator Ground Control Station. The bunker was a windowless, half-buried blockhouse on the edge of the Grand Forks Air Force Base, just outside of Grand Forks, North Dakota. A glass wall separated the control room from the pilot's positions below. There were three drones flying today, one over the British Columbia–Washington-Idaho-Montana border looking for 'humpers' carrying in loads of marijuana, another one cruising in a regular pattern over the Great Lakes from Duluth on Lake Superior to Rochester on Lake Ontario, and the third flying circles at 44,000 feet over the town of Winter Falls, New Hampshire. At that height the gray-blue, pilotless aircraft were invisible to the naked eye and even to binoculars. The drones were too small to show up on radar, turboprop operated to avoid being attacked by heat-seeking missiles and made out of carbon fiber rather than aluminum for further stealth.

General Angus Scott Matoon sat with Harris in the upper control room, smoking a cigar and watching the relay screens from the pilot's positions on the console in front of them. He'd been given a report by Major Neville, his adjutant, earlier that morning and he was feeling quite pleased. The prairie fire had been extinguished via a hiking accident in a State Park in the Catoctin Mountains. It had barely made the back pages of the Washington newspapers, and besides a single clip on Channel 4, there had been no TV coverage at all.

'Do you ever catch anything?' Harris asked. 'I've seen them used as hunter-killers in Pakistan and Afghanistan but that's a whole different kettle of fish.'

'All they get is smugglers out west. Most of the terrorist types feel uncomfortable in that kind of environment. Camping in the woods isn't for towel heads.'

Harris sighed. Matoon really was a bit of a stereotype, but the gruff, heavyset general was Sinclair's man, so he really didn't have any choice in the matter.

'We've picked up one or two persons of interest coming across the lakes, but it's mostly cigarette smuggling out there. The rag heads don't have too much experience with water, either. If you ask me the whole bunch of them are just a little on the lazy side. They fly over to Canada, which lets anyone into their stupid country, and then they try to fly into the States. That's how the 9/11 Arabs got in. They gotta know that any brown-skinned guy with a name like Yusef or Achmed's going to get pulled out of the line. The real stupid ones try to take the bus to save money. There's about three thousand miles of open border they could cross on foot, perfectly safely, carrying an A-bomb but they always do it the hard way.'

The 9/11 terrorists had not entered through Canada, despite the myth. They'd entered the country through New York, L.A. and Miami with U.S. documentation, but that was beside the point. Fiddling with the joystick to the left of the screen he could zoom, pan and tilt like any film camera, completely independently of the operator on the floor. Matoon watched him play, a smile on his jowled face.

'My grandson plays *Avatar* with a stick like that; makes people fly, guns fire, people move. It's all beyond me. The kid's eight years old and he could probably fly one of these better than the guys down there at the controls.'

'How many people in the town?' Harris asked, watching the monitor. He was flitting around like Peter Pan at rooftop level now. It was almost vertigo inducing. He could see the tops of people's heads as they trudged down the sidewalks in their winter clothes. A cop car drove down the main drag.

'About two thousand this time of year.'

'What do you figure as the collateral damage?'

'Couldn't tell you,' said Matoon, blowing a smoke ring. 'High, I expect. The whole idea is to scare the living crap out of the entire country, not just tell them the sky is falling.'

'How many cops in Winter Falls?'

'Eight on any shift. Shifts are twelve hours, so there're eighteen active officers. Eight are patrolmen on each shift. We know where all the off-duty officers live. He'll take care of them first.'

'What about the county sheriff?'

'Eleven miles away. Not a problem. Two roads into town. Pick the right weather situation and it's a lockdown.'

'So the whole thing is going down?'

'You having second thoughts?'

'No, not really,' said the CIA man.

'Sure you do. Anybody would think twice about what we're doing. This is the big time. We do this, we save the country.' The general made a snorting sound. 'Our president's a pussy. America's going down the toilet. We can't let that happen. We need a strong hand in the White House.'

'It's not far from being a coup d'etat,' said Harris. 'And we're talking about a lot of casualties.'

'How many people died in 9/11?' Matoon said.

'Twenty-eight hundred,' answered Harris.

'About the same here.'

'You know this is different.'

'Why? Because of how your asset is going to do it? Don't be a fool. There are always civilian casualties in war – it's a given, no matter how those casualties are inflicted.'

Harris stared at the monitor. He could see people ice fishing on the frozen lake, kids making a snowman on a lawn. Students at the Abbey School playing hockey. He'd read the reports, studied the dossiers, knew the town inside out even though he'd never set foot in the place.

'You realize if we stop him and "uncover" the plot at the last minute, we'll be heroes.'

'Sure.' Matoon grinned. 'The prez would give your boss a medal, but it wouldn't get anything like the coverage if we go through with it.' The general reached over and patted Harris on the shoulder. 'Like another president once said, "Stay the course," Mr Harris. We're doing this to make America great again.'

'You're sure this is going to work?' Peggy asked. They were driving yet another rental car, this one picked up at Montréal-Trudeau International after their arrival from Zurich. Holliday was behind the wheel, piloting the big Ford Explorer down the eight-lane, snow-blown freeway. They were more than an hour outside of Montreal, traveling due west, the St Lawrence River a quarter mile away on their left. It might as well have been Antarctica for all they could see. It was only two o'clock in the afternoon but they were driving with all their lights on, halogen fog lamps included.

'It's the only chance we've got,' Holliday answered. 'Homeland Security will have our passports, prints and pictures on file. We try to fly in and we'll be picked up in ten seconds. All the border crossings will have our names in their computers. That's why I picked up the

Explorer from that little local company. No U.S. affiliates, so they can't be scanned by the Men in Black.'

'Couldn't we have just waited out the weather in Montreal?'

'This is just the kind of weather Harry likes for this sort of thing,' said Holliday, peering down at the odometer. The vehicle had almost two hundred thousand kilometers on the dial and was seven years old. The only speed for the wipers was intermittent, and the only heat came from the defroster keeping the windshield clear. Both Holliday and Peggy had bought down ski jackets and winter boots in the little town by the airport, but despite bundling up, Peggy's teeth were still chattering.

'Almost there,' said Holliday. Through the thumping windshield wipers moving melting slush from one side to the other Holliday saw an exit sign for MacEwan Boundry Road and eased the Explorer into the far right lane. There was hardly any traffic on the highway, but even in a four-wheel drive vehicle one wrong move could be a disaster. The exit came up and he slowed even more, going around the small cloverleaf and passing over the wide, straight highway they just left. Holliday drove slowly along a two-lane blacktop that was now perfectly white.

'This is a blizzard,' said Peggy nervously.

'This is Canada in the winter,' said Holliday.

'This is life threatening,' said Peggy. 'Why are we meeting this friend of yours at a Subway in the middle of nowhere? And just who exactly is this mysterious Harry?'

'He's a Mohawk Indian.'

'So?'

'He and I were in the Rangers together. When he retired he went back to the rez, settled down, opened a business, got married, had two kids – the whole thing.'

'Is he Canadian or American?'

'Both. The reservation straddles the river, so he claims both nationalities. He likes to fight, so he joined the Rangers.'

'That still doesn't explain why we're meeting him in the middle of a blizzard at a Subway.'

Holliday laughed. 'He loves subs. That's all he used to talk about when we were in the bush. Meatball subs. As soon as he saved up enough money he bought a franchise.'

'And this has to do with our present predicament how?'

'He set up a little boatbuilding business for local fishermen, as well. Sold outboard motors, too.'

'So?'

'He sells snowmobiles in the winter.'

'Why am I getting this sinking feeling?' Peggy said. The familiar black-and-yellow sign of a Subway restaurant appeared through the whirling snow. Holliday pulled into the recently plowed parking lot. At the far end of the lot was a new-looking Land Rover Defender with a plow attachment.

'Nice ride,' commented Peggy. 'I didn't think there was that much money in cold-cut combos and Ski-Doos.'

'Harry has other sources of income,' said Holliday. He climbed out of the Explorer and pushed his way through the snow to the brightly lit entrance of the Subway. Peggy reluctantly followed him through the cold.

The inside of the sandwich shop was brightly lit and toasty warm. There were two men behind the long, high counter. One was an adolescent, mouth set in a constant teenage sneer, his chubby cheeks set into a square serious face. He was wearing a paper hat and smoking a cigarette. The other man was in his fifties, hard-faced, his long black hair gathered into a ponytail. He had a wrestler's body, and like the boy he was wearing a silly paper hat. He was sitting on a stool and reading a copy of the *Cornwall Standard Freeholder*. He jumped up when he caught sight of Holliday.

'One Eye!' He grinned. He came across the room and slapped Holliday on the back, and the two men went through a complicated ritual handshake.

'Act like two old geezers at a Masonic meeting,' grunted the teenager, scowling and sneering simultaneously.

The man with the ponytail turned away from Holliday and gave Peggy a long, appraising look. 'You must be Peggy.' His smile broadened. He had two eyeteeth capped with gold, which made him look like a wealthy vampire. 'I'm Harry Moonblanket.' He cocked a thumb in the direction of the chubby-cheeked teenager. 'The lump there is my American nephew, Kai-entaronk-wen.'

'What he means is, my name is Billy Two Rivers.' He turned to his uncle, the sneer still intact. 'Screw you, Chief Wears Depends.'

'Mouth like a rat trap,' said Harry proudly. 'Chip off the old block.'

'Hippie,' grunted Billy.

'You ready, One Eye?' Harry said, turning his attention to Holliday.

'I thought we were going to wait for nightfall. No moon and all that.'

'This is better,' said Harry. He removed his paper hat, took a fur-lined hooded parka down from a hook and shrugged it on. 'Nighttime, they fly helicopters with searchlights. Weather like this, they're deaf, dumb and blind.' He pointed toward the ceiling. 'Even the big eyes in the sky can't see anything.' He came out from behind the counter, turning once to give his instructions to Billy. 'We get any customers, give them their subs at half price. Meatball subs on special, two for one.'

'Anybody who travels in this weather just to get a sub is out of his friggin' mind,' Billy responded.

'Just mind the store, kid.'

'*Onen*, Uncle. Good luck,' said Billy

'*Onen* and *Niá-wen*, Nephew.' Moonblanket took

Peggy by the elbow. 'We'll take the Rover. You ride shotgun, sweetheart. Nothing like a pretty girl beside you for good luck.' They headed out the door.

'Where are we going?' Peggy asked.

'To a place where the streets are paved with gold, my dear – twenty-four carat.'

23

Seated at the counter in Gorman's Restaurant, Chief Randy Lockwood bit into his Denver sandwich. It was way past lunchtime but there'd been a minor drug bust at the high school that morning and the paperwork had taken him well into the afternoon.

An occasional dime bag of weed trickling down from the Quebec side of the border was one thing – he'd smoked and inhaled more than his share back in the sixties – but cocaine was something else again.

The locker bust had come on an anonymous tip, which meant it was one student ratting out another. By the time he'd gotten around to it, Tommy Horrigan, the owner of the locker in question, was in the wind. Making it worse was the fact that the kid had turned eighteen the week before, putting him in adult court whenever they managed to track him down.

Complicating matters for Lockwood was the fact that Mark Horrigan, the kid's old man, was chairman of the Wolf Run Golf and Country Club and the owner of Wolf Run Retirement Estates, an adult living development on the northern edge of town. A local bigwig. Going up against Mark Horrigan was not going to be pleasant. Horrigan was a shrimp with a severe case of short-man syndrome and far too much money. He'd been an obnoxious little bastard since grade school and nothing much had changed since.

Lockwood glanced out the big, half-steamed-over window and out on to Main Street. Anything moving by necessity had four-wheel drive. It was another one of those hell-born blizzards birthed somewhere in arctic Quebec for no good reason. Maybe it was one of the old Indian gods getting revenge for the arrival of the French in the 1500s. What had one of those early explorers called it? The Land God Gave to Cain. No kidding.

'Why does everybody in this town have to know everyone else?' said Lockwood. He put down the sandwich half and picked up his cup of coffee.

'That's what small towns are all about,' said Reggie Waterman, wiping his steel hook on his apron. 'Everybody knows how much money you've got in the bank, everyone is screwing or has screwed your wife at one time or another and everyone knows if you're using Viagra or not.'

'Small towns suck,' said Lockwood on the other side of the counter.

'Amen,' said Waterman. 'Speaking of which, Terry Jones over at the feed store says someone came in yesterday and bought eight hundred pounds of that Incitec fertilizer. Terry'd never seen the guy.'

'Who needs eight hundred pounds of fertilizer in the middle of winter?' Lockwood asked, suddenly interested. The Oklahoma City bombing had used a ton of ammonium nitrate and diesel fuel to take out the Murrah Building, yet more than fifteen years later there were still no federal regulations about buying the stuff. A couple of states required identification to be shown but that was about it.

'He get any ID?'

'Maine driver's license.'

Which didn't mean a damn thing. 'He say why he wanted it?'

'Said he was from a big greenhouse operation in Brunswick. They got caught short, he said.'

The Falls were a long way from Brunswick. Sixty miles or so. Surely there was some place closer to buy fertilizer.

'Which greenhouse?'

'He didn't say,' answered Waterman. A group of kids from the Abbey School with skates slung over their shoulders swept in on a blast of frigid air. Reggie came out from behind the counter, took their orders for French fries with gravy and cheeseburgers, then came back and went to work at the grill. Streak Lockwood took another bite of his sandwich. Bad weather or not he was going to have to take a trip out to Terry Jones's place when he was done eating. Just in case.

They stepped inside a tumbledown boathouse, but instead of boats there were two canvas-covered lumps on the frozen surface of the water. Someone was already waiting for them, an alien figure taller than Moonblanket and wearing what appeared to be a space helmet and a suit made out of dangling white strips of fabric.

'I don't see any twenty-four-carat gold,' said Peggy. 'Just the Abominable Snowman here.'

'Brandon Redboots – a friend of mine,' explained the Mohawk.

The figure in the white gillie camouflage suit nodded silently.

The blizzard wind outside was rattling the walls and roof like the Big Bad Wolf. Moonblanket went to a locker and took out three sets of loose, drooping gillie suits in pure white.

'Put these on,' the Mohawk said.

'I've never dressed up as a yeti,' said Peggy, slipping her legs into the one-piece suit.

'When I was a kid there was a book called *The Disappearing Bag*,' said Moonblanket. 'That's exactly what these are.'

'Hot,' said Peggy, her voice muffled inside the suit.

'Not for long,' said the Mohawk. He went back to the locker and brought out three full-face GMAX snowmobile helmets, once again in pure white. Holliday and Peggy jammed theirs on. Moonblanket stepped down on to the ice and pulled the canvas covers off the two lumps, revealing a pair of white snowmobiles.

'Arctic Cat Z1 Turbos,' said Moonblanket. 'Just about the fastest you can get.'

'How fast?' Peggy asked.

'About a hundred and ten or so on a good ice surface.'

'You're kidding, right?'

'We're usually going a little slower than that because we're towing cargo pods. Maybe sixty or seventy.'

'Cargo pods?'

'Ask me no questions, I tell you no lies,' said Moonblanket. 'Peggy, you ride with me. Doc, you go with Brandon.' Peggy dropped down on to the slick ice and climbed on behind Harry, who was straddling the front seat. Brandon Redboots got into the driver's position on the second machine. When they started up Peggy was surprised at how quiet they were and said so.

'Double mufflers on the engines. Polaris silent running chains and gears,' answered Moonblanket.

'How long is this going to take?' Holliday asked.

'On a good day, maybe three minutes,' said the Mohawk. 'It's about a mile and a half all told. Five hundred yards to the island, which is still on the Canadian side, then a little less than a mile to Raquette Point on the U.S. side. The only danger is in the first minute – from here to the island. From the island to Raquette Point it's Akwesasne land. The Feds can't touch us.'

'Don't they have tribal police?' Peggy asked, her voice blurred by the helmet but still understandable.

Harry Moonblanket pointed at the silent man sitting directly in front of Holliday. 'Meet Chief Brandon Redboots of the Akwesasne Tribal Police.' He laughed, gunned the engine and burst out through the open front of the old boathouse. Without a word Redboots followed them out into the whirling snow.

The wind roared all around them as they raced across the frozen river channel, the cold steadily leaking through the suit and then Peggy's ski jacket. Within thirty seconds she was freezing, teeth chattering inside the helmet. Suddenly, out of the corner of her vision she saw a shadow racing beside them, perhaps fifty yards away. She wouldn't have seen anything if the other snowmobile hadn't been bright yellow with a pulsing blue-and-red light on a short mast. It was slowly sliding in their direction. In front of her Harry Moonblanket let out a high-pitched yell and then a string of incomprehensible words that Peggy assumed were the Mohawk equivalent of swearing. She turned her head and saw a second blue-and-red light on their right.

'Who are they?' Peggy asked, yelling into the side of the Mohawk's helmet.

'Mounties!' Harry yelled back. 'The river's federal property! Hang on!' The Mohawk twisted the throttle and they surged forward, almost tipping Peggy off the back of the racing machine. The pulsing lights were getting closer. She had a flashing memory of some old movie with a Mountie singing on a horse and knew there'd be no singing cops out here. Directly ahead of them an angled ramp of packed snow appeared.

Harry hit the ramp at full speed, with Holliday and Redboots right behind them. Trees appeared at the top of the ramp and Peggy realized they were on land once again. Almost immediately Moonblanket throttled back and slowed. A hundred yards farther on in the gully he stopped and let Redboots come up beside him.

'Old Panthers,' grunted Redboots speaking for the first time, his visored face invisible.

'What's he talking about and why have we stopped?' Peggy asked urgently, looking back over her shoulder for the telltale red-and-blue flashing lights. There was nothing but blowing snow. 'Where are the Mounties?'

'This is Cornwall Island,' said Moonblanket, sitting in front of her. 'Akwesasne land. The Mounties can't set foot on the place without asking our permission and Brandon's not likely to give it under the circumstances.'

Chuckling, Redboots began to sing in a low, guttural voice: *'Teiohonwa:ka ne'ni akhonwe:ia Kon'tatieshon iohnekotatie Wakkawehatie wakkawehatie.'*

'What's he saying?' Peggy asked.

'It's his favorite song about paddling his canoe. He always sings when he beats the Flat Hats.'

'The Flat Hats?'

'The Red Jackets, the Mounties,' explained Moonblanket.

'How did they know we'd be there?' Holliday asked seriously.

'Billy phoned them up and told them. He's the tribe's official confidential informant.'

'Your nephew?'

'Sure. The Akwesasne survive on smuggled cigarettes. We even own our own tobacco farms. It's in the treaty from about two hundred years ago. Sometimes we get some serious criminal types down from Montreal, bikers mostly, try to horn in on our business. Billy informs on them. Makes a few bucks for himself. He goes to university now, so he needs the bread.'

'He did it on purpose?' Peggy asked.

'Sure. I told him to. We're on Z1 Turbos. The Flat Hats use old Panther 440s. If we'd been dragging a pod of smokes they maybe coulda caught us, but not with one passenger each. No contest.'

'It scared the hell out of me,' said Holliday.

'Speaking of which,' said Peggy, 'can we get to where we're going to sometime soon? I have to pee.'

Morrie Adler sat on one of the couches in the Oval Office and waited for the president to calm down. Outside the tall, bulletproof windows it was a winter-wonderland postcard, everything covered in a disguising mantle of snow.

'I won't do it!' the president steamed. He'd been a secret smoker until a secret checkup had told him in no uncertain terms that he'd better become a secret quitter, which he had, but the side effects of nicotine withdrawal were secretly making him very testy. It occurred to Morrie that wars could be declared or escalated on the basis of the president's physical condition. There was no doubt in his mind that Roosevelt would have done better at Potsdam if he'd felt better, and whether people liked to admit it or not the last couple of years of Ronald Reagan's term, the White House and the country had been run by his staff.

'They're plugging a hole,' said Adler. 'Nothing more.'

'They're not plugging a hole; they're reading polls,' said the president.

'Sinclair's the all-out favorite for the job.' Adler shrugged. 'You've put off appointing a vice president for too long already, kemo sabe. Make your choice or do what the party wants, but do it fast.'

'You mean do what that psychopath Kate Sinclair wants,' snorted the president. 'From what I hear, she's been whoring herself all over Capitol Hill for two weeks now, kissing asses, gathering in favors and blackmailing what's left over.'

'It's what the country wants, as well,' said Adler. 'Ever since *you know who* was in this office the nation's been polarized; there is no center line. That's a tightrope you can't walk along anymore. The people want guns and butter, give them guns and butter.'

'I'll think about it,' said the president.

'Think fast,' said Adler. 'Time's a-wasting.'

24

Bedford Mills, Virginia, was the perfect western Virginia town. Main Street really was called Main Street, the churches all had snow-white steeples and the red-brick courthouse in the middle of town had a white cupola and a bell that was once used to call out the volunteer fire department.

The population of Bedford Mills was slightly more than five thousand and more than two-thirds of the adult males owned rifles. Almost the same percentage owned handguns and half of them owned fly rods for catching trout in the cool, clear streams that fed White Mountain Lake. There were no Hispanic families in Bedford Mills and only a very small percentage of the population was African American. There was one family of Chinese descent, Ross and Katie Wong and their kids, but they were fourth-generation American.

The biggest employer in the town was Savage Trucks, which custom built water tankers, milk tankers, dump bodies and sanitation trucks. The other major employer was the Wolf Ridge Distillery, which made a variety of specialty liquors, the most popular being Stonewall 12-Year-Old Bourbon. All in all, safe territory for Senator Richard Pierce Sinclair to have a town hall meeting on the coming threat of domestic terrorism in America.

The town hall itself was located on South Tower Street on the far side of the old Norfolk and Western tracks. It was only a few minutes' walk from the old Liberty Depot, which was now a family restaurant with cute menu items listed under titles like Main Line, Water Towers and Cabooses.

Once upon a time the town hall had been home to the Bedford Mills Klavern of the Ku Klux Klan. It was briefly used as a headquarters building by Stonewall Jackson during the Civil War, and eventually became the local Masons' Lodge. The Masons faded away in the area, and in its final incarnation it was used as a recreation center by the Knights of Pythias.

Try as they might the Pythians couldn't keep up with the slow decay of the 150-year-old building and it was finally rescued by the Bedford Mills Historical Society, which bought it for a dollar, then brought it back to its former glory, then handed it over to the town. The ground floor was now the town library while the second-floor stage and auditorium were sometimes used for local theater productions, award presentations by local service clubs and events exactly like the one taking place this evening.

The original dressing rooms were located behind the stage and had been redecorated from the burlesque era for some unknown reason. There were posters of Fanny Brice everywhere and a couple of Moulin Rouge posters, as well. Each of the three dressing rooms had a small couch, a rotating makeup chair and a wall-to-wall mirror.

Kate Sinclair had chosen the middle of the three rooms and had waited on the couch while Chelsea, the hired movie hair and makeup girl, made her son look even more senatorial than he was. She added salt-and-pepper highlights to his temples and a few age crinkles around the eyes for wisdom, and then helped him insert the gray contact lenses that dignified his washed-out blue eyes.

As a final touch Sinclair's mother handed her son a very up-to-date pair of cherry-red half-glasses to pull from his pocket when he was reading something or appearing to, even though at forty-six he still had twenty-twenty vision. When Kate was satisfied with her son's appearance she gave the hair and makeup girl a hundred dollars and dismissed her.

'Is all of this really necessary, Mother?'

'It's television, dear,' answered the elderly woman. 'If Nixon had worn a little pancake that night in Chicago things might have gone very differently.'

'Local?'

'Network, cable, bloggers, the *New York Times*. Fox, looking for blood. The message is beginning to get through, darling, just as I knew it would.'

'I'm still not sure about this, Mother,' said the senator, a worried expression on his perfectly made-up face. 'With the Pope being assassinated and the vice president dying ... There's been so much violence, I don't think I should look as though I'm advocating more.'

'Not advocating, dear; warning about it. Our borders are like sieves; the economy is in the sewer; the poor, the homeless and the unemployed are at the end of their rope. There's bound to be a groundswell of grass-roots violence that will spread through the country like wildfire unless something is done about it, and quickly.' Since Kate Sinclair wrote her son's speeches it wasn't surprising that she could quote from them at length.

'That's like asking for martial law. A dictatorship,' argued the senator.

'We're not asking for either one. We're asking for the strong America of the past. Better security. Vigilance. The ability to find our enemies and destroy them before they do the same to us.'

'How about something like this,' suggested the senator, the timbre of his voice adopting its senatorial edge. 'Guantánamo was a failure because we didn't annex the whole damn island during the Spanish–American War and Kennedy didn't have the courage to invade properly at the Bay of Pigs in 'sixty-one. As for the Japanese, it's been almost seventy years since Pearl Harbor. It's ancient history and so are the internment camps. If a reporter or anyone else asks about places like Manzanar, we counter with Changi in Singapore.'

'Excellent.' Kate Sinclair beamed.

'When is it scheduled to happen?' the senator asked.

'Better if you don't know exactly, dear. It will seem more natural.'

'He knows what to do?'

'He's the best,' assured the senator's mother.

'And when it happens?'

'Act the part,' said Kate Sinclair. '*Sic semper tyrannis* but with a happy ending.'

The auditorium had seating for a 180 people and standing room under the balcony for 60 more. The balcony itself had long ago by default turned into a storage area for old props and costumes, since the hall was rarely used for theatrical productions now that the Mountain View Cinema had closed down and was the home of the Bedford Little Theater.

Tonight the auditorium was packed, mostly with locals but also with reporters and cameramen from all the national networks and newspapers. In the time since the assassination of the Pope and the death of the vice president, Senator Richard Pierce Sinclair had gone from being an obscure albeit handsome junior senator with a strident message that almost never made the news to a pundit on CNN when it came to issues of terrorism. He was a regular guest on everything from *Meet the Press* to Glenn Beck's TV and radio shows, and 'author' of an upcoming book titled *American Terror*, which had already been accepted for publication by Regnery Publishing, the foremost conservative publisher in the nation.

Tonight was Senator Sinclair's eighth town hall meeting, and the most heavily attended by the national press. When he was interviewed the week before on *Larry King Live*, the comment was made that in recent days it seemed as though the senator was campaigning for president. His reply was a nice, gap-toothed smile and the perfectly scripted response: 'Not this year, Larry. Being a senator is enough for any American.'

As usual, security at the meeting was provided by the Blackhawk Security, a subsidiary of Kate Sinclair's main corporation, the modern version of the original Crusader Pipe and Tile Corporation, now generally known as IPT International. There was a pair of armed guards at each of the four exits, and a metal detector and a wand-carrying guard at the main entrance. There were four more guards close to the stage and two out in the parking lot.

The guards were dressed like Secret Service agents, complete with lapel pins and wrist microphones. This was no coincidence; Kate Sinclair was well aware that presentation was everything these days and the Secret Service–style guards were nothing more than an extension of the makeup that Jack Kennedy used – and Richard Nixon didn't – during the debate in 1960.

Senator Sinclair appeared on stage at 8.15 p.m., exactly on time. He looked composed, with a slight touch of the humble in his demeanor. Tonight, given the small-town, essentially rural audience, he was wearing old lace-up shoes, well-worn blue jeans and a brown sports jacket over an open-necked, plain white shirt. His Yale ring was missing, and his usual Rolex President had been replaced by a Timex Indiglo.

The ruddiness and color of his cheeks, given to him by Chelsea the makeup girl, lent him the appearance of a man who spent a great deal of time outdoors. Educated at places like Exeter and Yale, the senator had long since lost any trace of his native Virginia accent, but like any good politician he was able to affect the twangy drawl of his youth any time he wanted – the help of a speech coach his mother hired for him every summer didn't hurt.

As usual Senator Sinclair's opening remarks took the form of a canned speech he'd given dozens of times before about the threat of domestic terrorism. It was peppered with sound bites for the networks, and while it never mentioned American-born Muslims as the generators of such terrorism the speech inevitably mentioned that there were 'as many as' five million Muslims in the United States, which provided a 'rich environment' for extreme political views. The overall feeling was that the Muslim community was growing by leaps and bounds and would soon surpass Christianity's slim numerical majority in the world unless something was done, and done soon.

The inference was clear, even if only subliminally stated: America was a Christian nation. The currency said it, the Pledge of Allegiance said it, the Constitution of the United States said it, and so did the Declaration of Independence. It was an old and very American principal: he who is not my friend is by definition my enemy.

At exactly eight thirty, as applause and cheers echoed around the auditorium, every camera in the room was either in tight close-up of the senator as he appeared on the stage, looking slightly embarrassed by the adulation of his audience, or wide on a shot of the enthusiastic crowd as it clambered to its feet in a standing ovation. Senator Sinclair moved to center stage and stood in front of a simple lectern to give his speech.

According to the time code on the endlessly analysed raw CNN tape it was 8:31:30:09 when someone on the far right side of the second row drew an odd-looking handgun from beneath his jacket and screamed out something in Arabic just before he fired. The man's voice was loud and clear in the high-ceilinged old hall.

'Bismillâh ir-rahmân ir-rahîm! allâhu akbar! lâ ilâha illâ-llâh!'

It took CNN in Atlanta barely five minutes to have the phrase translated: 'For the glory of Allah, most merciful and most compassionate! Allah is great! Allah is the one true god!' According to the translator the dialect was either Egyptian or Syrian.

Completely vulnerable behind the simple lectern, the stricken Senator Sinclair spun around and crumpled to the floor. The gunman, still screaming, ran toward the fire exit on the right-hand side of the stage. A total of six Blackhawk security guards fired at the man independently, striking him eleven times in the head, neck and chest. He was dead long before he reached the floor, bone, blood and brains spattering in every direction.

Two hundred and thirty-two people in the auditorium ran for the stairs and the emergency exits. The first person to reach the fallen senator was his mother, who had been watching from the wings.

She fell to her knees and gathered her only son into her arms. The CNN cameraman who was one of the very few who had remained in position caught the shot perfectly. So did a local freelance photographer named Patrick Henry Jefferson, who worked mostly, but not exclusively, for the *Bedford Mills Bulletin*, and who shot the scene from a slightly but crucially different angle that caught the scarlet blossom of blood on the senator's snow-white shirtfront and the perfect look of maternal shock and anguish on Kate Sinclair's aging, handsome, aristocratic face.

Within three minutes of the shooting a tape was uploaded on to YouTube and a tweet went out on Twitter purportedly from the group Jihad al-Salibiyya taking credit for the attack on the senator and telling the world that after striking abroad they were now bringing the fight and the cause to America.

By morning Jefferson's photograph appeared in every newspaper in the United States, from broadsheet to tabloid, including front page above the fold in the *New York Times*. For Kate Sinclair, the publicity was priceless.

Forty-eight hours after the event itself, reading a script hastily written by Morrie Adler, the president announced that Richard Pierce Sinclair had been appointed to the vice presidency of the United States. By the end of the week it was the cover of *People* magazine and *Time*. Within ten days Patrick Henry Jefferson had a New York agent and slightly more than half a million dollars in the bank.

25

'This is a very, very, bad idea,' said Peggy. She and Holliday were sitting in the cab of the old pickup truck they'd borrowed from Harry Moonblanket two days before. The battered old F150 was parked across from a plain white bungalow on West Federal Street in Bedford Mills. It was typical of most of the homes in the working-class Virginia town: slightly run-down, in need of paint and sitting on a half-acre lot crusted with a thin layer of old snow. A pink flamingo was frozen in place on the front lawn and the large area in the rear showed the hard, lumpy ruts of a vegetable garden. A carport with a fiberglass roof had been tacked on to the right side of the house like an afterthought. Sitting under the green, corrugated sheet of plastic was a brand-new, jet-black Porsche Turbo S.

'It's the only idea I have left,' said Holliday. He scratched at the heavy bristle on his cheeks and chin – his early attempt at a disguise. With the eye patch he looked quite frightening. 'We can't go back to the house in Georgetown, you can't go back to Rafi and I can't think of anyone else we can go to for help. We've got to figure this whole thing out by ourselves.'

'What good is this guy going to be?' Peggy asked. 'I still don't get it.'

'Neither do I,' answered Doc. 'There's something wrong about it, just like Brennan and Philpot and all the rest. This guy Jefferson was there. Maybe he saw something we missed. It's worth a shot.'

'And if he turns around and blows the whistle on us?'

'Then we're no worse off than we are right now,' said Holliday. 'On the run with no place to go.'

The gun used to shoot the newly appointed Vice President of the United States had been a short-barreled Walther P22 semiautomatic pistol that had been purchased quite legally at a local Bedford Mills gun store. The identification provided by the purchaser had identified him as Theodore Douglas Trepanik, a resident of Bocock, Virginia, a double-wide trailer park suburb of Lynchburg. Further investigation had uncovered that Trepanik was employed as a technician for Falwell Aviation at the nearby Lynchburg Regional Airport.

As it turned out, Theodore Douglas Trepanik had passed away ten months previously and his trailer home in Bocock had been ransacked during the funeral. Although his wife, AnnieRuth Trepanik, had taken care to cancel all of her late husband's credit cards, she hadn't noticed that both his driver's license and Social Security card were missing from his wallet. The wallet had been on his bedside table along with his keys and reading glasses on the night of the massive heart attack that killed him.

Subsequent to the shooting, investigators from the FBI and Homeland Security discovered that the assassin had been registered at the Bedford Mills Super 8, using the Trepanik identification. Searching the room they found a Kuwaiti passport in the name of Shamed Khalil Zubai, as well as a Dutch passport in the name of Ismael Aknikh. The Kuwaiti passport showed an entry into the United States four months previously while the Dutch passport showed an entry into JFK in New York only two weeks before.

On that basis it was assumed that the name on the Kuwaiti passport was an alias and that Ismael Aknikh was the man's real name. According to the Dutch authorities Aknikh was thirty-two years old, born in Amsterdam of Moroccan immigrant parents. Both his parents were dead and he had no other known family in Amsterdam or anywhere else in the Netherlands. Beyond that the killer was a cipher, as was the group who took credit for the Sinclair shooting, as well as the assassination of the Pope: Jihad al-Salibiyya.

Ismael Aknikh and the Jihad al-Salibiyya were the fulfillment of Richard Sinclair's most dire predictions: an extremist Muslim terrorist organization centered in the United States; a festering wound that up until the night of the shooting had gone unnoticed.

At a press conference held at Walter Reed hospital in Washington the day after the shooting Kate Sinclair stated unequivocally that the attempt on her son's life was a call to action. All the intelligence, counterterrorist and federal police agencies, including Homeland Security, had failed to identify either Jihad al-Salibiyya or the threat that it represented. According to her, the attack was nothing less than an early warning of much worse to come, a clarion call to the American people and their government that another 9/11 was in the making. In closing Kate Sinclair then made her own ominous prediction: Jihad al-Salibiyya's next attack would almost certainly come sooner rather than later.

'What if Jefferson is under surveillance?' Peggy asked nervously.

'Where?' Holliday laughed. 'The street is empty, the houses are a hundred yards apart and there's no one around. It's too damn cold. There's no place to hide around here and, besides, why would anyone want to put a newspaper photographer under surveillance?'

'So far we've had the CIA, the Secret Service, the Italian police and the Royal Canadian Mounted Police coming after us. Why not the Bedford Mills Police force?'

'Only one way to find out,' said Holliday. He zipped up his ski jacket, then climbed out of the car. Peggy followed, muttering under her steaming breath.

Holliday reached the rickety front steps and climbed up to the equally rickety stoop. The closed curtains on the front windows looked as though they'd been made from *Star Wars* sheets – tiny images of C3PO and R2D2 repeated endlessly. He glanced over at the Porsche. It was so new you could still see little scraps of the dealer's label on the passenger's side window. Give this Jefferson credit; he'd established his newfound wealth in record time. Holliday knocked on the door.

From inside the house he could hear the sound of a television blaring, the Brain telling his friend Pinky of yet another plan to take over the world. Hearing the Animaniac cartoon, Holliday realized that it was Saturday. Suddenly the door was jerked open by a man in red-and-blue pajamas, holding a half-eaten Pizza Pop in one hand. It smelled revolting and was oozing red sauce over the man's hand. He was in his forties, with thin brown hair and an oval face pitted from adolescent acne, and was wearing heavy wire-framed spectacles. He had a small mouth and no chin at all.

'What?' said the man.

'I'd like to talk to you about the town hall meeting you covered a few nights back.'

'Screw off,' said the man. 'I'm watching TV.' He slammed the door but Holliday managed to get his foot in first.

'It's important,' said Holliday, trying to keep his voice even.

'I told you, screw off!' said the man, pushing as hard as he could against the door. Holliday reached into the pocket of his jacket and pulled out the ancient Beretta Storm that Brennan had lent him. He poked the heavy barrel through the space in the door, aiming the old automatic at the man's midsection.

'Step inside the house,' said Holliday.

The man's eyes widened behind the glasses and his hands shot up in the air, squeezing the contents of the Pizza Pop out on to his hand and arm. He stumbled backward into the house. Holliday followed. Peggy came last, shutting the door behind her.

'Is this a robbery?'

'No.'

'Who are you? All the money's in the bank.'

'I told you it wasn't a robbery.'

'Then what do you want?'

Holliday sighed. Back to square one.

'We want to know what went on at the town hall meeting.'

'Can I sit down?'

'Certainly,' Holliday said with a nod.

Jefferson's living room was a slum. Newspapers were everywhere, Chinese take-out containers and pizza boxes were scattered around on tables and chairs, and the long, gold-colored couch had crumpled clothes draped over the back. He popped the empty shell of the Pizza Pop into his mouth, licked most of the goop off his hand and arm, then wiped off the rest with an old shirt hanging over the couch. He sat down. The television, a huge flat-screen on the opposite wall with equally massive speakers, blared out the Brain's most famous expression: 'Are you pondering what I'm pondering, Pinky?'

'Turn it off,' said Holliday, raising his voice over the

sinister musings of the hairless mouse. Jefferson manipulated the remote and the Brain cut off in midponder.

'The town hall meeting,' prompted Holliday.

'The senator got shot. The shot made him vice president. He got lucky; I got lucky.'

'How many pictures did you take?'

'Lots.'

'What does that mean?'

'Maybe two hundred or so. It's easy with digital.'

'What camera?' Peggy asked.

'Nikon D90.'

'How were you shooting? Single-frame or video?' The D90, Peggy knew, was one of the very few single-lens-reflex cameras capable of shooting something as complex as a full-length feature film. It had already been used to shoot more than one television commercial.

'I was shooting single frames in the beginning. Establishing stuff – you know, crowds, a few local big guys 'cause they want to feel important. You know. For the speech I went to video. That's how I caught the shot so well, the one of the senator and his mom. I just isolated that single frame and sold it.'

'Where's the rest?'

'On my computer.'

'Get it,' Holliday said.

The computer turned out to be a Sony Vaio Z with a gigantic 358-gigabyte hard drive. Peggy gingerly picked up the assorted garbage on the coffee table in front of the couch and carried it to the kitchen. She came back a moment later with a stricken look on her face.

'It's a war zone in there,' she whispered to Holliday. 'There are things *growing* in the sink and there's a nest of little spiders in the cutlery drawer.'

'Fruit flies, too,' said Jefferson, overhearing her comment. 'I got a real problem with them, as well. I don't know where all the damn bugs come from.' He frowned. 'Maybe I should call an exterminator or something.'

'Buy some Venus flytraps,' muttered Peggy

'Show me the pictures,' said Holliday.

Jefferson brought up a file and opened it. He began running through the pictures he'd taken. The first several dozen were taken from somewhere in the town hall parking lot and showed various individuals arriving. There was nothing of particular interest until Jefferson took up a position along with several other photographers in what had once been the orchestra pit. From that position he took a series of panoramic shots of the audience and then turned his attention up to the stage as Senator Sinclair appeared and took his place behind the podium.

'Go back,' said Peggy, looking over Jefferson's shoulder. 'Five frames or so.'

'Sure.' Jefferson clicked back through the pictures.

'There,' said Peggy, 'there's your man.' The photograph showed a man in his early thirties, blank-faced, white and beardless. He was dressed in chinos and a red nylon, quilted ski jacket, and was sitting on the far right of a middle aisle. He didn't look anything like the classic, wild-eyed jihadist. He looked like he worked as a checker at a Piggly Wiggly store and Peggy said so.

'Just the kind of freak the senator's been talking about,' said Jefferson. 'He was right enough about that.'

'Run the pictures ahead,' said Holliday.

Jefferson did as he was told. Twenty frames further on Holliday stopped him. 'This is the moment he gets hit.' In the photograph Sinclair was halfway through a clockwise pirouette, thrown backward away from the podium, almost pushed to the floor by the impact. The camera swerved, searching through the audience for the shooter, then went back to the prostrate senator, sprawled on the floor, left hand clutching his right shoulder.

'Back, slowly,' Holliday instructed.

Jefferson went back through the shots, back to the moment when Sinclair began to spin and fall.

'Stop.'

Jefferson stopped.

'There's the problem,' said Holliday. 'Our friend the Dutch Arab is sitting to the right of the stage. With Sinclair facing the audience he should have been hit on the left, not the right. And if he was shot from the right the force of the impact would have turned him counterclockwise, not clockwise. Not to mention the fact that this man Aknikh was sitting below the senator. The bullet's trajectory would have been up, not down. He would have been pushed off his feet and backward by the shot, not straight down.'

'Sounds like a lot of Kennedy-conspiracy gobbledy-gook,' snorted Jefferson.

'A lot of that gobbledygook, as you call it, still hasn't been logically answered,' Holliday said.

'So he wasn't shot by Aknikh?' Peggy asked.

'He couldn't have been,' answered Holliday. 'He was definitely shot from above and from the left.'

'The balcony,' said Jefferson.

'What balcony?'

'There's a balcony in the town hall. It's used for storage now.'

'Then he wasn't the shooter,' Peggy said. 'The whole thing was a setup.'

'It looks that way.' Holliday nodded. He turned to Jefferson. 'Who else has seen these photographs?'

'A guy from the FBI came around and said he had a warrant to impound them all as material evidence. He asked me if I had copies but I said no.'

'You lied?' Peggy asked.

'They're my pictures, aren't they?' Jefferson huffed.

'They may be your death warrant,' said Holliday. 'If I were you I'd hop in that new Porsche of yours and get the hell out of town.'

'Why? I haven't done anything wrong. I have my rights.'

'Maybe they'll put that on your tombstone,' said Holliday. 'The fact is, people in high places are laying in a cover-up and you and your pictures are a loose end.

These people snip off loose ends without even thinking about it.'

'Take his advice,' said Peggy. 'Pack your bags and run like hell.'

'Kate Sinclair had a script all along,' said Holliday as they drove away. 'First the Pope, which gets the vice president to travel to Rome, then the VP gets killed and then her son plays the wounded martyr.'

'And now *he's* the VP,' said Peggy.

'I've met Kate Sinclair,' said Holliday, his tone grim. 'She'd never go to all this trouble to wind up settling for second-best. The script doesn't have an ending . . . yet.'

They were less than a mile out of town when they were pulled over by a red-and-gold West Virginia State Police cruiser. Holliday waited for the inevitable; he had only his own identification and no papers for the old pickup truck. When they ran his name through the computers, all hell was going to break loose.

As the trooper approached, bundled up in his uniform parka, Holliday rolled down his window. The trooper bent down and looked inside the car. The man had a hard, lean face, his eyes hidden behind aviator-style mirrored sunglasses.

'Afternoon,' said the trooper. Out of the corner of his good eye Holliday saw the cop's partner approaching Peggy's side. A woman. The female trooper rapped on Peggy's window with the knuckle of her index finger. Peggy rolled down the window.

'What's the problem?' Holliday asked.

'No problem, Colonel Holliday.' He lifted up his hand and shot Holliday in the chest with an X3 Taser. In the passenger's seat Peggy was already going into convulsions. Within twenty seconds they were both unconscious.

PART THREE

Intermezzo

26

He knew very little. Wherever he was, it was windowless, utterly dark and concrete. He knew it was concrete because he could feel its surface under his hands. By his count it was twenty paces long and twelve paces wide. With his arms outstretched he couldn't touch the ceiling, which meant it was taller than eight feet. In the center of the unreachable ceiling was a blower vent that cycled off and on regularly. The air was cool, maybe a little less than seventy degrees. Chilly but bearable. There was a single door, a slab of metal with a felt strip glued to the foot to blot out any ambient light, with hinges on the outside. There was a metal, lidless, tankless toilet and a sink built into the end wall. He was in a large, purpose-built holding cell.

He knew a few other things. There was a vague but clear scent of aviation fuel blown in through the vent system, which meant his jail bunker was part of or very close to an airport facility of some kind. They'd taken his clothes and he seemed to be dressed in some oversized boiler suit and rubber thongs. Prison garb. By his own estimation he'd been under for close to forty-eight hours, but it could have been longer. He had no recollection of anything after the powerful jolt of electricity he'd received.

He didn't actually know but he was pretty sure what happened after that. The diplomatic term the State Department used these days was 'extraordinary rendition' and it had been around since Reagan's day. The simple term was 'kidnapping.' Take a subject off his home turf and do whatever you wanted to him in places just like this: black sites. Another euphemism, for 'torture chamber.'

He knew he could be almost anywhere. The CIA and the Joint Chiefs maintained black sites in almost every country in Europe and in a dozen or more sympathetic countries around the world. They used everything from Gulfstream Vs to Lears and even a couple of Boeing 'Biz' Jets wearing phony tail numbers and registrations.

The whole system had a whiff of Nazism to it and from the first time he'd encountered it back in Afghanistan it had offended Holliday's sense of military honor. You fought wars out in the open, not by skulking under rotting logs and damp stones. The CIA for its part was supposed to gather intelligence, not act like a modern-day version of the Spanish Inquisition.

Suddenly a wire-covered fluorescent fixture in the ceiling flickered to life, buzzing and clicking for a few seconds before giving out a steady light. Holliday blinked and covered his eyes in the sudden glare. A moment after the light came on the metal door opened and three men appeared dressed in generic BDUs that didn't look like any American camouflage pattern he'd ever seen. The caps were a little odd, too – the bills were quilted and they had fold-up earflaps. The design was clearly Eastern European – Russian, Czech or Bulgarian. He was somewhere behind what used to be called the Iron Curtain.

The first two men were carrying a small metal table. The third man carried a pair of metal straight chairs. They set them down in the center of the room directly under the light fixture.

'*Holloa.*' Nothing. Not Bulgarian.

'*Csak keveset beszélek magyaru.*' No response. Not Hungarian.

'*WyliÂż mi dupe, matkojebca.*' Definitely not Polish.

'*Dobra Den. Do prdele.*' A slightly turned head and a small look of surprise on one of the men carrying the table.

Gotcha, thought Holliday. They were Czech. The last time he'd been in the Czech Republic had been more than a year ago with the Sinclair girl on a wild-goose chase that had almost killed him.

The three men left the room. They also left the door open. Holliday didn't move from his position on the floor. A reed-thin figure, cigarette in hand, appeared in the doorway.

'Mrs Sinclair,' said Holliday as Kate Sinclair walked into the dungeonlike room. The tip of her cigarette glowed. She was wearing a very expensive Chanel pin-striped power suit.

'So nice to be remembered.' The elderly woman smiled.

'You must be very pleased,' said Holliday. 'A heartbeat away from the White House. Too bad he didn't earn the position on merit.'

'We're not here to talk about my son, Colonel. We're here to talk about you and something that rightfully belongs in our family.'

'How did you find us so quickly?' Holliday asked, avoiding the subject of Brother Rodrigues's notebook.

'We've had you watched for weeks.' She paused, blew smoke and inhaled again. 'Now, let us get down to business.'

'This is the second time I've been kidnapped by your little group,' said Holliday, stalling. The Sinclair matriarch sighed.

'I'd hardly call it a "little" group,' she answered. 'The membership of Rex Deus is considerably larger than you might think. We have a great many members in high places.'

'People who can make other people disappear? People who can fake assassination attempts?'

'You mean my son?' Sinclair shook her head. 'That was easy in comparison to killing the Pope.'

'If you were setting me up as some kind of patsy, why make me vanish now?' Holliday asked. 'I should be brought down in a hail of bullets somewhere, with the media invited to the finale.'

'All in good time, Colonel. We all have our parts to

play in our little production.' She dropped the short end of her cigarette on to the concrete floor and ground it under her heel. 'The notebook,' she said. 'The Templar notebook. My notebook.'

'It's not yours, and you know I'm not going to tell you anything about it.'

'Of course you will,' said the old woman. 'Eventually. We have leverage, you see. Your cousin.'

'What have you done with Peggy?'

'Don't worry, Colonel. She's as much a part of the story as you are. You'll be reunited later, I assure you.'

'Your assurances don't impress me much, Mrs Sinclair. You and Matoon and the rest of your crazy friends are all traitors.'

'Patriots,' answered Sinclair.

'Crap,' snorted Holliday.

'We're taking this country back, Colonel Holliday.'

'Back from who, exactly?'

'Back from the mongrel hordes that have been bringing our nation to its knees without us even knowing about it, much less caring. It's bread and circuses. People are watching reality shows about stupid women having eight or ten children at a time, parents are putting their children in balloons for publicity and meanwhile the country's going to hell. They watch pansy movies about trees that are alive or trees that can walk and talk. Half the country is Mexican, Jew or Arab. Our borders are leaking blood in one direction and drugs and illegal immigrants in the other, our money's been devalued and our foreign policy is all about appeasement. No one even speaks English anymore!'

Holliday saw something in her eyes then and he suddenly knew there was no point in trying to have a rational discussion or argument with this woman. Whether borne out of too much power or from something carried in the blood, Kate Sinclair was utterly and irrevocably mad, as mad as any fundamentalist Muslim putting out a fatwa on a cartoon show, as paranoid as Richard Nixon had been at his worst moments, as crazy as a loon.

'You're insane,' he said quietly. 'And you're an accessory to murder. You're no better than Charlie Manson.'

'I am the avatar of destiny,' said the Sinclair woman ponderously. 'And history will absolve me.'

Fidel Castro's final remark in his own defense at his first trial, and a sentiment expressed by Hitler, Stalin and Rasputin. Good company. All dictators, all with God complexes and all utterly insane.

'So what's the plan?' Holliday sighed.

'I intend to recover my birthright from you. To that end we are moving you to Pankrác Prison immediately.' Sinclair smiled blandly and lit another cigarette. 'You've heard of it?'

'A nineteenth-century hellhole on the outskirts of Prague,' said Holliday. 'The Nazis used it and later on it was a KGB interrogation center.'

'It's now owned by Blackhawk Security.'

'You, in other words,' said Holliday. He smiled wanly.

'Presumably I can expect a little in the way of advanced interrogation techniques – a little waterboarding, maybe?'

'Certainly.' Sinclair smiled. 'But you won't be the recipient. Miss Blackstock will.' She called out a single harsh command in Czech. Three guards suddenly appeared, two carrying automatic rifles, one carrying shackles and chains.

'Your chariot has arrived, Colonel,' said Kate Sinclair. 'Time to load you on to the bus.'

The windowless old prison bus took the road from the old Příbram airport at Dlouhá Lhota north through the old forests of the foothill country in central Bohemia. The bus was like something out of an old chain-gang movie: driver and guard segregated from the prisoners by a chain-link grating with apertures just big enough to poke the barrel of a shotgun through.

The prisoner entrance was through a heavily secured door in the rear of the bus with its own little caged enclosure for a second guard, who was also armed with a short-barreled riot gun and controlled the master lock that opened the threaded shackles and chains that secured the prisoners.

The prisoners themselves occupied long benches that were bolted to the floor on either side of the bus. The benches in turn were divided into narrow cubicles by sheets of gray steel etched with the handcuffed graffiti of a thousand previous occupants. It was, in effect, a jail on wheels, walls made of armor plate, the windshield made of bulletproof double-thickness glass and the heavy tires puncture proof.

Tonight there were seven people from the black-site bunker on the bus: Peggy, Holliday and five rumpled-looking young men with black cotton bags tied securely over their heads, babbling blindly together in Farsi, their voices strained with panic.

Holliday was shackled directly across from Peggy on the bus in the forward section.

'Are you sure about this Pankrác place?' Peggy asked.

'There's no reason for Sinclair to have lied.'

'But what's the point?' Peggy asked. 'Why doesn't she just get rid of us?'

Holliday shrugged. 'She will, as soon as she gets the information she wants.'

Peggy shuffled her feet, pulling slightly on the shiny steel shackles threaded through eyebolts along the length of the bus. Her movements pulled on the chain around one of the hooded men's ankles and his head jerked in her direction.

'Ann ru sar et, kiram tu kunet cos eh lash jende!'

'Torke char, arabe kassif!' Peggy yelled down the bus. The man who'd cursed at her turned his hooded head around and the other four laughed at her quick and unexpected comeback to the man's insult.

They could hear the ringing of a railway-crossing bell and the bus slowed to a stop. After several long minutes the guard and the driver began talking. Holliday leaned forward on the hard metal seat and peeked around the edge of the metal divider. He could vaguely make out the flashing red lights of the railroad crossing and the lowered red-and-white-striped barriers.

'What's up?' Peggy asked from the other side of the bus.

'Some glitch at a railway crossing,' answered Holliday. 'The lights are flashing and the barriers are down but there's no train.'

'What are they arguing about?' Peggy asked.

'Whose responsibility getting off the bus and checking it out is, at least as far as I can tell,' replied Holliday.

'Who's winning?' Peggy laughed,

'The driver, I think,' said Holliday.

Sighing melodramatically the guard got up from his seat and the driver pushed a button on his control panel. The hydraulic double doors hissed open and the guard went down the three steps to the outside.

The high, explosive round came through the open door, vaporized the guard and kept going until it detonated against the far side of the driver's compartment, sending a long spray of blood, debris and yellowish bony shrapnel the length of the bus.

'Oh, crap,' whispered Peggy, ducking back into her narrow little cubicle.

Holliday knew what she meant. Someone was trying to break the hooded men – probably Afghani Talibans or Al-Qaeda – out of custody, and to their rescuers he and Peggy would be useless baggage, and infidel baggage at that. Holliday pulled hard at the chains of his shackles but nothing budged. A second explosion rocked the bus on its heavy wheels. Holliday risked a peek. Someone had blasted open the rear prisoners' doors. The rear guard, protected in his cage, poked the barrel of his riot gun out through the grate and fired blindly. There was a brief moment of silence and then Holliday heard the familiar rasp and ping of a hand grenade pin being pulled. There was a faint knocking sound and then a flat, crumpling explosion. The chains shackling him to the floor went slack.

There was a final, smaller explosion from the front of the bus and then absolute silence. In a single, surreal moment Holliday could actually hear the sound of crickets outside in the forest. He stayed well back in his little metal enclosure and silently motioned Peggy to do the same thing.

The strange silence went on for a long minute, and then there was a harsh whispering voice: *'Yellah! Yellah!'* Someone speaking Arabic.

The hooded prisoners began to chatter, some of them laughing, and Holliday felt a slackness in the chains threaded through the I-bolt at his feet. There was more chatter and then silence. Only a few seconds passed and then there was the stuttering hammer of an automatic weapon.

'What's happening?' Peggy whispered.

'I don't think our Farsi friends got the reception they were hoping for,' said Holliday.

There was another period of silence and then the sound of booted footsteps coming in their direction. Three men appeared, all carrying folding stock Czech Skorpion submachine guns and all dressed identically in black, wearing Kevlar body armor and black balaclavas covering their faces. One of them appeared to be a woman.

One of the men stopped in front of Holliday's little enclosure. He slung his light machine gun over his shoulder, then took a pair of heavy-duty bolt cutters off his belt, silently snipped the shackles at Holliday's feet and threaded the chain through his handcuffs. He took the bolt cutters and slid them back on to his belt, then reached into the side pocket of his combat trousers and took out a small key. He unlocked the handcuffs and took a step back.

'You're free, Colonel Holliday.'

Holliday looked at him strangely. There was something in the rasping voice that seemed familiar.

'Don't recognize me, Colonel?'

The man reached up and pulled off the knitted balaclava that covered his head. He smiled down at his old adversary and quoted from the New Testament: *'And when he thus had spoken, he cried with a loud voice, Lazarus, come forth. And Lazarus walked.'*

The man standing over him laughed, the scar on his

throat as thick as a curled red worm. 'I was in bandages for months.'

It was Antonin Pesek, the Czech assassin he'd shot and killed in Venice more than a year before.

27

The Penzion Akát was a tobacco-colored, stucco-fronted hotel that overlooked the railway tracks and the streetcar terminal at the Smichov metro station in western Prague. The building was without any architectural distinction whatsoever – one step above a flophouse where a noisy night's sleep could be had for a few crowns, and where the cracked china rattled on the tables in the cafeteria-like dining room every time a streetcar rumbled by. It was totally anonymous, a place for traveling salesmen and tourists without much money.

'He's dead?' Holliday asked, coming out of the hotel room's coffin-sized bathroom.

'Double tap: one to the heart; one to the head. Very professional,' said Pat Philpot, munching on a chicken leg from the KFC down the road. Peggy was sprawled in an overstuffed armchair on the opposite side of the room and Antonin Pesek, their savior on the road to Pankrác Prison, stood beside the grimy window, watching the street below.

'But why kill him? He didn't know anything. He was a local photographer who didn't know what he had.'

'Jefferson knew *you*, Doc. That's what got him killed.

Originally you were meant to be a fall guy. Now you and Ms Blackstock are flies in the Sinclairs' ointment.'

'The whole thing is too Byzantine,' said Peggy. 'It's a fairy tale, something out of the Brothers Grimm.'

'The world is a Grimm place.' Pesek smiled, briefly turning away from the window. 'In the sixteenth century a Bohemian countess named Elizabeth Báthory liked to bathe in the blood of virgins she lured to her castle. As a serial killer she was much more prolific than your Theodore Bundy. Now that is truly Byzantine, my friend.'

'So, where do you fit in the grand scheme of things?' Holliday asked Philpot.

The CIA analyst picked up a piece of chicken, then thought better of it and dropped the battered lump back into the bucket on the table. He wiped his lips with a napkin and belched discreetly.

'The Sinclair family has been a plague in D.C. since the beginning. They've got links and connections that go back to Donovan and Dulles and the old OSS boys – the Ivy League spies. They stuck themselves on the intelligence community like a flea on a dog and they never let go. There's been a cadre of Rex Deus members in Congress, the Senate, Justice and the Pentagon for decades. The old senator was too corrupt to ever make a move on his own – like Joe Kennedy and the bootlegging years. But he had the right connections and before he died he passed the mantle on to his grandson, and he passed it on to his wife, the venerable

Kate. Now she's finally making the move that the old man dreamed about.'

'Putting her son in the White House.' Holliday nodded.

Philpot gave a hollow laugh and tossed a chicken bone into the wastebasket beside him. 'The White House? That's just the beginning.'

'What's that supposed to mean?' Peggy asked.

'There was a movie a long time ago, back in the early sixties,' said Philpot. 'It was called *Seven Days in May*.'

'Never heard of it,' said Peggy.

'Ah, youth.' Philpot smiled, judiciously plucking another piece of fried chicken from the bucket.

'I remember. It was about a military coup d'etat,' said Holliday. 'A general doesn't like the way a milksop president is dealing with the Russians over some missile treaty, so he plots to take over the United States by force of arms.'

'That's the one,' said Philpot. 'And Kate Sinclair's about to do the same thing with the help of her little buddies in the Central Intelligence Agency and the Pentagon, General Angus Scott Matoon in particular. She doesn't care much for the way the present administration is giving away the store. She thought she had the power on Capitol Hill to get the poor bastard impeached. Now she's trying a back door to put her son on the throne and her behind it.'

'In the movie the reason for the coup d'etat was a lily-livered missile treaty the general honestly believed was crippling America's power. What's Kate Sinclair's excuse?'

'What do you think was the best thing that ever happened to George W? What got him elected for a second term and allowed him to start a phony war in Eye-Raq. The best thing that could happen to any president you can name?'

'Bin Laden and 9/11,' offered Peggy. 'Saddam Hussein and the phantom weapons of mass destruction.'

'A common enemy,' said Holliday.

'A rallying cry. One if by land, two if by sea, the English are coming! The English are coming!' Peggy said. 'Jihad al-Salibiyya.'

'The whole thing's crazy,' said Holliday. 'Does she really think her son getting winged by a fake terrorist is enough leverage to overthrow the government?' He shook his head. 'There isn't one politician in the U.S. of A. who is that stupid.'

'Which is saying something,' rasped Pesek, still standing by the window. 'Since there are many very stupid politicians there. More than here.'

'She'd need another 9/11 to pull it off,' said Peggy. 'Something huge.'

'Which is precisely what she intends.' Philpot nodded, leaned back in his groaning chair, wiped his hands on a napkin and lit a cigarette. 'Except this time it won't be a rich Saudi Arabian with daddy issues and a teeny-tiny weenie. This time it'll be a homegrown, Kansas-corn-fed, little-mosque-on-the-prairie domestic rag head, just like the poor martyred Senator Sinclair has been fog horning about for the past couple of years. The prez will be pressured by Matoon to declare martial law and if he won't do it he'll be impeached and replaced by the young senator. He's already in the VP's chair. There's only one thing left.'

'Tom's Hill,' whispered Holliday.

'What the hell is Tom's Hill?' Philpot scowled, irritated that the flow of his narrative had been interrupted.

'When we tossed Tritt's house in Lyford Cay –'

'*You what?*' Philpot stared, owl-eyed.

'We tossed Tritt's place at Lyford Cay. . . . I'll tell you about it some other time. Anyway, I found a CD with a whole lot of information about a place called Tom's Hill. I didn't think much of it at the time, but now . . .'

'Now what?' Philpot asked.

'According to Tritt's CD, Tom's Hill has a population of only a few thousand but almost all of them are employed by a company called the King Fertilizer Corporation. King Fertilizer is the largest manufacturer of ammonium nitrate in the United States.'

'Dear God,' said Philpot, looking horrified.

'What's so bad about that?' Peggy asked. 'What does fertilizer have to do with any of this?'

'Because ammonium nitrate is the basic ingredient for ANFO,' said Pesek. 'The explosive that was used in your Oklahoma City bombings.' The dapper-looking assassin shook his head sadly. 'You Americans really are crazy. The sale of such fertilizer has been regulated in

Europe for years, but still anyone in your country can buy it by the ton, no questions asked.' He poked back the sheer curtains and looked down at the street again. 'Speaking about crazy Americans, it looks as though we have company.'

Philpot was instantly alert. 'What are they driving?' He drew a Glock 9 from his shoulder holster and jacked a round into the chamber.

'Lincoln Navigator,' answered Pesek. He drew his own weapon, a Beretta 92, and took a stubby little suppressor out of his suit jacket pocket.

'Blackhawk,' said Philpot. 'Either that or our guys. How many?'

'Four,' said Pesek. 'Three in a group; one trailing.'

'What are they carrying?'

'Backpacks.'

'What kind of ordnance, do you think?'

'Probably FN P90s. Suppressed. The BIS uses them.'

'BIS?' Peggy asked.

'*Bezpečnostní informační služba*,' said Holliday. 'The Czech Secret Police.'

'How do we do this?' Philpot asked.

The Czech assassin didn't hesitate for a second. 'We need to contain them. The trailing man will come up the stairs to block any attempt at escape. The other three will take the elevator and come into the room. They'll have a key card.'

'How can you be so sure?' Peggy asked.

'Because you can bribe anyone in Prague, Ms Blackstock. Hotel clerks come very cheap, young lady, I assure you.' He nodded to Holliday. 'You and your cousin into the bathroom. Lie down in the bathtub. Mr Philpot, you take the stairwell.'

'And you, *Pane* Pesek?' Philpot asked.

Pesek smiled and briefly touched his well-groomed mustache. 'I shall be in my own room across the hall.'

Philpot nodded and left the room.

'Quickly,' said Pesek. 'It will be soon now.'

Holliday grabbed Peggy by the elbow and they headed for the bathroom. Pesek left the room, locking the door behind him.

'Didn't he try to kill you once?' Peggy asked, kneeling down in the old cast-iron tub.

'More than once actually,' said Holliday, climbing in after her. 'Not to mention the fact that I tried to kill him. I thought I had, as a matter of fact.'

'And you still trust him?'

'I don't have to,' said Holliday. 'Philpot's paying for his services.'

'What does that have to do with it?'

'Pesek's a pro. He survives on his reputation. He betrays the people who pay his fee and he never gets another job. He's blackballed for life and probably winds up getting a hit taken out on him.'

'Murderers with ethics. What's next?' Peggy sighed.

'Shut up and bend down,' said Holliday, crouching lower. 'The bad guys will be here any second.'

There was nothing but the faint clicking sound of the magnetic lock popping to announce their arrival and then a dull rattling sound like fifty ball bearings in a washing machine. Holes appeared in the bathroom door, the medicine chest mirror exploded and then there was silence.

'*Do prdele!*' said an angry voice.

'*Do piče!*' said another voice.

There was a brief silence and then the sound of Pesek's voice. '*Dobrý den, Zdvořilí pánové,*' said the assassin politely. There was a startled exclamation and then three clicks, like someone slowly winding an old-fashioned alarm clock, followed by three more.

'What the hell was that?' Peggy whispered, crouched down like a frog in the tub.

Holliday stood up. He could have been melodramatic and told her it was the sound of death, but he stayed silent.

'It's safe,' said Pesek. 'You can come out now, Colonel Holliday.'

Holliday stepped out of the tub and opened the bathroom door. Peggy followed him.

'Holy crap!' Peggy said.

There were bleeding bodies all over the floor.

Pesek stood in the short hallway leading to the front door, unscrewing the suppressor from his weapon.

'Don't touch anything,' he said. 'And come with me

quickly. There are probably more where these came from.' He nodded at the corpses bleeding into the worn carpeting. 'If not more of them, the police will arrive eventually. We must get you on your way.'

'Where are we going?' Holliday asked. 'We have no papers, no passports – nothing.'

'Aix-les-Bains,' said Philpot, stepping into the room and surveying the damage. 'I have a friend there.'

28

Billy Tritt and a boy named Stephen Barnes, one of the more technically minded of the skinhead, psychopathic members of Maine's Right Arm, stopped the stolen AT&T Southwest van beside the big junction box on Highway 18, a mile from the Tom's Hill plant of the King Fertilizer Corporation. Tritt switched off the engine and turned to the young man beside him. Both Tritt and Barnes were wearing official AT&T uniforms and hard hats taken from the bodies of the former occupants of the van.

'You know what to do, soldier?' Tritt asked firmly.

'Yessir.' Barnes nodded. 'Open the junction box and look for a yellow T1 line cable. Where the yellow cable joins the main bundle I insert a three-way and run a secondary line back to you in the van.'

'Good,' said Tritt. 'Got your tools?'

'Yessir.' Barnes patted the weighty belt around his waist.

'The three-way?'

Barnes nodded and dug into the upper pocket of his slightly bloodstained uniform pocket and found the large, chrome connector piece. He held it up. 'Right here, sir,' the young man answered proudly. He hadn't graduated from Lincoln Technical Institute because of money and some drug problems, but he knew what he was doing. If he'd graduated he could have worked for any cable TV company in the state, although the two years at Wyndham Correctional really screwed him when it came to getting jobs.

'Good. Off you go, then, soldier.'

Barnes, eager as a 260-pound, muscle-bound puppy, clambered out of the van and set up the traffic cones just like he'd been told, even though there wasn't a car for miles. The scenery was bleak – endless stretches of windswept, dirty snow over stubbled cornfields that went on forever.

The junction box was a big green thing just off the shoulder. Barnes took a short crowbar out of his tool belt, snapped the lock and got down to work, looking for the T1 line that fed the fertilizer plant's routing information to the servers at the API Logistics center in Wichita. API was the dedicated contract carrier that shipped King Fertilizer's product to its various locations.

It took Barnes fifteen minutes to find the T1 line and another ten to feed a line from the box to the little porthole in the side of the van. Tritt took the cable, crimped on a connector and fit the line on to his Hewlett-Packard laptop. Within a minute or so he'd made his way on to the server at King Fertilizer and had diverted four container loads of ammonium nitrate prills to the dedicated King Fertilizer International docks in Baltimore.

A few more keystrokes and he set the proper authorization codes for the drivers he would send for the shipment, routing the fertilizer from Baltimore to Maine via Triskip Carriers, a container barging service that served multiple shippers carrying mixed cargo from Baltimore to New Jersey, New York, Boston and Portland, then connecting onward to Halifax and Montreal.

With those few actions in the middle of the frozen Kansas hinterland, Tritt had put 270,000 pounds of the primary explosive element for the biggest truck bomb ever made into the system. Within the next seven days it would arrive in Portland. During those seven days the other members of Maine's Right Arm would collect the 2,700 gallons of diesel fuel necessary to add to the explosive-grade prills in the containers. The resulting explosion, effectively ignited, would be roughly one thousand times greater than the Oklahoma City bombing.

When Tritt was done, he disconnected the computer and rapped on the side of the truck. The cable snaked out through the little porthole and disappeared. Tritt opened the driver's-side door of the truck and stepped out into the cold, his breath hanging like fog in the still air. He watched as young Barnes gathered up the extra cable, then closed the door of the junction box. He replaced the combination lock he'd snapped off with the crowbar with an identical one from his jacket pocket.

'All done,' Barnes said, grinning at Tritt. The assassin

looked up at the dull gray sky. It was beginning to snow. Big, wet flakes. Perfect.

'Good job. Now drop the extra cable on to the ground.'

'Beg pardon?' Barnes said.

'Drop it, soldier.'

'Sure, sir,' the young man said, frowning and obviously confused. He did as he was told, however, dropping the extension cable on to the snowy ground. Tritt unzipped his jacket, took the Mossberg Bullpup shotgun out of its sling and shot Barnes in the head. From the neck up Stephen Barnes vanished, pieces of flesh, brains and skull as small as shining pennies went rising into the air like a cloud of spray, settling invisibly on the snow behind and beyond the rest of the young man's body.

The corpse crumpled like a Kleenex. Tritt replaced the shotgun in its sling under his arm and went to the corpse. He took a pair of large biohazard bags out of his pocket and the small hatchet off the dead boy's tool belt. He neatly hacked off the boy's hands, putting one into each biohazard bag.

He sealed the bags, put one in each pocket of his down jacket and then picked up the wound-up length of cable. He used his toe to nudge the corpse into the ditch by the side of the road. Eventually, after a few more nudges, the boy's body toppled over into the ditch.

Tritt kicked snow into the ditch until the headless,

handless body was roughly covered. With luck the boy's decomposed and leathery remains wouldn't be discovered until spring planting time. It would probably be longer than that before the corpse was identified, if ever.

He gathered up the cones, got back into the truck, switched on the engine and the heater, then tossed the coil of cable and the traffic cones into the back of the vehicle. He headed east, toward Wichita Airport. He'd park the truck in the long-term lot, wipe it down and that would be that.

His basic kit was in an overnight bag in a locker there. He'd rent something from one of the big agencies, drive a couple of states over and buy a food processor in some anonymous Wal-Mart. He'd grind up poor Steve's hands and flush the pureed remains down the toilet in an equally anonymous motel at least one state over from where he'd shopped at the Wal-Mart.

He'd rinse the food processor in a bath of Clorox in a motel one state farther on, and finally he'd donate the food processor to a Goodwill in some big city he was passing through. It was overdoing it, Tritt knew, but better too much than too little, as his old grandma used to say, whether it was for making pies or anything else in life.

'You've got to be kidding me,' muttered Chief Randy Lockwood of the Winter Falls Police Department. 'Why is he coming here?'

Mayor Dotty Blanchette sighed and leaned back in her chair. 'Because Mr Know-It-All went to the Abbey School and it's his fortieth graduation reunion.'

'I don't think you're supposed to call the President of the United States that kind of name.'

'Just stating a fact. And, anyway, he's the lame-duck President of the United States.'

Lockwood sighed. 'When exactly?'

'Ten days. Advance team arrives in a week. Apparently it's the annual grudge game scheduled between Winter Falls High and the Abbey School and he's been invited to drop the puck. A photo op, I guess. I'm supposed to be his escort since his wife is off in Thailand or somewhere, trying to save twelve-year-old hookers from AIDS or something.'

'He was hockey, right, not football?' Randy asked. 'I barely remember him.'

'Yeah, he was captain of the Abbey School hockey team. The only reason they made him captain was because his old man bought the hockey rink for the school,' said Dotty. 'He got into Andover, but the Abbey had a better hockey team so he spent four years there before he legacy'd his way into Yale. Thought he was God's gift to women, too, which he was, of course. Handsome as hell and all sorts of charisma. He could smile a girl into bed. Not me, though. Too charming by a long shot.'

'Women can be so cruel.' Lockwood grinned.

'Water under the bridge,' she said. 'The good old days. Best forgotten.'

'How's he getting here?' Randy asked. 'When his dad came up in the summers he always took a float plane. The lake is frozen, so that's out.'

'In their great wisdom the Secret Service haven't seen fit to tell me a goddamn thing at this point,' said Dotty. She leaned forward in her big, old, leather swivel chair and took a long sip from her stainless-steel Starbucks cup. The coffee was obviously cold and old and she winced as she sucked down the bitter brew. 'Sometimes I think I'm pickled in caffeine,' she said. 'It's the only thing keeping me alive. Not easy running this town, even in the winter, let alone without presidents tripping over their own feet.'

'I think it would be a good job,' said Lockwood with a twinkle in his eye. 'All those perks – chain of office, getting to ride in one of Mark Horrigan's Cadillacs at the head of the Trout Parade every year.'

'Speaking of Horrigan, did you ever find his kid?'

'Vanished into the clear blue,' said Randy. 'Word is his dad sent him down to his mother's place in Florida.'

'Going to go after him?'

'Why rock the boat?' Randy shrugged. 'He'll get into trouble down there soon enough. Let them handle it.' He got up from his seat in front of Mayor Dotty's desk. City Hall was in the old Municipal Building and through Dotty's arched windows he could see across the square to the parked cars on Main Street. Time to give out a few parking tickets to swell the town's treasury. 'Besides,' he said, smiling, 'I've got more important things to think about than Tommy Horrigan. I've got to look after the GD President of the United States.'

29

The first person to see Aix-les-Bains for what it was worth was probably a Roman centurion on his way into Gaul from Italy to conquer the unruly barbarians. When he mustered out of the army he returned to the pretty lakeside spot, built a pool over the hot springs, called it Aquae Grantianae and a tradition was born.

Located under the shadow of Mont Revard by the shores of Lake Bourget, the largest body of fresh water in France, the little town of Aix-les-Bains has been soothing the arthritic joints of its wealthy patrons for the last two thousand years. It came into particular favor in the 1880s after a visit from Queen Victoria of England. She decided she liked it so much Her Royal Majesty attempted to buy it from the French government. They graciously declined and then built a casino and a racetrack to further fleece the charming resort's guests, renaming the hot springs Royale-les-Bains.

Special trains arrived from Paris full of high society who came to paddle on the plage. Steamers churned their way across the English Channel, filled with the straw hat–and-tennis set, intent on whiling away the hot summer months in the refreshing Alpine air as wives cheated on husbands, husbands on wives and best friends on each other while Clara Butt sang 'The Keys of Heaven' on the gramophone. It was la belle epoque, and as with all epoques, it faded away like an old soldier, the gilt in the ceilings beginning to peel, the marble floors cracking and the pipes carrying the hot springwater making a terrible clanking noise and sounding much like the joints of the patrons it had once serviced. The small and ancient town hidden away in the mountains was virtually forgotten, which was exactly why Mr Richard Pyx, the document provider, lived there. That and the town's proximity to his numbered bank accounts less than a hundred miles away in Geneva, Switzerland.

Peggy Blackstock awoke as the first pink rays of the sun rose over the mountains and craggy hills that marked the edge of the French Alps of the Haute Savoie. She had made her way to the backseat of the Prague rental Mercedes somewhere along the way and Holliday was now sitting in the front with Philpot, who was still behind the wheel.

'Good morning,' the chubby man said brightly as she sat up, blinking and looking around. 'Almost there.'

'Where is there?' Peggy yawned. She stared out the window. They were on a high mountain road. To the left banks of heavy forest tilted upward; below, in the reaching light she could see the geometric outlines of a town nestled at the far end of a long, wide lake.

'Aix-les-Bains,' answered Philpot. A narrow gravel road appeared on the left and Philpot took it, guiding the old Mercedes up between the scruffy pines, the road winding around outcroppings of rock until they reached a broad, flat meadow on a small plateau. Directly ahead of them was a classic French country house right out of *Toujours Provence*: a rectangular building of old whitewashed stone, a few deep windows and a steep-pitched tile roof. At the end of the lane a roughly constructed carport with a green, rippled fiberglass roof sagged against the side of the house. Under it, gleaming in deep, dark blue was an expensive two-seater Mercedes SLK 230.

'Whoever this guy is, he must do pretty well for himself.' Holliday grunted, spotting the car.

'Pretty well indeed,' Philpot agreed. 'The war on terrorism declared by our recent leader had much the same effect as Woodrow Wilson declaring war on alcohol. It's always been the same way: one way or the other war is good for business. There's a great deal of demand for Rich's skills these days.'

'Rich?' Holliday asked.

'Richard Arbruthnot Pyx. It's too absurd to be anything but his real name.' Philpot laughed.

There was a wooden sign over the door, a name chiseled out in neat letters: LE VIEUX FOUR.

'The Old Kiln,' Philpot translated, without being asked. He pulled their Mercedes in behind the sports car and switched off the engine, the old diesel dying with a shudder and a cough. They climbed out into the cool of early morning, Holliday and Peggy stretching and yawning, Philpot lighting a cigarette. Pyx must have had some kind of early warning system because he was already waiting at the door, a broad smile on his friendly face. He certainly didn't look like a forger to Peggy. In fact, he looked more like a rock star on vacation than anything else. He was tall, slightly stooped, wearing jeans and a white shirt with the tails hanging out. There were sandals on his bare feet. He had thick, tousled, dark hair and two days' growth of beard, and behind round, slightly tinted glasses a pair of extraordinarily intelligent brown eyes. He looked to be somewhere in his late twenties or early thirties.

'Paddy!' Pyx said happily. 'Brought me some business, have you? Or just stopping in for a *pain au chocolat* and a cup of my excellent coffee?' On top of the good looks he had an Irish accent like Colin Farrell's.

'Business actually, but I don't think we'd turn down pastry and coffee.' He turned to Peggy and Holliday. 'Would we?' He introduced them, one after the other, and Pyx stood aside and ushered them into his kitchen. It was relentlessly low-tech with the exception of a bright red Gaggia espresso maker that was hissing and steaming on a simple plank countertop that looked as old as the house. The floor was dark flagstone, the ceiling plaster with exposed oak beams, the walls whitewashed stone. There was an ancient refrigerator, a freestanding pantry, a separate oven and a large, professional-looking set of gas burners.

Herbs hung from nails, copper-bottom pots and

cast-iron frying pans hung from the beams and early morning sunlight poured in through a single, multi-paned window with rippled old glass set into the wall beside the grill. Outside Peggy could hear birds chirping. At any other time it would have been an idyllic moment in the country; right now it was edged with fear, worry and terror. Pyx sat them down at a yellow pine kitchen table in the middle of the room, brought out a plate of warm and aromatic chocolate croissants from the pantry and busied himself at the exotic-looking coffee maker for a moment, making them each a large, foaming cup of cappuccino, which he then brought to the table. He sat down himself, dunked one end of a croissant into his coffee and took a bite of the soggy pastry. Peggy did the same. There was so much butter in the flaky crust that it really did seem to melt in her mouth. Philpot took two.

'So,' said Pyx. 'You don't look like the kind of people Paddy here usually brings to me, but I've learned that appearances can be deceiving.'

'Passports,' said Philpot, his mouth full. 'And all the other paraphernalia.'

'Talk to me,' said Pyx, turning to Peggy.

'What do you mean?'

'Say something – Peter Piper picked a peck of pickled peppers.'

'I don't understand.'

'I'm trying to see if you have an accent.'

'I don't.'

'Depends on your point of view. In Castleknock I wouldn't have an accent but here I do. Speak.'

Peggy did as she was told.

'Westchester, New York, but you've recently spent a lot of time in Israel.' Pyx nodded.

Peggy stared. 'How did you know that?'

'Vast experience,' he said, grinning. 'It's what I do.' He turned to Holliday. 'Now you,' he said. 'Same thing.' Holliday grudgingly repeated the line of doggerel.

'Born in West Virginia but raised in upstate New York, right?'

'Close enough.' The man was dead-on, of course. He'd spent his first four years in Norfolk after his father came out of the navy and before he joined the railway.

'Neither of you have an accent that anyone's going to be able to pick up unless they're an expert, which most U.S. passport control officers aren't. We'll make you Canadians. Either of you done much traveling there?'

'I've been to Toronto a few times, and Montreal,' said Peggy.

Pyx turned to Holliday. 'You?'

'Same.' He frowned. 'Why not make us Americans?'

'They've got access to U.S. databases. I'm presuming you're persona non grata there at the moment or you'd be using your own names.'

'It's a long story.'

'Aren't they all?' said the Irishman. 'Ontario, then.

Easy. They've got simple birth certificates and driver's licenses. You'll have to have a health card, as well.'

'Health card?'

'It's free. Ontario government. Very efficient about having the cards, and for some sort of privacy-act reason they're not allowed to cross-index the databases between the bureaucracies. Good photo ID. I can do the health card, the driver's license and the birth certificate right here.'

Peggy didn't understand a word of what the man was saying.

'The passports,' Philpot prodded.

'Even simpler.' Pyx smiled. 'But first the photographs.' He stood up and led the way to the rear of the house. They turned into an L-shaped hallway lined with bookcases leading to the bedroom, but instead of moving on Pyx stopped at the turn of the L and pulled out a volume from the bookcase. There was a faint clicking sound and the case swung open on a completely invisible hinge.

'Open sesame,' said Pyx, and stood aside to let them enter. He followed and shut the bookcase doorway behind them. Peggy looked around the secret room. It was large, fifteen feet on a side, and windowless. Work-height counters ran around three walls with built-in shelves above. There were dozens of neatly labeled binders on the shelves, color coded, and in one corner there was an array of half a dozen large, flat-screen monitors. Beneath the monitors on steel racks there was a row of featureless black computer servers, each one with a blinking green light on its front surface. The counters were loaded with an array of peripherals from large flatbed scanners to photo light tables and several very professional-looking color printers and photo printers. Along the far wall was a complex three-screen LightWorks computer editing console for motion pictures.

'You're awfully free with your secrets,' said Holliday. 'We could have been cops.'

'You're not,' said Pyx. 'Paddy would have killed you by now if you had been. He also let me know you were coming, and if he hadn't I would have known about it from the moment you turned off the main road.' He smiled, clearly taking no offense at Holliday's comment. 'And I wouldn't have greeted you with coffee and chocky croissants, believe me.' He shrugged and nodded toward the LightWorks console. 'Besides, I have a perfectly valid film-editing enterprise going on. There's nothing here that's particularly incriminating except on the drives, and I can dump data faster than any copper could ever get into this room.'

Holliday frowned. 'I didn't see him call you.'

'He text messaged me from Pilsen. I gather you had a little trouble in the land of bad Czechs.'

'Some,' said Holliday.

Peggy's attention was suddenly drawn to a large camera mounted on a professional tripod against the wall, facing the bookcase doorway. 'That's a Cambo Wide

DS with a Schneider 35 XL Digitar lens, and a Phase One P25 medium-format back.' Her eyes widened. 'That's, what, thirty grand?'

'More like thirty-five,' said Pyx. 'Just about the most expensive point-and-shoot you can buy.'

'I'd hardly call it point-and-shoot,' said Peggy.

To Holliday it looked like a fat lens attached to a big, flat, square piece of metal. It didn't really look like a camera at all.

'It's in line with the digitizing equipment governments use,' said Pyx. 'Which is how they make passports now, at least in the United States and Canada. It's supposed to be foolproof. Instead of photographs being glued and laminated, they're digitized, then thermal printed right on to the page.'

'Must make your job harder,' Holliday said.

'Much easier, as a matter of fact.' He gestured toward the back of the bookcase door. It was painted a neutral off-white and a pair of low-level lights placed high on either side of the doorway effectively washed out any shadow. 'Stand there, would you?' he asked. Holliday positioned himself against the doorway. 'Head up, no smile, mouth closed,' he instructed. There was a snapping sound and a bright flash, and Peggy realized the lights on either side of the door were photographic strobes. 'Now step away and let Ms Blackstock take your place.' Holliday moved and Peggy stood against the door. Pyx adjusted the tripod down to compensate for the difference in their heights and the strobes flared again. 'Great.' Pyx nodded. He took the flash card out of the camera, slipped it into a special drive unit beside one of the flat screens, then typed a set of instructions into the computer. 'Any name preferences?'

'No,' said Holliday.

'Me neither,' agreed Peggy.

'Okay, you'll be, uh . . . Norman Peterson, and Ms Blackstock will be Allison Masters.'

Pyx went back to the keyboard and started typing again. 'Place of birth, Toronto, Ontario, Canada. Date . . . 1981 or so. Mother's maiden name . . . Father . . . Documents provided. Guarantor.' He typed on, humming under his breath, and finished the online form a few moments later. 'Next thing is the routing, so it doesn't come back to me here,' he explained. 'First I grab an appropriate Canadian consulate – Albania, say – and put in their address as a point of origin.' He read it off the screen, 'Rruga, Dervish Hima, Kulla, Number Two, Apartment Twenty-two, Tirana, Albania, and finally the packet-switching code.' He finished typing with a flourish.

'What does all this accomplish?' Holliday asked.

'This will tell the passport office computer in Ottawa that Mr Norman Peterson and Miss Allison Masters, both presently in Paris, France, which is the closest actual passport-issuing office in the area, are renewing their passports, and have, in fact, already done so. It is telling the computer that the new passports are actually waiting at the embassy in Paris. Meanwhile a different set of instructions has been sent to new files, along with a request for a JPEG digitization of two new passport pictures. Everything gets backdated by a few days, the passports get printed during today's run and they'll be ready and waiting for you when you get to the embassy. Show them the birth certificates, driver's licenses and Social Insurance Numbers I'll provide you with and they'll give you two perfectly authentic Canadian passports, hot off the press, orchestrated by yours truly. If one of their electronic forensics people tries to reverse analyse the transaction it will dead end at the Albanian consulate, which is probably located in a dirty little hole-in-the-wall office above whatever passes for a convenience store in Tirana. It's a little convoluted, but it's a perfect hole in the system. Bust into their own database, they assume that the instructions are their own and thus legitimate and authorized. Hasn't failed me yet.'

'Don't you mean Social Security Numbers?' Peggy asked.

'Don't make that mistake at the embassy in Paris if anybody happens to question you, which they won't. Social Security is American; Social Insurance is Canadian.'

'But we're not going to Paris,' Peggy argued.

'Oh yes, you are,' said Paddy Philpot.

With the exception of their passports, they had all the documents they needed by two in the afternoon. As a bonus Pyx had thrown in two valid Bank of Nova

Scotia Visa cards in their new names, each with a ten-thousand-dollar limit that, according to the Irishman, would somehow be skimmed from the huge Canadian bank's vast stream of invisible wireless transfers that pinged off satellites around the world each day.

They spent most of their day at Le Vieux Four drinking ice cold Sangano Blonde beer, nibbling on cheese and pâté and listening to Paddy Philpot spin tales about his old cloak-and-dagger days. Holliday could almost forget why they were in this beautiful place. Almost.

In the early afternoon, documents in hand, they thanked Pyx for his hospitality and the speed and quality of his work, then climbed back into the Mercedes and headed down the mountain to the valley below. Finding the auto route, they made the sixty-mile trip to Lyon in a little over an hour and Philpot dropped them off in front of the modern Part-Dieu railway station.

'There are fast trains all the time. The trip to Paris takes about two hours. You should be all right. You remember the name of the hotel I told you about?'

'Hotel Normandie. Rue de la Huchette between Rue du Petit Pont and the Boulevard Saint-Michel on the Left Bank,' said Holliday, repeating Philpot's instructions.

'Good man.' The CIA analyst smiled.

'We owe you for the passports,' said Holliday grudgingly. 'I haven't forgotten, you know. We'll pay you back.'

'Think nothing of it, Doc. Consider yourself back on the Company payroll.'

'What about you?' Holliday asked.

'I have some people to see back in Prague. But we'll meet up again back in the States.' He took a small black cell phone out of his pocket and handed it to Holliday. 'I'll call you.' He smiled again, rolled up the window and drove off.

Holliday and Peggy turned, crossed the broad sidewalk and went into the low-ceilinged modern terminus. They bought a pair of first-class tickets on the next high-speed train to Paris, a brand-new TGV Duplex double-decker with big, airplane-style seats, lots of legroom and a top speed of 186 miles per hour.

They boarded the train, found their seats and settled in for the relatively short journey. So far they had seen nothing suspicious, but without passports and only forged documents to identify themselves they both felt vulnerable. The train was packed, mostly with tourists of various nationalities on their way back to Paris, but they had seats together and no one paid them any attention.

The train headed smoothly out of the station, right on time, and a few minutes later they were gathering speed as they raced through the suburbs of the big French city. Neither one of them had spoken since leaving Philpot at the entrance to the station.

'You want something to eat?' Holliday asked. He had taken the aisle seat, giving Peggy the window.

'No, thanks.'

'Drink?'

'No, I'm not thirsty,' said Peggy, shaking her head. 'Maybe later.'

'Yeah, maybe later,' said Holliday awkwardly. Another moment passed.

'What do you really know about Philpot?' Peggy asked finally.

The train began to sway and vibrate slightly as they hit the open countryside and continued to gain speed. 'I know he and Pesek got us out of a lot of trouble yesterday. He's arranged for passports today. Stuff we couldn't have done ourselves.'

'Like some kind of guardian angel – is that it?'

'I'm not sure.'

'You ever wonder whose side he's on?' She frowned. 'He could be part of Sinclair's scheme. He could be part of the rogue group within the Agency. Lies inside lies inside lies.'

'Yes.'

'Well?'

'I can't give you an answer because I don't know. I only know what he's done for us so far.'

'There's something wrong with the world when you suspect that *everybody's* out to get you.'

Holliday was silent for a moment. He stared at the striped fabric and the pull-down table on the seat ahead.

'You ever watch a TV show or read a book and come to a place where you stop and ask yourself, why don't they just go to the cops?'

'Sure,' Peggy said. 'It's like in a horror movie when the girl goes down into the dark basement and everybody but her knows she should turn and run.'

'But if she did, the movie would end right there,' agreed Holliday. 'That's where we are,' he went on. 'We're at the place where the movie should just end, because if we had any brains we'd run to the cops.'

'But we can't,' said Peggy.

'What are you getting at?'

'Philpot's keeping the movie going.' She paused. 'And you can GPS us off that phone with the right equipment.'

'So?' Holliday asked.

'Why is he doing it?' Peggy said. 'He and Pesek's people save our bacon after they kidnapped us, and now he gets us passports. He wants us back in the middle of it all. Why?' She paused. 'Is he setting us up like Brennan did?'

'That thought had crossed my mind,' Holliday said abjectly. 'But what are we supposed to do about it now?' He turned and looked at Peggy. 'I should send you back to Rafi in Jerusalem.'

'Don't be so retro, Doc. And besides, Rafi's not in Jerusalem; he's in Ethiopia or somewhere, looking for some lost Roman Legion or King Solomon's Mines or something. And, anyway, I wouldn't go. You need me.' Peggy looked out the window, then back at Holliday. 'So, what do we do now?'

'I might have one more card to play,' Holliday said thoughtfully.

'It better be an ace,' said Peggy.

Kate Sinclair was over the mid-Atlantic on her way back to the United States for her son's formal investiture as vice president when her companion's satellite phone pinged insistently. Excusing himself, Mike Harris took the call. He listened for less than a minute and then ended the call.

'Anything important?' Sinclair asked, smoking a cigarette and sipping a glass of her own red wine.

'Pyx reporting in as you requested. He's given everyone passports and Visa cards. The Visas have GPS locators under the hologram, just as he said. We can find them anytime we want.'

'Good,' said the old woman. 'I always knew bribing that man was a good idea. Knowing who's looking for false IDs can be quite useful at times.'

30

Holliday and Peggy picked up their passports at the Canadian Embassy in Paris, took a cab to Charles de Gaulle Airport and arrived in New York twenty-three hours after boarding the TGV in Lyon. Surprisingly, everything had gone without a hitch. The passport officer at the embassy gave them smiles as he handed them their phony passports, the cab driver to Charles de Gaulle talked about how much he had enjoyed a recent trip to New York to visit his married sister in Brooklyn, and the food on the Air France jumbo was terrific. The security people at JFK barely gave them a second look even though they didn't have any luggage, and they waved down a limo heading into the city on their first attempt. They booked two adjoining rooms at the newly refurbished Gramercy Park Hotel and by lunchtime they were in the Rose Bar, snacking on Kobe beef burgers with hand-cut fries and green tomatoes.

'So who exactly is Max Kessler?' Peggy asked, dipping a fry into a blob of ketchup. 'And why are we going to see him?'

'He's kind of like a shadow Henry Kissinger,' answered Holliday. 'He was a geek before the word was invented. An information freak, a people collector, a scholar, a schmoozer. On top of that he's been a private counsel and intelligence adviser to the last four presidents.'

'I've never heard of him.' Peggy frowned. She popped the fry into her mouth and chewed appreciatively.

'That's the point,' said Holliday. 'He's like the phantom of the opera, always the behind-the-scenes guy.'

'Why so secretive?'

'I think it has something to do with his father.'

'Who was his father?'

'An SS Colonel, Rhinehard Gehlen's executive assistant.'

'You lost me. Rhinehard who?'

'Gehlen. A Nazi spymaster in charge of their Soviet desk. He traded his information to the OSS in return for him and his family being brought to the States under Operation Paperclip. He worked for the CIA for decades. He went back to Germany and became head of West German Intelligence until the late seventies. Hugo Von Kessler stayed here along with his wife and his son. Max just carried on the family tradition. There are still whispers about Max's access to secret information but nobody really cares as long as he comes up with the goods.'

'How do you know him?'

'We helped each other out a few times over the years,' said Holliday vaguely. 'The point is, Max Kessler knows everything and everybody when it comes to the CIA and anything to do with intelligence. If Philpot's playing us or Tritt is involved with some kind of plot he'll know about it.'

Max Kessler occupied what had once been Boris Karloff's gloomy apartment on the sixth floor of the Dakota, overlooking Central Park. The building was famous for being the location used in *Rosemary's Baby* and the place where John Lennon was assassinated.

Kessler's apartment had a living room, a dining room converted into an office, two bedrooms and an enormous kitchen. There were an awful lot of dark wood paneling, crystal chandeliers and heavy Victorian furniture that was brought over from England by the container load and sold as 'important antiques' during the fifties and sixties. There were doilies and dusty-looking Persian carpets everywhere and bad paintings of horses and battles from forgotten wars on expensively papered walls. It could have been the home of somebody's dowager aunt.

Kessler looked like an undertaker. He greeted them at the door, wearing a three-piece, dark blue pinstripe suit, a blue-and-gold Harvard Law silk tie and expensive-looking, tasseled shoes. He wore round horn-rims balanced on a long nose that mimicked his overlong chin. The cheeks were a little sunken, and his forehead arched up into thinning steel gray hair swept straight back in shiny Prussian perfection. The eyes behind the glasses were like lumps of coal, and when he smiled a greeting it looked as though the slight movement of his thin lips would crack his entire face like a boiled egg.

He led them into the small living room and gestured toward a sofa upholstered in black and yellow stripes that might have suited someone's grandmother. He lowered himself into a tall-backed armchair upholstered in the same fabric, tenting his fingers like an old-fashioned schoolmaster surveying a roomful of students. Peggy suddenly realized the role he was playing: it was a combination of Basil Rathbone and Jeremy Brett doing Sherlock Holmes. When he spoke he even had a faintly British accent, when by rights it should have been German.

'It has been some time, Colonel. I was rather surprised by your telephone call.' He smiled thinly. 'Presumably it is a matter of some urgency.'

'That remains to be seen.'

'Before we begin, there is the matter of the telephone given to you by our mutual acquaintance Mr Philpot.'

'I took out the SIM card and the battery.' Holliday said.

'A wise precaution. The use of GPS transponders in most telephones these days is a matter of some concern to me. It seems faintly Orwellian. A bit too *1984* for my tastes.'

'What's your take on Philpot?' Holliday asked, getting to the point.

'He could easily be playing both sides.'

'But both sides of *what*?' Peggy asked.

'You were involved in that affair with Rex Deus and the Sinclair woman some time back, were you not, Colonel?'

'I didn't think it was common knowledge,' answered Holliday, surprised.

'Common knowledge isn't my stock-in-trade,' said Kessler, his voice dry.

'What about Sinclair?' Holliday said.

'A murdered Pope. A priest and his male lover found dead on a back road in suburban Virginia. Two dead Blackhawk Security operatives in an apparent fatal automobile accident in Rock Creek Park, but with a dozen bullet holes in the remains of the immolated vehicle. An assassinated vice president. A national warrant for your arrest in Italy; an incident at the Canadian border involving a man and woman who match your descriptions. An assassination attempt by an unknown terrorist group on a United States senator, a murdered photographer burned to death in his new Porsche, and finally a federal warrant here, which begs the question of how you returned to the United States without alerting the authorities. You and Ms Blackstock have cut quite a swath in the past week, Colonel.'

'You left out the part about being kidnapped and flown to an American black site in the Czech Republic,' said Peggy.

'Ah yes, the melodramatic rescue by *Pane* Pesek and his little ninja crew. I didn't think it was worth mentioning.'

'Easy for you to say,' snorted Peggy.

'I am a spider in a web, Ms Blackstock. I stay in my little lair and morsels of information eventually make their way to me. Sometimes the morsels add up to a tasty meal; sometimes they do not.'

'And in this case?' Holliday asked.

'In this case they add up to Kate Sinclair, which in turn leads us to her Rex Deus compatriot in the Central Intelligence Agency.'

'And who might that be?'

'Michael P. Harris, deputy director of operations. The *P* stands for Pierce. He's Kate Sinclair's brother. As I said, crumbs of fact that sometimes go unnoticed.'

'That could explain a great deal,' murmured Holliday, trying to piece it together.

'Or nothing at all,' replied Kessler. He smiled. 'In this case, however, it explains almost everything.'

'Do tell,' said Peggy.

'By this time, at least according to Mr Philpot, you are aware of Madame Sinclair's ambitions for her son, and thus for a Rex Deus hegemony in the United States. But Kate Sinclair needs more leverage. Having her son receive a flesh wound from a so-called terrorist and playing second lead in the White House isn't good enough to push her agenda over the top. I would suggest that she needs a bigger bang, and she needs it to come soon.'

'Who, what, where and when?' Holliday said. 'Those are the missing crumbs, as you call them.'

'The who is simple,' said Kessler. 'Kate Sinclair can do nothing on her own and neither can her son – not that he has the sense. No. The who is definitely Mr Harris. As to the rest – look for an event or a person, a time or a place where havoc would reap the most benefit. And look for it soon. Time is of the essence. It must come before our new vice president leaves the news cycle. Put Mr Harris in such a place at such a time and you will have your answer.'

'Any ideas?' Holliday asked.

'One or two,' said Kessler, smiling thinly.

PART FOUR

Finale

31

The Abbey School in Winter Falls predated the entire concept of tourism, and had been established in the early 1800s by a group of monks fleeing from the charred remains of what had once been the Petit Clairvaux Abbey in France. Over the previous centuries Petit Clairvaux had been ravaged by everything from plague and murderous kings to the destruction of the Templar Order, Napoleon Bonaparte's distaste for the monastic life and organized religion in general, and finally by fire.

The twelve remaining monks set sail for the new world, found an out-of-the-way spot in the forests of New Hampshire and settled down to a contemplative life and the making of cheese from sheep's milk.

Unfortunately the rich, smoky cheese they produced proved to be unpopular, and by the early 1900s St Joseph's Abbey transformed itself into a tuberculosis sanitarium and survived as such until most of the monks and their patients died during the deadly second wave of the Spanish flu epidemic of 1918.

In 1920 the Abbey transformed itself once again and became the Abbey School, a Catholic boarding school with the explicit mandate to produce priests and monks who would extend the Benedictine creed in America. That didn't work any better than the sheep's milk cheese, and in 1930, as Winter Falls itself became a popular summer retreat for the rich and powerful, the Abbey School, by now a sprawling compound of hundred-year-old buildings and more modern structures, opened its doors to the children of anyone with the means to pay the hefty tuition and boarding fees, regardless of race, creed or color – with the exception of members of the Negro race, the Chinese and above all members of the Jewish faith. It was, in fact, relentlessly male, white, Anglo-Saxon Protestant for the next half a century.

During those fifty years the Abbey School attained a certain level of prominence as a prep school where A-list celebrities, politicians and the superwealthy of nations around the world sent their not-quite-A-list sons. The school had a number of advantages: it stressed sports – or games, as the school called them – rather than academics; it was in out-of-the-way New Hampshire, which meant it was both difficult for the school's privileged students to get into too much trouble with drugs, sex or alcohol, and it was distant enough to provide an excuse for parents not visiting except under the most extreme circumstances.

By the sixties there was regular limo service from New York and Boston and there was floatplane service from both those cities for parents who couldn't wait to see their sons ensconced behind the mossy granite wall that surrounded the old monastic compound.

It was the perfect spot to send a World War Two naval hero and retired admiral's son with a relentlessly B-plus average and utterly average SAT scores whose father wanted him to become president. Likable, handsome and with a great smile, but basically just an ordinary guy with a good haircut and great hockey skills.

Hockey was the only thing he'd ever excelled at, beyond being heir to a billion-dollar oil fortune on his mother's side. The game was, in the end, the real reason for his attendance at this fortieth reunion. More than his eventual graduation from the Abbey and his nudge-and-a-wink entrance into Yale, it had been his win over the Winter Falls Wolves as captain of the Abbey Argonauts and the winning of the coveted St Joseph's Cup that had been the proudest moment of his pre-presidential life. As Morrie Adler had once put it in a Charlie Rose interview, 'It gave him the green light for the rest of his life.'

In his heart of hearts he'd known it was the single thing that finally spurred him on to success; if he could win that game he could win anything. It was one of his biggest benders, too, as he got bombed out of his gourd on the foul crabapple moonshine Morrie Adler made in his hidden basement still, and compounded by Lucky Strikes rolled in Polaroid film emulsion, a dimethyltryptamine, acidlike high discovered by his cousin, Mickey Haines.

Now, with his presidential library being built in San Diego, his $200,000-a-year pension, travel budget, office expenses, a decade's worth of Secret Service protection and top-of-the-line health insurance coming out of the taxpayer's pocket all ready to go and waiting for him at the end of his term in a year and a half, it only seemed right to cap it all off with a visit to the Abbey.

The President of the United States thought about that while seated in the luxuriously appointed passenger's compartment of Marine One as it droned across the late-afternoon Vermont sky on its way to Winter Falls. Beside him, Morrie was going over the most recent intelligence reports on the jihad slayings, trying to make sense of it all and coming up empty. Below them the snow-mantled forest stretched to the horizon. Morrie lit a Cohiba, took a deep drag and leaned back in the butter-soft leather armchair, a cut-crystal glass of 107-proof Pappy Van Winkle's Family Reserve on the rocks in the holder by his right hand.

'You think Shannon O'Doyle will be at the game?' Morrie asked wistfully.

'The Snow Queen?' The president laughed. Shannon O'Doyle had been the sexual fantasy of every boy at the Abbey and at Winter Falls High. Naturally ash blond and shy, her nylons made that terribly erotic whispering sound when she crossed her legs. 'She's probably a gray-haired old lady by now.'

'So what?' Morrie replied. 'Some dreams go on forever.' He smiled around the fat Cuban cigar. Those really were the good old days. 'And, anyway, we're gray-haired old men.'

The president sighed. Why was it that it took so long to get where you were going but the time spent after arriving was so brief? It was the one real problem with the American Dream: inevitably you woke up. The helicopter rumbled onward over the trees and the president stared out the window, thinking about Shannon O'Doyle's nylons and the shivering, dangerous sound of skates rushing on ice.

'What are the odds this Kessler guy is right?' Peggy asked. They were sitting in the back booth at Gorman's, overlooking the dock and the flat, bright white of the lake ice, turning gold now with the fading light of the winter sun. The iceboats were drawn up in a row, their sails furled, the roaring wind off the lake sending up a strange, cicadalike hum through their taut rigging.

Holliday sipped his coffee and stared out the window at the bleak, frozen scene. In the summer the docks and the lake probably looked about their best at this time of day. 'Pretty good,' he said, feeling as bleak as the frigid scenery. 'He seemed pretty convincing.'

'He sounded convincing in his living room at the

Dakota in New York,' said Peggy. 'Reality is a little different.' She lifted her shoulders. 'It could just be coincidence. There's nothing going on here, I swear.'

'Kessler doesn't believe in coincidence any more than I do,' answered Holliday. 'He believes in synchronicity.' He put down the coffee and began to tick off points on his fingers. 'A president is coming to visit. Conveniently assigned to the event is Mike Harris, who's also a direct relation of Kate Sinclair. The timing is right – these days it's a short news cycle, and our new, distinguished vice president, Richard Pierce Sinclair, is soon to go off the radar. Winter Falls was voted the safest place in America, which makes it a perfect target. Easy to crack and shocking to see destroyed. If Sinclair and Rex Deus want to make a statement, this is the moment and this is the place.'

'And if we're wrong?'

'Then we're wrong and we look somewhere else. Nothing wasted.'

'Except time,' muttered Peggy. 'Time we could have spent elsewhere.'

'JFK said something about assassination: "If anyone is crazy enough to want to kill a president of the United States, he can do it. All he must be prepared to do is give his life for the president's."'

'What's your point?'

'This country has spent a trillion dollars on antiterrorism since 9/11 and yet we couldn't stop a guy with a bomb in his crotch on a flight to Detroit. You just have to do your best. Nobody appointed us the president's saviors; that's what the damned Secret Service is for.'

'And what if Kate Sinclair and Rex Deus have infiltrated the Secret Service? It's not impossible, you know. She seems to have wormed her way into everything else in Washington. Why not the Presidential Detail?'

'Does that make it our responsibility?' Holliday said.

'Officially, no. Morally, maybe.'

'I'm not the nation's moral arbiter,' said Holliday, a note of bitterness in his voice.

'Maybe you should be,' said Peggy. 'We certainly need one. And even a voice in the wilderness eventually gets heard.'

'Kessler's given us a bit of an edge – believe me, Peg, he knows more than he's telling. Max Kessler's manipulated his way through every administration since Reagan. He *wants* us to be here. He knows something's going to happen in Winter Falls tonight and he's hoping we can stop it.'

'How? What are we looking for?'

'Tritt. He'll be here somewhere – I guarantee it. And this time it won't be just an assassination. If Kessler's right he'll amp it up. Kate Sinclair needs something big enough to trigger Matoon and all the rest of it.'

'I think we're both nuts. I feel like I'm in the middle of one of those conspiracy theories you read about on the Internet,' said Peggy. 'It's like . . . this can't be real and we can't be in the middle of it. Why us? A couple of ordinary people in the middle of a military coup, *here*, in the United States? It's crazy.'

'Tell that to John Wilkes Booth,' said Holliday. 'He was a second-rate actor who changed the course of American history when he assassinated Abraham Lincoln. Adolf Hitler was a failed artist and a lowly corporal in World War One, but he was eventually the driving force behind the death of fifty million people. Sometimes the conspiracy theorists are right, kiddo.' Holliday glanced at his watch. Two more hours to the face-off. They were running out of time. Holliday touched Peggy on the arm. 'Come on,' he said quietly. 'Time we were on our way.'

Chief Randy Lockwood sat in his small office in the Municipal Building, hemmed in by the three mongooselike agents who'd been glued to him since eight o'clock that morning. Dotty had told him to wear the dress uniform out of respect for the president, but he felt a little ridiculous. Besides the fact that typically it only came out for cop funerals in other towns, it also happened to be freezing cold outside and beginning to snow, and the wind blew through every stupid brass buttonhole. If that weren't enough to make him extremely uncomfortable, he found all the medals and citation bars a little embarrassing.

Only one of the agents, Special Agent in Charge Saxby, spoke to him. The other two were apparently there to watch Saxby, or maybe even Lockwood himself; he still wasn't sure. 'It's all unnecessary,' snapped Saxby. 'Someone should talk to them.'

'I didn't have anything to do with it,' said Lockwood. 'The headmaster at the Abbey School suggested it to the principal at the high school and they extended the invitation jointly to the president.'

'Nobody checked with us, no one checked with Homeland and no one said a word to the Secret Service,'

Saxby grumbled. 'The stupid son of a bitch drops a puck and the operation costs the taxpayers over a million dollars and takes us away from what we should be doing, which is tracking terrorists, not escorting lame ducks on junkets into the damned bush.'

'Don't blame me,' said Lockwood. 'I didn't vote for him.'

'After the attack in Virginia the current threat level is Orange. You know what that means?'

'Sure,' said Lockwood dryly. 'It's like ordering a Venti White Chocolate Mocha Frappuccino at Starbucks. Defcon One and Broken Arrow and Bent Spear and all that James Bond–coded bull puckie terminology you guys throw around. It's a big deal, right?'

'You can call it what you want, Chief Lockwood, but it means there is a high risk of terrorist activity in the homeland at the moment. That's something we take very seriously. You should, too.'

'I'm old-fashioned, Agent Saxby. What my dad used to call a bonehead, a practical guy. So listen up when you're in my town, all right? I was a quarterback in football because I wanted to impress the girls. When I went to Vietnam I realized the idea wasn't to kill Vietcong; it was to survive the tour. When I went back for the second tour it was to get rank and up my pension.

'When I came back here it was to give out parking tickets and go fishing. The last murder we had in Winter Falls was twenty-five years ago when one of the cottagers found out her husband was screwing a girlfriend back in New York. She got off with provoked manslaughter and three years' probation. She's one of the school trustees to this day.

'I'm not going to get all hot and bothered about your Code Reds or whatever you call them. The game is being played on the Abbey School rink, not the World Trade Center, and the president will only be here for a couple of hours. If you can't spot a jihadist in this crowd, then you don't deserve your job.'

Saxby gave him a sour look. 'Do you know why those planes flew into the Trade Center towers, Mr Practical Policeman?'

'Why don't you tell me, SAC Saxby?'

'They were a target, Chief Lockwood,' said Saxby. 'And they were easy. The two tallest buildings in New York City. They were also arranged so that when you looked at them from due north or due south, which was how they were attacked, they looked like a solid slab. Even with that the first one almost missed. A practical target. And that's what you are, parking tickets or not, fishing or not. This place, with the president in it, has a target painted on its back whether you like it or not. You're the safest town in America with the President of the United States in the bull's-eye. Osama bin Laden couldn't have had a better wet dream.'

'Let's hope you're wrong, Agent Saxby,' he said. 'I've done the best I could under the circumstances. I've got both shifts of my men out; I've given half of them to the Secret Service guys and your people to pair up with.

Everybody knows everybody else in town. Strangers stand out like sore thumbs.

'It's not like it's summer, with tourists coming and going all the time. They brought in sniffer dogs to check out the seats at the rink for bombs; they've put up metal detectors anywhere His Honor will be going. They've cleared a landing spot for the chopper in the park in front of the Municipal Building, there's two Secret Service Escalades waiting that arrived this morning and your guys have had that little helicopter of yours buzzing around all day, looking for snipers on rooftops. I'm not sure there's not a hell of a lot more we can do.'

Suddenly Saxby's expression changed. From sour it went to worn and barren. He looked as though the weight of the world was bearing down on him, grinding him down, making him old before his time. 'That's always the problem, Chief Lockwood. You always do whatever you can, you cover every base, you look in every nook and cranny but it's never enough. Most of the time this kind of thing is the most boring duty in the world.

'You read all those Tom Clancy books and watch all those hard-ass shows on TV but it's all a load of crap; looking for terrorists is a lot of crap. I've been doing this job for thirty-two years and seven months. Five months away from mandatory, and from day one it's been nothing but nerves because sometimes it's just never enough, and sometimes you overlook something, and sometimes before you know it, the whole thing blows up in your face and you're half a second too late. You oooh when you should have ahhhed, you go left when you should have gone right, and for thirty-two years and seven months my nerves have been cocked like a loaded gun, just waiting for that one mistake.'

He paused. 'My insurance agent once told me that everyone has a freight train and a railroad crossing in his or her life and you never see it coming until it's too late.'

'Nice, uplifting insurance agent you have,' said Lockwood, trying to lighten things up. But he knew exactly what the gray-haired FBI man meant. You never knew where the bullet that hit you came from. One of these days he could stop a rowdy summertime DUI and find himself looking down the barrel of some punk's Saturday-night special and wind up in the uniform he was wearing right now, except flat on his back in a satin-lined wooden box. Outside the front of the building a big Sandri Sunoco fuel truck rumbled by on its rounds. The wind was rising and the snow was falling even more heavily. It was going to be a nasty night in Winter Falls.

Saxby gave a twisted little smile. 'I just want this whole thing to be over and the ex-president to be on his way, and then, Chief Lockwood, maybe you and I can find a place to have a cold beer and a big steak and tell each other old war stories.'

'Amen to that,' agreed Lockwood.

33

Malcolm Teeter, who liked his friends to call him Stryker, his favorite character from the video game *Mortal Kombat*, sat alone at the wheel of the Sunoco oil tanker parked behind the Winter Falls Shopping Center on Crooked Pond Road. The detonator for the nine-thousand-gallon, twenty-eight-ton ANFO bomb that filled the red, white and blue tank was on the dashboard in front of him. Made up of a radio-controlled servo from a toy motorboat purchased at a RadioShack in Portland, the detonator was connected to four six-volt batteries and a PerkinElmer slapper blasting cap like the kind used in antitank rockets.

The new dude had showed them how to order things like that online. He'd even managed to get them all what appeared to be perfect replicas of New Hampshire National Guard uniforms so they'd fit in during the Winter Falls operation.

He called himself Barfield, and he was nice enough but he was too quiet. And, anyway, Malcolm wasn't stupid, was he? In no more than a week, even though nobody said anything, you could tell who was boss now and it sure as hell wasn't Wilmot *goddamn* DeJean anymore. He had the rank, sure, and walked around the compound with that 'I am the principal of this school' look on his face, but it was Barfield who showed them all the new tricks – like getting rid of all that hot-dog stuff, about shooting pistols on the side, like how to mix in and not give people clues like showing your tats or wearing shit-kicker boots, like the difference about looking and actually seeing, and most of all about patience.

Malcolm didn't like driving in the smallest load, but just like this Barfield guy said, it was the most important because it was the first. It would draw away the heat from the real ground zero – the school – and bring it up here, to the north of the town. According to Barfield, there was going to be a lot of heat in town, and driving down Main Street you could almost feel it.

Going by the park in front of the cop shop and fire hall, you could pick them off everywhere. Like, what kind of idiot wears a topcoat and carries an attaché case and just stands on the corner in the middle of a snow-storm? Secret Service or a Fed, that's who. Nobody noticed Malcolm, of course, which was the whole point. Sunoco was just about the biggest heating oil distributor in the state and there were Sunoco stations all over the place. Who saw a fuel truck in the middle of winter? They were *supposed* to be driving around at all hours of the day and night.

But still, he didn't like the waiting around. Of the six trucks his was the only one that wasn't going to be close to the rink. It was fine that he was key man or whatever

Barfield called him, but it didn't do much for his – what was it? – his self-esteem. He felt a bit like the odd man out.

Teeter looked out the half-frosted windshield. The parking lot in front of the big P&C supermarket. Almost closing time. Teeter picked up the simple little radio control that would detonate the bomb parked next to the side wall of the shopping center. He might be the odd man out, but he knew the stats.

He grinned. He could see the estimates and the comparisons in the newspapers. The Oklahoma City bomb had been three thousand pounds; this one was fifty thousand pounds. The Oklahoma City bombing created a thirty-foot-deep crater and took out half an office building, causing damage for blocks around. This one would vaporize the entire supermarket and half a dozen other stores in the shopping center.

He would get a cell phone call from Barfield. That was the signal to climb out of the truck with the detonator, press the switch and then run like hell. He'd have five minutes to get himself out of range and to the rendezvous on Pine Street. He checked his watch again. Twenty minutes. He turned up the Tina Turner cut on his iPod. Now *there* was an old bitch who could sing.

General Angus Scott Matoon sat in his E Ring office in the Pentagon and fretted. It was eight o'clock in the evening and so far there was no news from Winter Falls. That could mean nothing or anything, but if

Crusader was to succeed he needed to take the men of Prairie operational, and soon. He had enough men in place to take over the small but vital command-and-control units of the nation's telecommunications satellites, but to gather the reins of that power into a single fist would take time. Crusader was a tightrope; America had to be briefly thrown into chaos before Vice President Sinclair came to the rescue. As well as being Chairman of the Joint Chiefs and Chief of Staff of the Army, Matoon also had personal command of the little-known and even less-documented USNORTHCOM, the United States North American Command – a million-member strong homeland defense force controlling the land, sea and air in and around the continental United States, Canada and Mexico, and essentially occupying both the United States and those two sovereign nations under an iron-fisted martial law that came from the Oval Office and the commander in chief. It had been quietly established just after 9/11 and further augmented during the economic crises of 2008 to 2010, with the fear of a banking collapse and the threat of a new civil war.

As soon as word came down that Crusader was in motion, Matoon's main job was to take over the euphemistically named Consequence Management Response Force, a massive, military-manned national police force from USNORTHCOM's headquarters at Patterson Air Force Base in Ohio. None of this could be accomplished until he had control of the satellite systems and Rex Deus became the de facto leadership of the nation. He looked at his watch. He couldn't wait any longer. He picked up the red telephone in front of him on the big oak desk that had once belonged to General Robert E. Lee and punched in a number.

'We have a prairie fire.'

Everything went off like clockwork. The chopper landed square in the center of the big canvas target that had been pegged out on the snow-covered grass of the little park in front of the Municipal Building on Croppley Street. The smiling president, bounding down the short steps, shook hands with Mayor Dotty Blanchette, and together, before they froze to death, they got into the middle Escalade in the nine-car procession and headed for the Abbey School.

The Abbey School rink, named for the president's late father, was located on the foundations of what had once been the main animal pen for the Abbey's cheese-producing sheep and that had later been converted into what had been pretentiously referred to as the Big End – the main cricket field for the school. Cricket had gone over like a lead balloon and the large area to the east of the main school building had been converted into a baseball diamond. With New Hampshire regularly having as much as five months of winter, hosing down the baseball field in late October or early November and turning it into a skating rink seemed like a natural thing to do, and with the prez's prowess at hammering his opponents blindsided into the boards and making power plays, covering the rink and putting in seating followed equally naturally.

Previously the classic game between Winter Falls High and the Abbey School had taken place on the schoolyard rink at the latter, but that meant the game had to be played in daylight and attendance was usually pretty low. With the covered rink at the Abbey the game changed dramatically; there were cheerleading squads for both schools – all-male for the Abbey, all-female for Winter Falls – and with seating for 2,500 you could get half the population of the town and the faculties and student bodies from both schools into the building.

Marching bands played, programs and hot dogs were sold to raise money for the two schools' favorite charities – in the case of the Abbey School this meant sending twenty dollars a month to a child of indeterminate sex named Sui Sang in Hong Kong, and in the case of Winter Falls High it was twenty dollars a month to the Salvation Army.

The whole thing had the nice, American ring of sportsmanship and charity about it, and in its own way the dropping of the puck ceremony developed its own cachet, like being made a Hasty Pudding Man or Woman of the Year at Harvard University. Celebrities of both real and dubious distinction had been given the invitation, from Dick Cheney and Wayne Gretsky to Pee-wee Herman and Howie Mandel. To drop the puck at the Abbey–Winter Falls game was a hot photo op, especially when the *New York Times* was doing a magazine cover story on you timed to coincide with the announcement of your political autobiography, *Promises, Promises*, which the prez knew he was going to have to write sooner or later.

The ride to the old gray wall surrounding the Abbey School took less than ten minutes, even at motorcade speed – more than enough time for Morrie to inquire about the whereabouts of the luscious Shannon O'Doyle, who, Dotty was sad to inform him, had died of breast cancer almost ten years gone by.

They drove through the main gates, manned by two patrol cars with their flashers going just to show people how serious they were, then drove around the long, curving driveway past the main building and the old cloisters to the rink, a glass-and-steel flying wedge that had nothing to do with the nineteenth-century, gothic pile of the dark, gloomy school.

Another three minutes and Dotty, Morrie and the president were being escorted to their center-ice seats by two Eagle Scouts, one from the Abbey and one from the high school. Flashes flashed, the PA system boomed and the two teams were introduced and lined up on the ice to shake hands with the man who held the throttle of the world. At seven fifteen the festivities began. Forty-five minutes of high school bands and stupid speeches and the puck would drop.

No one noticed the big Sunoco heating oil truck parked beside the main building, a man in a Sunoco uniform with a nozzled hose in his hand in front of an ordinary-looking standpipe. No one, it seemed, realized that if any truck should be parked beside the school that night it should have been a big green Hess Natural Gas truck, not a big, yellow Sunoco fuel oil tanker.

Kate Sinclair's Gulfstream landed at Manassas Regional Airport and taxied toward the cluster of 1930s-style buildings that marked the terminal area. Just as the pilot cut the engines to a dull throb, Mike Harris's satellite phone pinged again. He took the call, a slow grin wreathing his features.

'What?' Sinclair asked, irritation in her voice; she hated when other people knew things she didn't.

'According to the GPS, they're in Winter Falls.'

'Put out an APB or whatever it's called. Have them picked up,' said Sinclair. Her smoky breath rattled in her throat and she felt her heart swell with expectation.

She smiled her own private smile. It couldn't have worked better if she'd planned it. With Matoon's people in charge and habeas corpus suspended in the face of martial law, getting the whereabouts of Holliday's invaluable notebook could be done legally and on American soil. With that notebook and the enormous wealth it represented, the Rex Deus line would rule in the Western world for a thousand years. 'Have them held in custody until I figure out exactly what to do with them.'

34

William Tritt had dispatched small units of Maine's Right Arm in their National Guard uniforms to the homes of all off-duty members of the Winter Falls Police force, all members of the Carroll County Sheriff's Department who lived within a twenty-mile radius of the town and the homes of all off-duty firemen in the area. By now those potential threats would either be bound and gagged or dead if they gave any resistance.

The remainder of his small force was dispatched to the woods surrounding the Abbey School. It was virtually a suicide mission, of course, but he'd spun enough tales of the population rising up in sympathy that the men of Maine's Right Arm were positive of their success.

Tritt, of course, didn't give a damn; he was doing a job that he was getting paid for. What happened after the job was done was none of his affair, nor did he want it to be. Until the detonation occurred there, they were to keep anyone and everyone from exiting the rink. For his own part, Tritt was in his room at a local bed-and-breakfast on South Main Street, his laptop open on the bed, waiting for the confirmation that the last payment had been deposited into his Swiss account. He had no intention of being near any of the fireworks when they went off. In fact, he intended to be some miles away.

Dean Crawford piloted his cruiser through the falling snow, doing his regular run up North Main along the lake up to Goose Corner, then back again, winding up at the shopping center where he'd Code Seven for a meal at Denny's and then do it all over again until the end of his shift.

Tonight everyone was getting hot and bothered by all the security around the president's visit, but Crawford had been a cop for far too long and in far too many places to care. Red Balls were something to be avoided no matter what form they took. A tour to Iraq during the Gulf War plus a decade on the Miami-Dade force, then the Baltimore force, had taught him that. Even marriage was a Red Ball, as he knew only too well after three wives had left him. Not that he wasn't a good cop. He was; he prided himself on it, in fact, but you had to slow down eventually.

No, for now at least he was perfectly happy just to do his regular shift up to the sewage plant and around again, keeping his eyes out for the bad guys that never showed up at this time of year. For the most part crime was seasonal in Winter Falls, just like it was most other places. Crooks don't like the cold any more than they like it too hot. On a night like tonight the worst he was going to get was a stalled-out car in a snowbank or a DUI, and that was just fine with him. He'd book out at the end of his four-to-midnight, go back to his little bungalow on the pond and catch a little late-night TV with a beer or maybe two. Alone. Quiet. Peaceful.

Crawford turned the cruiser off Willow on to Crooked Pond Road then turned into the shopping center parking lot. Just about everything was closed except the P&C and Denny's. Everything else was dark. The snow was coming down heavily now, the wind off the lake sending it into whirls and eddies that caught in the yellow vapor lamps like bizarre, miniature tornadoes. A big Sunoco tanker was servicing the P&C, and Crawford found himself wondering if the drivers of those hulking things got extra bucks for night work or for driving through blizzards. Probably, the lucky bastards. The way the chief made it sound you were supposed to take the occasional midnight-to-eight shot if you were unmarried and you were supposed to do it without overtime.

On the other hand, he'd had worse bosses than Lockwood. If nothing else the old graybeard knew what combat was like, which was a plus. Coming back from any war wasn't easy. It did things to you and did them to you young, things most people who hadn't done it couldn't understand. Lockwood did, so the occasional temper flare or sour mood was taken with more than a grain of salt. He also understood that sometimes a man had to put himself to sleep with something stronger than a beer or two to keep away the dreams and that was a bonus, too.

Crawford parked the cruiser in front of Denny's, then coded himself out with dispatch. He made sure the bulky Motorola portable PDA was tucked into its little holster on his belt, then climbed out of the car. He took a few seconds to stretch, then trudged through the soft, deepening snow and stepped inside the restaurant. The place was almost empty except for a couple way in the back and two or three more customers hunched at the counter like regulars at a neighborhood bar. Workers coming off shift; maybe the driver of the Sunoco truck. Who knew? Most of the locals were at the hockey game – a game he could take or leave.

A bored-looking waitress came around with a menu, but he ordered from memory what he had every night on this shift: country-fried steak and eggs with hash browns and coffee. There was a copy of the *New Hampshire Gazette* on the bench seat of the booth he was in and he browsed through it until the big plate with his dinner came.

The waitress put it down in front of him, and for a while he read while he ate. Halfway through an editorial on setting a Robin Hood tax on the banks he stopped eating and put his fork down. Coming down Crooked Pond he'd seen a car with rental plates and a JFK Hertz license holder going in the opposite direction. He even remembered the number: ABC 2345, like a kid had chosen it. Why would somebody renting a car at JFK come to northern New Hampshire on a day like this? There were a hundred legitimate reasons, of course, but his cop sense was twitching and his appetite was gone. He took out his PDA, typed in a Code Five wants-and-warrants request and got an answer back almost instantly.

'Son of a bitch,' he whispered.

'Pardon?'

Crawford looked up. The waitress was standing there with a pot of coffee in her hand. He dropped ten bucks on the table. He looked at the PDA screen, took a deep breath and switched the machine off. 'I gotta run,' he said. *Who'da thought, a goddamned Red Ball in Winter Falls, New Hampshire.* He put the PDA back into its little holster and stood, his meal forgotten. He headed out of the almost-empty restaurant at a run.

They drove down Sugar Hill Road on the outskirts of Winter Falls with Holliday behind the wheel. They'd spent most of the day searching for some evidence of Tritt, but had come up empty. What they had seen was a town crammed with Secret Service. Holliday had even seen what appeared to be National Guardsmen here and there, which he thought might be a little extreme. He headed the rental car toward South Main Street and the highway out of town. Kessler had been wrong; there was no threat here.

'I can't believe the press swallowed that whole Jihad al-Salibiyya thing. Don't they have investigative reporters anymore?' he mumbled in frustration.

'It's all blogs and opinion these days.' Peggy shrugged,

shivering in the seat beside him. The car's heater had died long ago. 'The Internet bled newspapers dry and real journalism dried up with it. The news cycle is all about razzmatazz, not story. An autistic kid getting found in a swamp or a guy hiding under the pulpit of his church, surviving a hurricane, outrates the outbreak of a foreign war or a disaster somewhere else killing tens of thousands. Live outside the United States like I have and you start to realize what a bunch of navel-gazers we are.' Beside Peggy, Holliday suddenly tensed. 'What's the matter?'

'I think that's a cop car behind us.'

'Maybe it's nothing. There are cops everywhere in this town tonight.' Suddenly the cop car's flasher came on and his siren whooped once.

'He wants us to stop.'

'Can we outrun him?'

'In a Ford Escort?'

'We've got ID.'

'Let's hope Pyx did his job right,' said Holliday. He pulled over and stopped. Behind him the police car did the same. Nothing moved; no cop climbed out of the cruiser.

'What's he doing?' Peggy asked.

'Something's wrong.'

'FREEZE!' said a bullhorn voice out of the snow-white darkness.

And then all the lights in the world came on.

35

'I'm getting too old for all this,' Holliday said with a sigh. He and Peggy were sitting handcuffed on opposite sides of a metal desk in an interrogation room not much larger than a toilet cubicle. It smelled that way, too, pine disinfectant not quite masking the tang of old urine, passed gas and drunkards' vomit.

It appeared that Winter Falls liked its interrogations straight and to the point. There was a retro video camera with a built-in mike looming down from a bracket in the corner and a piece of one-way glass that was so old the aluminum film was wearing off and you could see a ghostly image of what passed for the Winter Falls PD squad room.

The scene on the road leading into town had been like something out of a Bruce Willis movie. Cops of all shapes and sizes pouring out of cars and vans, some in uniform, some plainclothes, and some very definitely Feds of one kind or another. At one point they were standing handcuffed, freezing in the falling snow, while Homeland Security, the New Hampshire State Police and the FBI argued over jurisdiction.

Finally a cop in a dress uniform appeared, bundled them into a Winter Falls cruiser and gave everyone at the scene the hairy eyeball before he whisked them off to the station. It was a show of very large and very brass cojones, and no matter what the interrogation room smelled like, he found himself if not liking, at least respecting the grizzle-haired cop. Holliday was willing to bet that there was either the Marine Corps or the Rangers in the man's background.

'Now what?' Peggy asked.

'We get quizzed by the locals and then passed up through the chain of command until we get to the big guys. Either that or we get sent to Gitmo.'

'I thought it would be closed by now.'

'Hard to keep a good idea down,' said Holliday.

'You know anyone who can get us out of this?'

'I know lots of people.' Holliday shrugged. 'I just don't know which side anyone is on anymore.' He looked around the room. 'We'll just have to wait it out, I guess.'

'I've never been in jail before. Don't we get a lawyer or something?'

'We're way past lawyers, kiddo. We are now deep in the swamp of National Security.'

The cop in the dress uniform appeared, minus his brass-buttoned jacket. He shut the door behind him and sat down in the only other chair in the room.

'Comfy?' asked the policeman. He looked irritated.

'Peachy,' replied Holliday.

'Which one of you can tell me why I'm not sitting

with the President of the United States, watching a hockey game and having my picture taken?'

'Because something terrible is about to happen to your town if you don't get really busy right now,' Holliday said bluntly.

'Is that right?' the cop said.

'That's right.'

'Explain.'

'A man I know named Max Kessler, who has been an adviser to every president all the way back to the first Bush, said your town was the likely target for a major domestic terrorist attack, which is actually a front for an eventual takeover of the presidency and the country itself by Kate Sinclair; her son, the vice president; and Army Chief of Staff General Angus Scott Matoon, all of whom are members of a semisecret religious organization known as Rex Deus. They were also behind the assassination of the Pope by an American triggerman.'

'You've got to be kidding me,' said the cop. 'That's a Dan Brown novel. Tom Clancy on steroids.'

'Not even a little bit,' said Holliday. 'It's *very* real. All of it.'

'You expect me to believe that?'

'No,' said Holliday. 'Which doesn't change the fact that it's true. Lots of people didn't believe Paul Revere, either.'

The cop sighed and rolled up the sleeves of his dress shirt. Cop body language for 'Now we get down to business.' Holliday burst out laughing. It wasn't the reaction Lockwood had expected.

'What's so funny?'

'I was right.'

'About what?'

Holliday nodded his head at the ribbon-and-death's head tattoo on the man's forearm. 'Rangers lead the way,' he said.

'I was First Battalion,' said Lockwood.

'Lurp,' said Holliday. Which meant LRRP, or Long Range Reconnaissance Patrol.

'Where?'

'Chu Lai, Ah Shau Valley. Those nice beaches at Nha Trang.'

'Same here. You must have known Nyguen Coung, then.'

'Kit Carson Scout – one of the best. Sure, I knew him.'

Peggy was lost.

'You're the real thing, then,' said the police chief.

'I am,' said Holliday. '*Sua Sponte* and all that. Eighteen and full of beans.'

'So, then, what's this about you and your friend here being tagged as all sorts of terrorists and killers? Bodies everywhere. Shoot on sight; federal warrants.'

'Long story,' said Holliday.

'I don't have time for long stories. The Feds are going to come barging in here any minute now and I'll have to hand you over. No choice. Just give me a condensed version and I'll see what we can do.'

'You ever hear about a guy named Billy Tritt?'

Malcolm Teeter had seen the cop bolting out of the Denny's and he didn't wait around to see who he was going to take down. As quietly as he could he climbed down out of the cab and booked out of the neighborhood. There was no doubt he was deserting his post and that he'd catch hell from that guy Barfield, but he knew perfectly well that this was just a dry run, anyway, so what did it matter? The first ass you saved was your own.

When nothing happened after ten minutes, he started to rethink his position, huddled as he was in somebody's backyard behind a fence, freezing half to death and smoking his last three cigarettes. He knew there was a pack of Luckies in the glove compartment and in the end that's what took him back to the truck, not fear of Barfield's wrath.

He got real lucky then. He'd just eased himself back into the seat when the cell phone rang. If he'd waited another minute he would have missed the call. He let out a long, relieved breath, picked the phone up off the dash and flipped it open.

Twenty-two and a half inches from the back of Malcolm Teeter's head, the cell phone—activated initiating explosion ignited the twenty-seven tons of ANFO, turning the tanker truck into an enormous grenade that vaporized Teeter before he had a chance to say hello.

The shock wave expanded exponentially, flattening the supermarket and the rest of the shopping center within less than a second. Shrapnel from the blasted stainless-steel truck leveled trees and cut through the surrounding houses like mutilating scalpel blades, killing anything alive within a thousand feet of the detonation.

A monstrous fireball blossomed like some brilliantly colored tumor, suddenly erupting from the snow-covered ground as the secondary blast wave expanded. The sound was like a crack in the world, a freight train rushing into a tornado, Joshua's trumpet at Jericho shattering windows for a mile in every direction. The earth literally shook. The two-way mirror in the interrogation room at the Winter Falls Police Station cracked from side to side and then crashed to the floor as the entire building shook.

'Christ!' yelled Lockwood, who'd almost been thrown from his chair. 'What the hell was that?'

The overhead light dimmed, flickered and died. Everything went dark.

'The beginning,' said Holliday, out of the blackness. 'Now get us out of these cuffs before it's too late.'

36

The positioning of the first of the tanker trucks beside the shopping center had not been accidental. A hundred feet away, tucked in behind the P&C supermarket, was the main substation off the 132-kilovolt grid that powered the entire town of Winter Falls. The eight-foot-high chain-link fence topped with razor wire was no protection at all from the ANFO bomb and was obliterated during the first seconds after the explosion.

Unfortunately for the residents of the town, the main switching station for Granite State Telephone stood fifty feet from the electrical substation and transformer, and the two nearby cell phone towers on Pine Hill Road were also rendered inoperable. Within an instant almost all methods of communication in Winter Falls were destroyed.

The sound of the explosion even penetrated the hockey arena at the Abbey School, the arched rafters shaking as the pressure wave rolled over the town. Within seconds the Secret Service had begun their standard extraction procedures for the president, but they were startled and more than surprised to find themselves pinned down by what sounded like small-arms fire coming from the woods. The president and his party were taken to the Abbey dressing room, a below-grade concrete bunker where they would be safe.

'Where's the president right now?' Holliday asked as they struggled to find their way through the squad room. Half the ceiling had collapsed and the air was full of plaster dust. They could hear voices and the sound of coughing, but they couldn't see anything. Holliday and Peggy kept close on Chief Lockwood's heels as he followed the wall around toward the entrance to the squad room.

'Hang on,' wheezed Lockwood, trying to spit out the cloying, ancient plaster from his mouth. 'I'll get a hand-held.' The policeman reached out blindly, his hand finally finding the rack of charging radios the officers used when they weren't in their cruisers. He hit the ON switch but there was nothing but static. 'What the hell?' He hammered the radio set with his palm but there was still nothing. They could hear the sounds of people trapped in the rubble from the fallen ceiling. 'Flash-lights,' said Lockwood numbly. 'We need flashlights so we can get these people out of here.'

'There's no time!' Holliday insisted. 'That was just the start! You think it's a coincidence with the president here?' He clutched at Lockwood in the darkness. 'Where would he be?'

'The rink. The Abbey School.'

'Where would the Secret Service take him in an emergency? A blackout?'

'Back here.' Lockwood said. 'His chopper's on a temporary pad in the park.'

'We've got to stop him before it's too late,' Holliday said firmly. He tugged hard on Lockwood's arm. 'Get us out of here. Now.'

'There are people injured here. My people. I can't just leave them.'

'You can't help them, either. This son of a bitch murdered the Pope and blew up the vice president. He just took out all your lights, power and communications, and I guarantee you, he's not finished yet.'

Lockwood stumbled out into the hallway with Holliday and Peggy close behind. Plaster dust hung like a cloud and in the haze shadowy figures made their way to the shattered glass-front door. Finally they stood outside the building in the blowing snow. The entire town was dark except for the headlights of slow-moving vehicles across the park. There was no sign of the presidential motorcade.

'We're going to freeze to death like this,' said Holliday, shivering.

'Come on,' said Lockwood. He led them down the street that ran in front of the building to a row of shops on the square. Lockwood stopped at the largest one and Holliday read the old-fashioned sign on the front: UNCLE JIMMY'S SPORT PARADISE. Lockwood didn't hesitate. He put his boot through the metal-and-glass-front door, reached in and twisted the lock, then stepped inside. Holliday and Peggy followed. The place was dark and silent, a wide, long, low-ceilinged room divided into aisles. Lockwood found a big twelve-volt lantern and swung the beam around the room. Racks of antlers, a moose head, a stuffed lynx head and a lacquered blue marlin hung from the walls.

Lockwood shone the light down the middle aisle. At its end there was a rack of orange and camo quilted hunting jackets. They followed the policeman down the aisle and each of them pulled on one of the jackets.

'Now what?' Peggy asked.

'Weapons,' said Holliday.

'I'm not sure I want you armed,' said Lockwood.

'I don't care what you're sure of. I'm not going after Billy Tritt without something with a very large caliber in my hand.'

'I could lose my job,' said Lockwood.

'I could lose my life.'

'Point taken,' said Lockwood. 'Gun up, I guess.'

Holliday chose a secondhand AR-15 with a sling and put it over his back. He stuffed his pockets with magazines, then chose a Mossberg 12-gauge autoloader, crammed five slug shells into the automag and stuffed his pants pockets with twenty more. For a handgun he chose a Colt M1911 .45-caliber semiautomatic pistol exactly like the one he'd used in combat from Vietnam to Somalia. He found a web belt with a pouch and loaded half a dozen magazines, while Peggy and Lockwood armed themselves.

'This is like an audition for *Rambo Six*,' Peggy said,

choosing a rather unladylike Ruger Blackhawk. 'What kind of bullets does this thing use?'

Lockwood had picked a Remington 480 Bushmaster to go along with the Walther on his hip. 'Casulls, .454-caliber. You fire that thing, young lady, you be sure to hold it in both hands. He handed her a box of the large shells and she methodically began to load the cylinder.

'Young lady, my ass,' she muttered.

'What if the good guys see us wandering around like this?'

Lockwood took out his badge and ID wallet, slipped out the badge and pinned it on the front of the camo-patterned hunting jacket. 'This will have to do,' he said. 'Now, what exactly are we looking for?'

'The explosion was a distraction,' said Holliday. 'It's almost certainly designed to draw away local law enforcement and get the Secret Service to exfiltrate the president. That means they'll bring him back to the chopper and get him the hell out of here. That's the obvious protocol.'

'So you think this Tritt character will be close by?'

'I can almost guarantee it.' Holliday nodded. 'He'll have night-vision equipment and something big enough to bring the helicopter down before it gets very far off the ground. A Stinger or something like it. And that won't be the end of it, either.'

'That's not enough?' Lockwood said.

'The whole idea is to create enough chaos to justify

Matoon pressuring the White House into declaring martial law. I'm guessing Tritt's got more truck bombs that he's going to let off, probably using some kind of remote detonator.'

'Cell and radio are out. How's he supposed to set these things off?'

'Cell phones are out, but satellite phones aren't.'

'How do we know this guy if we see him?' Lockwood asked. 'My town's being blown to hell and it's pitch-dark.'

'Look for the guy carrying a surface-to-air missile,' said Holliday.

'This is just like the good old days,' grunted Lockwood. 'Trying to kill an enemy you can't see.'

'I hated the good old days,' said Holliday.

'Me too,' answered Lockwood. They went out into the cold again.

At the Abbey School the Secret Service had found and routed the half dozen men in phony National Guard uniforms, killing four and wounding two, who were now being held prisoner. The two survivors quickly told the Secret Service about the plan to blow up the entire school with an ANFO bomb, and the president and his entourage were immediately removed from the premises, leaving the evacuation of the other people at the stadium to the local police. Twenty-five minutes after the explosion that had turned out the lights all over Winter Falls the presidential limousine was on its way back to the center of town and the waiting Marine One helicopter.

Billy Tritt sat in his room in the inn and tried to control his anger. The first explosion had gone off perfectly, sending Malcolm Teeter to whatever hell awaited his shriveled, mindless soul.

Windows had blown out in half of Winter Falls, there was panic everywhere and a huge fire was developing on the eastern edge of town. It had been distraction enough to draw the fire trucks out of their hall on the west side of the Municipal Building and from the looks of it from his position, part of the roof of the police department had collapsed. With the cessation of communication resulting from the triple threat of the destruction of the electrical substation, the telephone switching hub and the two cell towers serving Winter Falls, both the Headquarters Emergency Management unit of the New Hampshire State Police in Concord and the F Troop station in Twin Mountains would have automatically been alerted, but F Troop was sixty miles away and Concord ever farther. At the very least it would take F Troop the better part of an hour to appear and the HQ SWAT team about half an hour longer.

However, the second truck bomb at the Abbey School had not detonated for some reason and Tritt had been forced to go to his Plan B alternative. The second bomb should have demolished the main building of the school, the stone debris in turn destroying the relatively flimsy construction of the arched shell enclosing the hockey rink. By now Tritt should have been halfway across Lake Winnipesaukee, riding on the snowmobile he'd left behind Gorman's Restaurant earlier in the evening.

Reaching the other side of the lake and his rental car, Tritt would have detonated the other four truck bombs spread around the town via satellite phone, and while Winter Falls burned he'd be climbing aboard the little Cessna he'd chartered at Laconia Airport and heading into oblivion once more.

Instead he was on the third floor of an old brick bed-and-breakfast in a snowstorm, awaiting the inevitable arrival of the president and his retinue. It would make his own exfiltration considerably more dangerous, but he'd contracted for the president's death and, if nothing else, he always fulfilled his contracts.

Tritt shifted slightly in his chair beside the window. They'd be coming from the west and they'd be coming fast, lights flashing and sirens wailing. The security they used for once-upon-a-time presidents was definitely second-tier – new Secret Service types as well as old burnouts – but it was enough to give him trouble. There'd be a few local cops and a squad of state police from the VIP protection bunch, but that would be about it.

They'd all heave a sigh of relief once the chopper rose into the snowy air, and that's when he would strike.

He reached over and laid his hand on the tube of the ATC Confined Space Anti-Tank weapon. Unlike the weapon he'd used in Italy, the ATC was unguided, but from his window the chopper was no more than 150 meters away. He could hardly miss. The two-kilo, high-explosive warhead would turn the VIP helicopter into scrap metal in a split second.

He had timed it roughly and it would take him about thirty seconds to get out through the main-floor kitchen of the hotel and another minute to reach Gorman's Restaurant and the dock that ran out to the ice beside it. It was really the only way out.

Whatever was left of the Maine's Right Arm bunch he'd brought with him were to escape by road, but if the state police were any good at all they'd have expanding perimeter roadblocks established very quickly, especially with a President of the United States involved, soon-to-be-ex or otherwise.

If the MRA types were dumb enough they'd try to shoot their way out, which would mean even more fuel to Matoon and the Sinclair bitch's fire. The whole plan was insane, of course, but so was Hitler, and it didn't matter, anyway, since they paid well. He could and would retire on what they were paying him for this night's work.

He heard the sirens now, approaching fast. He parted the curtains slightly and opened the old-fashioned casement window. He picked up the antitank weapon from the side table on his left, balanced it on his right shoulder and used the index finger of his right hand to disengage the two safeties. He moved the index finger from the safety switches on the side of the tube and laid it firmly on the firing button that was located just in front of the optical night sight. He waited and for a moment he let himself see the clear Caribbean blue of the water just offshore from his place at Lyford Cay. He slowly let the air out of his lungs, imagining himself snorkeling above a school of darting spotted drums. Below him the motorcade came into view. They were here and it was time to end it.

37

'Shit,' said Randy Lockwood. Out of the whirling snow he could see the lead car of the motorcade, light bar flashing, the sound of its siren muffled by the storm. If Tritt was nearby they had no more than a few seconds to find him. Behind the Winter Falls cruiser he could see the trailing line of Escalades, one of them with the president inside. He gritted his teeth and prayed that this man Holliday was wrong.

As a rule the average person rarely looks higher than the horizon directly in front of him. This is a natural instinct bred into the human race for millions of years, since man's predators almost inevitably approached him on the same level, whether from the front or the rear. It is also the first instinct to disappear very quickly among military personnel and even civilians in places like Iraq and Afghanistan; like the unofficial motto of the Eighty-second Airborne in Vietnam, death very often came from above.

Holliday knew that if Tritt was nearby he'd go for the high ground. The square in front of the Municipal Building had two-story, Victorian-era buildings on the east side and the same on the west, with the Municipal Building forming the northern side of the square. The south, or Main Street side, was taken up by the Dominion Hotel, a squat, seven-story, flat-roofed brick building that looked down on to the park that formed the center of the square.

As the motorcade swept around the eastern side of the square Holliday looked up. At first nothing seemed out of place. The Dominion Hotel, like every other building in Winter Falls, was dark.

'Anything?' Lockwood said.

'No,' said Holliday, squinting through the heavy snowfall. The motorcade was pulling up in front of the Municipal Building.

'There!' said Peggy, pointing.

'What?'

'Third floor, fourth from the left. The window's open! Who the hell would have a window open on a night like this?'

Holliday stared upward, following her pointing finger. He caught a flutter of movement as the wind billowed the curtains. It was Kandahar, before he'd lost his eye. A fluttering window and a shadow with a cell phone. The Humvee stopped just in front of the IED before it exploded and the .50-caliber machine gun on the vehicle shredded the window frame around the twitching curtain and the shadowy figure behind it. He didn't hesitate and neither did Lockwood. They fired simultaneously just as Tritt's finger pushed down on the firing button of the antitank rocket.

The world exploded all around them. A flame trail

from the rocket arced down from the hotel window, catching the Super Puma helicopter squarely between the sliding door and the slightly sagging multiple rotors, striking the big twin Turbomeca engines and rupturing the fuel lines. For a fraction of a second there was silence and it seemed as though little or no damage had been done. Then the explosive warhead of the rocket detonated and the entire helicopter was enveloped in a growing fireball. The blast wave knocked Holliday, Peggy and Lockwood to the ground as fractured pieces of rotor spun off in all directions, one piece slicing through the front entrance of Uncle Jimmy's Sport Paradise, while a second, larger piece sawed through the middle of the lead police cruiser in the motorcade, instantly killing both the driver and his partner.

Through the smoke and flames there was no way to know what had happened to the president. A cloud of choking smoke drifted over the square as Holliday, Lockwood and Peggy picked themselves up. Combined with the heavy snowfall, visibility was now almost zero.

'He was on the third floor,' said Lockwood.

'Which way would he go?' Holliday asked.

'If he's smart he'll figure on roadblocks.'

'What does that mean?'

'He's probably got a snowmobile someplace. They use them to get out to the ice-fishing huts. It wouldn't look out of place down by the docks.'

Holliday nodded. 'He cuts across the lake and he's gone before anybody has time to think. Somewhere along the line he dials his sat phone and blows Winter Falls to hell.'

'Something like that.'

Holliday turned to Peggy. 'Find the top cop in charge over there,' he said, pointing toward the flaming remains of the helicopter. Tell whoever it is that the chief and I are going after Tritt, and they should start looking for more truck bombs before it's too late.'

'You're not just trying to get rid of me are you?'

'Don't be an idiot. I'm trying to save lives. Go!'

She went.

'Now what?' Holliday said.

'Follow me,' said Lockwood. He turned and disappeared into the smoke and snow, heading across the street to the inn.

It had been too soon, but Tritt didn't have any choice. He fired the rocket, dropped the hot metal tube unceremoniously off his shoulder and headed for the door, patting the pocket of his heavy parka to make sure the satellite phone was still there. He ran out into the dark hallway, ignored the elevator to the left and turned right until he reached the door leading to the stairwell.

A minute later he reached the lobby, which was now swarming with guests and hotel employees. People were calling out to one another, someone was crying and flashlight beams were cutting through the haze that had started filling up the main-floor reception area.

Everything smelled of smoke and jet fuel. No one noticed as Tritt headed into the restaurant at the rear of the hotel, then pushed through the swinging doors leading into the kitchen. Ninety seconds after destroying the helicopter in the square he was racing down the alley behind the hotel, and two minutes after that he was turning the key in the ignition of the big, silver Yamaha Vector snowmobile parked behind the patio of Gorman's Restaurant. He twisted the throttle, turned the snowmobile into a tight circle and headed west, out on to the frozen lake.

Tritt smiled behind his heavy woolen balaclava mask and stared out into the snow-filled emptiness of the night. The job was done. With a top speed of seventy miles an hour, no one could catch him now. At the halfway mark he'd stop the vehicle, take out the satellite phone and punch the preset number. It would be the largest non-nuclear blast since the Texas City explosion in 1947, which virtually leveled the entire town.

'We're too late,' said Lockwood. Both men stood at the bottom of the steps that led down to the dock behind Gorman's Restaurant. They could see the imprints of Tritt's boots in the fresh snow and they could faintly hear the sound of the receding snowmobile. There were three more of the vehicles parked at the foot of the stairs, all three surrounded by the pungent odor of freshly spilled gasoline. Tritt had ripped out the fuel lines. 'We'll never catch him. The son of a bitch is going to blow up my town and there's not a damn thing I can do about it.'

'I wouldn't give up quite so quickly,' said Holliday. He walked across the ice to where the line of iceboats was parked. He ran his hand over the sleek, jet-black fiberglass body of one of the water-bug-shaped boats. 'These are Monotype-XVs,' he said. 'I didn't even know they had them in the States.'

'You know how to sail one of these things?' Lockwood asked. The drag-racer bodies were about thirty feet long, with masts almost as high and a broad outrigger with a long bronze-and-steel blade at each end.

There was a third blade at the rear of the body, and the insectlike boat was steered with a large automobile-style wheel in the snug back cockpit. The pilot of the boat also handled the movement and adjustment of the sail through a system of lines and pulleys, while the front cockpit for the copilot essentially provided ballast and a counterweight to prevent the front end of the craft from taking to the air.

'I was stationed in Helsinki for a while. My people had this crazy idea to get assets out of St Petersburg using iceboats like these across the Gulf of Finland. We never tried it but I learned the basics.'

'How are we supposed to catch up with a snow-mobile in a sailboat?' Lockwood said. 'I've seen guys racing these but not at that kind of speed.'

'Top-end record for one of these boats is close to a hundred and twenty-five miles an hour,' said Holliday.

'You ride shotgun up front and I'll see if I can get you within range of the guy who's screwing with your town.'

'How do we get this thing rolling?' Lockwood said.

Tritt slowed the snowmobile, then pulled to a halt and checked the big dial on his watch. The wind was worse than he'd expected and he was going to be late. Not that it mattered; no one was waiting. But punctuality had always been a professional watchword with him and a point of personal pride. He remembered and abided by his German grandfather's favorite platitude: 'Anything worth doing is worth doing well.' He checked the GPS locator taped to the handlebars and made a slight adjustment.

Tritt was old enough and came from a time when GPS, satellite phones and most kinds of twenty-first-century technology were still things to be marveled at and not taken for granted, so he pulled out his old-fashioned Bézard military marching compass and checked that the electronic data from the GPS unit was accurate, which it was. He wound up the throttle of the snowmobile, then switched it off, suddenly aware of a strange sound coming from somewhere behind him. He lifted off his helmet and listened, then put one booted foot on to the windblown, virtually black surface of the ice.

Something. A distant, hollow rumbling. Not any kind of tracked vehicle like his snowmobile. The tone rose and fell erratically, the sound of it even vibrating through the ice. He didn't have the faintest idea what was producing the far-off, odd-sounding roar, but he knew that it didn't belong and for that reason alone he didn't like it. If he had to guess it sounded like somebody dragging a heavy wooden box across the ice at high speed. He looked at his watch again. It was a little too early but he decided to make the call anyway. He took the satellite phone out of his pocket and switched it on.

The silent snowmobile appeared in front of them without warning as Holliday struggled with the wheel, trying to keep the rushing, daggerlike iceboat under control. He had no idea how fast they were going, but up until a few seconds before they'd been trying to follow the sound of the snowmobile when it suddenly stopped. Whatever speed they were going the rush of the wind and the blowing snow made it impossible to communicate with Lockwood, hunched in the tiny forward cockpit, his big Bushmaster jutting toward the front of the boat.

Tritt turned at the sound of the boat, his eyes widening in his snow-rimmed, balaclava-covered face. He reached down with his right hand and brought up a squat little MP5 submachine gun. Lockwood fired, the shot from the big-caliber rifle striking the forward nacelle of the snowmobile and sending up a shower of sparks.

Holliday hauled on the wheel and tightened the sail line simultaneously, veering away in a sliding arc as the bullets from the MP5 stitched into the side of the boat and clanged off the long forward blade as it lifted into the air.

Holliday put the boat into a scraping, one-bladed turn, almost turning the craft over, but by the time they swung back in Tritt's direction the snowmobile was on the move again. Following him, Holliday hammered on the side of the hull to get Lockwood's attention. The cop turned in his seat and gave Holliday a death's-head grin and an okay sign. He hadn't been hit and apparently nothing vital to the operation of the boat had been hit, either.

Tritt was moving in a straight line now, gathering speed and pushing the snowmobile to its limits. In the distance Holliday could see the darker line on the night horizon that marked the far shore of the lake. Once on land Tritt would be lost. The snowmobile could travel over the snow-covered ground, but when the ice ran out the boat could go no farther.

Holliday saw one of Tritt's hands dropping off the handlebars to dig into the pocket of his parka. Initially he expected some kind of weapon, but then he saw the heavy rectangular shape of what had to be a satellite phone. Winter Falls was almost out of time. Holliday twitched the line, stiffening the sail, and the boat gathered even more speed. He could hear Lockwood firing but it was no use – there was too much movement and the shots were going wide.

Ahead of them Holliday could see Tritt twisting slightly in the saddle, driving one-handed, the other hand gripping the satellite phone. Behind the balaclava Holliday knew damn well the assassin was smiling. Holliday pulled the line through the pulleys even more tightly, his speed increasing once again. As the iceboat came up behind the snowmobile Holliday let go of the tugging wheel and let the boat have its head, the whole thing rising off the ice like a yacht heeling over in a high wind.

As the boat rose into the air so did the sharpened, three-and-a-half-foot-long bronze-and-steel blade. Holliday dragged the wheel around farther and the iceboat swung behind the snowmobile at close to a hundred miles an hour, the blade lifting even higher as they swung around the back of the speeding vehicle, turning in a single, sharp tack back on to its original course. The blade sliced into Tritt's body just above his bent hips, tearing through his down jacket, cutting through the spine and belly, severing trunk and torso in an instant. Blood gushed into the air and froze, dropping like tiny scarlet hailstones on to the night-black ice.

The snowmobile, the lower portion of Tritt's dismembered body still in the saddle, roared off into the snowy darkness. Holliday let the mainsail halyard loose and the boat luffed, settled and then stopped. He turned back in his seat, waiting for the distant roar of explosions and fireballs rising from behind them that would mark the destruction of Winter Falls. Ten long seconds passed. Then twenty. Then thirty.

Nothing.

'We did it!' Lockwood hooted.

Holliday closed his eyes and let out a long steaming breath.

They'd won.

38

Winter passed. Over the previous weeks a number of events had occurred abroad, particularly in the United States. As things turned out, the wound incurred by the new vice president had been much more serious than they'd first thought and he'd been forced to resign his position in favor of a healthy candidate better able to serve his country. A grateful president had given Richard Pierce Sinclair the Presidential Medal of Freedom in the Oval Office in absentia, the medal received instead by his mother, Kate Sinclair. William Sinclair was thought to be recuperating at his mother's vineyard estate in Switzerland.

Jihad al-Salibiyya fell out of the news cycle and was never heard from again. Wilmot DeJean, putative leader of a fringe militia group known as Maine's Right Arm, was found dead of a heart attack in his room at the Brac Beach Resort in Cayman Brac. According to several of his disgruntled followers DeJean had fraudulently embezzled most of the organization's 'war chest.'

Angus Scott Matoon disappeared on a helicopter hunting trip in northern Alaska. His body was never found. Randy Lockwood retired as Police Chief of Winter Falls shortly after testifying at a closed Senate hearing on the somewhat unorthodox activities of Lieutenant

Colonel John 'Doc' Holliday and Peggy Blackstock, although there was a rumor that he'd be running for mayor during next year's election. Following the Senate hearing all three were invited to the White House for a private lunch with the president and his wife.

The explosion that occurred during the president's nostalgic trip back to the town of Winter Falls was later discovered to have been caused by a man foolishly lighting a cigarette while topping off the heating tanks at a local shopping center. The resulting explosion destroyed the nearby electrical substation, plunging the town into blackness. The president was successfully evacuated and, according to White House sources, was never in any danger.

In the Bahamas Mary Breau, the real estate agent, had several people inquire after the Lyford Cay property belonging to Mr William Tritt, but she was having a great deal of difficulty getting in touch with the owner.

Spring came to the Vatican. Gentle breezes rustled through the olive trees and citrons along the garden pathways. The rush of Rome's frenetic traffic was a dull, distant roar behind high stone walls. For the moment all was calm in the home of St Peter's Church.

Cardinal Secretary of State Antonio Niccolo Spada and Father Thomas Brennan, head of Soladitum Pianum, the Vatican Secret Service, strolled through the Giardini Vaticani, the famous Vatican Gardens, enjoying the warm sunshine, the plaintive, understated call of the common redstart coming from the branches of the trees around them, a single, predatory kestrel flying high above them, its dark wings like a skirling warning of things to come. Passing a lemon tree, Spada plucked one of the small yellow fruits and held it to his nose, breathing in the rich, tart scent.

'So in the end very little has changed,' said the cardinal, his long robes brushing the gravel of the pathway as he walked.

'We have something of what we wanted.' The black-suited priest shrugged, the rancid odor of his fuming cigarette in harsh contrast to the lush, earthy perfumes of the gardens around them. 'At least we have a new Pope.'

'And a tractable one, as well,' murmured Spada. 'Unlike his predecessor. He was coming far too close to secrets that were none of his concern.'

'Sinclair didn't get the notebook,' Brennan said quietly.

'And neither did we,' snapped the cardinal. 'While the world watches our moral compass disintegrate into a tawdry sex scandal, the Holy See is on the verge tof bankruptcy.'

'Better to have the distraction of a sex scandal than an auditor's report,' answered Brennan.

'Holliday neither uses nor abuses the wealth of the Templars, wealth that rightfully belongs to the Church, not a single man.'

'He sees himself as no more than the steward of the treasure, not its owner,' said Brennan. 'Like the monk Rodrigues before him.'

'I couldn't care less about Colonel Holliday's perception of himself; I want what is rightfully ours.'

'Kate Sinclair would say the same,' reponded the black-suited priest. 'For her this has been a single battle in a longer war.'

'A war that we *must* win,' said Spada. 'Whatever it takes, get me the Templar notebook!'

Doc Holliday discreetly unbuckled his seat belt and gazed out the window as the big El Al 747 lumbered into the sky over Kennedy Airport and headed east. He settled back into his comfortable first-class seat, sipped his glass of freshly squeezed orange juice and turned to Peggy Blackstock, who occupied the seat next to him.

'So, tell me again why I'm coming back to Israel with you?'

'Because we both need a rest, because they fired you from your temp job at Georgetown University for missing too many classes and because Rafi found something on his trip to darkest Africa that he thought might interest you.'

'Great,' said Holliday. He finished his juice, put down the glass, eased his seat back lower and closed his eyes. 'Just as long as it's warm, there's a beach and I can get a little peace and quiet.'

'I guarantee it,' said Peggy.

'Famous last words,' muttered Holliday, and then he was asleep.

Read on for a taste of
Paul Christopher's new thriller

THE TEMPLAR LEGION

Available from Penguin in October 2012

Prologue

A.D. 1039
The Nile River at Karnak
One hundred leagues from Alexandria

His name was Ragnar Skull Splitter and his ship was the *Kraka*, named for the daughter of a Valkyrie and a Viking chief. *Kraka's* carved wooden image, eyes closed in dreaming sleep, long hair covering her naked body, graced the bow of his warship. It was said that Kraka, like her mother before her, had the power to interpret dreams and see the future. Ragnar fervently prayed that it was so and that she would guide him home once more with her prophecies, because for the last ten days he had traveled a river that seemingly had no end and for five of those days had traveled through what he now knew, despite the blistering heat from the relentless sun, was nothing less than *Niflheim*, the dark and eternally frozen land of the dead.

Ragnar was the cousin of Harald Sigurdsson, the head of the Varangian Emperors Guard in *Miklagard*, the Great Walled City, or Constantinople, as the local people called it. Ragnar was Harald's greatest warrior, and before setting out from that wondrous city at the neck of the world he had vowed to his cousin that he would not return until he had found the secret mines of the ancient king and taken their vast riches in Harald's name.

If he failed it would not be for the lack of a good ship and good men to sail her. From his position on the steering platform at the high end of the stern he proudly looked down *Kraka's* length.

She was eighty feet from the carved effigy of her namesake in the bow to the high, elegantly curved line of her sternpost. She was eighteen feet wide and barely six feet deep from the gunwales to the keelson that ran the length of the ship. She was made of solid oak from the shallow slopes of Flensburg Fjord, her clinker-built hull created by overlapping planks attached to the heavy ribs with more than five thousand iron rivets, roved between each plank with tarred rope. The planks became progressively thinner as they rose toward the gunwales, making the boat light, strong and flexible. She drew less than three feet and could be rowed right up on the shallowest beachhead.

At sea with her big sail set, *Kraka* could make an easy ten knots and could travel more than fifty leagues in a single day. Here, on a river as black as night, its waters populated by swimming monsters of dizzying variety, she could barely do two knots and travel six or seven leagues before her thirty-two rowers could no longer lift the ponderous eighteen-foot oars.

Ragnar looked fondly down at his men from the steering platform. Like Ragnar, they were stripped to the waist, the muscles of their backs and shoulders gleaming with sweat as they pulled the ship through the ominous waters. Also like Ragnar, each of them wore the linen head coverings bound with strips of cloth the local people called *nemes*.

In the bow, on a smaller version of the steering platform, stood the strange, high-ranking *negeren* court slave pressed on him by Harald, and the slave's even stranger companion, a gigantic eunuch named Barakah who took care of the *negeren's* personal needs as well as recording their whereabouts with fantastically detailed maps, sketches and drawings, made at his master's order. The black man's name was Abdul al-Rahman and it was he who suggested that Ragnar and his men adopt the *nemes* after two of the warriors collapsed over their oars, stunned and terribly sick with the sun.

Just below the steering platform, Aki, the last oarsman on the starboard side, called out the cadence with an old kenning chant:

> Most men know that
> Gunnbjorn the captain
> lies long buried in this mound;
> never was there
> a more valiant traveler
> of the wondrous-wide ground of Endil
> his tale told proudly and with honor

> in the skalds
> till Njörðr, god of oceans,
> Drowns the land.

Ragnar turned to his steersman, a gruff, powerful man named Hurlu who'd been steersman on *Kraka* for years before Ragnar became her captain. 'How long have the men been rowing?'

'Since the morning daymark.' Hurlu squinted up at the sun, which was almost directly overhead. 'Six hours at least. Too long.'

Ragnar nodded. He'd done his time at the oars often enough and knew the weight of the heavy blade digging through the water. His shoulders ached at the memory. 'We should pull into shore,' said Ragnar. 'Let the men rest.'

'I agree.' Hurlu nodded.

Ragnar let it pass. In a younger man it would have been an insubordinate response, but Hurlu was as old as the planks in *Kraka*'s bilge and he'd been piloting ships since Ragnar had played with balls of yarn in his mother's lap.

'We'll need shade,' said Ragnar. He looked out at the bleak, arid land on either side of the river. There was nothing to see but bare rock and high ridges of sandstone baking in the relentless sun.

Hurlu made a brief sound of disgust and spat over the sternpost. He nodded toward the bow. 'Ask your pet monkey up there; maybe he'll know where we can find some.' Hurlu had a superstitious mistrust of the black man and made no bones about it to anyone, including Ragnar.

Ragnar whistled shrilly, and when al-Rahman looked back he gestured for the black man to join him in the stern. Al-Rahman said something briefly to Barakah, who nodded, then stepped off the little platform down on to the narrow plank gangway that ran the length of the ship. As he moved, his long white robes swirled elegantly around his ankles.

Al-Rahman had the grace of a dancing girl but he was no simpering *rassragr;* Ragnar had seen evidence enough of that when they were loading stores in Alexandria. That same dancer's grace had turned to a warrior's brutally agile fury when a gang of cutpurses had confronted him in an alley and demanded payment for passage through to the street beyond, making it clear that he would suffer the consequences if he refused. Al-Rahman had sliced all four ragged men to ribbons in a few short seconds, a short, curve-bladed Saif appearing magically in his right hand from beneath those same swirling robes.

'*Aasalaamu Aleikum*, Ragnar; you wished to speak with me?'

'*Wa-Aleikum Aassalaam, Abdul,*' said Ragnar, using the response he'd been taught by al-Rahman. Beside him, Hurlu scowled and spat over the side again, just as Ragnar knew he would. Ragnar grinned; he enjoyed getting the older man's goat whenever the opportunity presented itself. Al-Rahman's ornately tattooed face broke into a smile as well; he knew just what the tall, blond Dane was thinking. They were a strange pair: Ragnar as broad as an oak, al-Rahman as slim as a willow, but both equally strong, each in his own way. They were too different ever to become real friends but over their time together they'd developed a mutual trust and respect.

'We need shade and freshwater, and soon; my men are wilting like flowers, Abdul. How likely are we to find it in this oven of a place?'

'Flowers,' grunted Hurlu. 'Huh.'

Al-Rahman turned and pointed. 'We will pass this ridge and the Great Snake will make a sudden turn. In its coils you will find a *waha* the old Greeks called Chenoboskion.'

'*Waha?*' Ragnar asked.

'A watering place in the desert, a sanctuary,' explained al-Rahman.

'How long?'

'At this rate?' Al-Rahman shrugged. 'An hour perhaps.'

Ragnar turned to Hurlu. 'You hear that, steersman? It seems we're not dead yet.'

'No,' said Hurlu, 'just dried-out old corpses like they use for their cooking fires in that pigsty of a city back there.' He nodded his head downriver.

'Al-Qahira,' said Ragnar, remembering the name

of the squalid place and its ironic meaning: 'the victorious.'

'That'd be the one,' said Hurlu. 'Using the corpses of their forefathers for kindling, pah!'

'Well, Hurlu, can our wilting flowers do it?'

The grizzled older man spat over the side again. 'Can they do it?' He turned and called down to the stroke oarsman seated on the bench below him. 'Aki! A war song for our lord and master here! Battle speed!' *Kraka* leaped forward.

In less than half the time al-Rahman had predicted, they came within sight of their goal, the dark river churning white under *Kraka*'s stern as the oars bit smoothly into the water. The *waha*, as al-Rahman had called it, was a few rudely built huts of mud and daub huddled under the protection of a gathering of date palms, their high, broad leaves bright green in the dazzling sun. The dark windows of the huts had the blank, sightless look that marked long abandonment.

Ragnar shaded his eyes and looked toward the shore. Perhaps a few fishermen had lived here once, but like everything else in this forsaken country, that was long past. The huts would be home only to scorpions and spiders now, seeking shade, just like *Kraka*'s crew. Ragnar could also see a small stream tumbling down the shallow bank of the river, coming from some spring hidden within the stand of trees. Back home, on the shores of Flensburg Fjord, the stream, barely a trickle, would have been ignored; here it was a life-giving torrent.

The men scarcely needed the order to pull toward the shore. Grunting a little with the effort, Hurlu turned the long steering oar against the current. According to al-Rahman this was the time of full flood for the river, and the water was high. A few moments later *Kraka* ran easily up on to the muddy bank. The two forward oarsmen hauled up the stone-heavy wooden anchor and heaved it over the side to hold *Kraka* against the flow. The landing was done silently and with ease; these men had beached their ship a thousand times on a thousand different shores, and the operation went with almost mechanical smoothness, but even so the men sat with rigid discipline until Hurlu called out the order; their throats were parched and their lips cracked with thirst but, as always, the ship came first.

'Ship oars!' Hurlu bellowed. The oars rattled through their leather-slung tholes as the men pulled them inboard until all thirty-two stood like a forest above the gunwales.

'Rack oars!' Moving from bow to stern the men swung their oars inboard and dropped them into the forward and aft cradles that already held the stepped mast, furled sails and boom as well as an entire set of replacement oars. In bad weather the filled racks sometimes acted as ridgepole for a tentlike space above the stores to keep dry under.

'Out you go, lads!'

With weak, croaking shouts of approval the men went forward to the bow and jumped down on to the mud- and pebble-strewn beach. Usually, if the water was shallow enough, the men would simply jump over the side where they rowed, but not here.

They'd all seen the gigantic, long-jawed, scaly creatures that lived in the shadowed waters of the Great Snake, and watched in horror as a pair of them took down a bullock calf quietly drinking at the shore just outside the town al-Rahman called Al-Qahira. The two creatures, acting in concert, had nearly bitten the bullock in half before they hauled it into deeper water, still bleating piteously until its cries were swallowed up and drowned.

With *Kraka* empty, the men staggering into the trees to find the hidden spring, Hurlu turned to Ragnar.

'Good enough?'

'Good enough.' Ragnar nodded.

Hurlu jumped down from the raised platform, stomped down the long gangplank and heaved himself over the side. Finally Ragnar and al-Rahman went ashore themselves, followed by Barakah, the silent eunuch.

The source of the tiny trickling stream turned out to be a large pool of almost unbelievably cool freshwater sparkling beneath the little forest of palms. Some of the men dropped down on their bellies and stuck their heads into the water; others simply stripped off their tunics and boots, then flung themselves naked into the pool.

Ragnar and al-Rahman slaked their thirsts with a little more decorum, then watched the men.

'Man needs; Odin provides.' Ragnar laughed, quoting an old saying his mother had taught him at her knee.

Al-Rahman smiled. 'Not Odin or any other god,' he said. 'This pool is the gift of time.'

'I thought you believed in your own god, Allah,' said Ragnar.

'I believe in the teachings of his great prophet Muhammad, may he be blessed, but Allah is not for man to know or pretend he understands. The Hebrews will not even speak their own god's name for the same reason.'

'And *kuffār*, like us. Infidels?' Ragnar smiled, remembering the word al-Rahman had taught him.

Al-Rahman smiled back at the burly Dane. 'Muhammad commands us to pity you and teach you the True Way.'

The two men left the pool and strolled through the stand of palms. The grass grew long here, and where rotted dates had fallen more sprigs of greenery grew. Ragnar realized that it was the first time he had relaxed in days. On the edge of the little grove of trees, with nothing but the open desert sands before them, they discovered a great slab of rock jutting from the soil. It was black and smooth as glass except where it had been deeply etched with lines and figures. Some of the figures were clearly meant to be men but others were pictures of strange, fantastic animals: huge horned bulls, some sort of gazelle with a neck so long it looked over all the other figures and additional, smaller creatures: a cat with enormous fangs, and something with gigantic ears and legs like tree stumps, two horns jutting from between its lips. Smaller lines had been scratched to indicate fields of grass and below everything was a thick black snake that could only be the great river behind them.

'Some man's fever dream from long ago?' Ragnar said, letting his fingers trail over the lines.

'Or a memory,' said al-Rahman. 'Perhaps this place was once a paradise of green grass and trees and hunters' game. Perhaps the pool your men are bathing in is nothing more than rain that fell ten thousand years ago and now springs up here and there to remind us of the past.'

'How can paradise become a desert?' Ragnar asked.

'How can the civilization that built the great pyramids and the ancient temples we passed have vanished?' al-Rahman responded. 'Nothing is impossible; everything fades away.'

Ragnar turned back and stared through the stands of trees at the river.

'Is our quest possible? Will we really find the Mines of Solomon?'

'The Romans thought it was real enough.' Al-Rahman shrugged. 'There are other stories.' The black man paused. 'There was once a great king named Sogolon Djata who could have been mistaken for Harald's

Solomon. His children grew very rich and it is said their very houses were made of gold. There are also tales of their great city in the desert, called Timbuktu, a place of vast wealth and a storehouse of even greater knowledge.'

'Could such a place really exist?' Ragnar said.

Al-Rahman laughed loudly, then clapped Ragnar on the shoulder. 'I think we shall find out, Ragnar Skull Splitter, the two of us, and perhaps even return to tell the tale.'

I

'Except for that one unfortunate trip we made into Libya to rescue cousin Peggy, Africa isn't really my thing,' said Colonel John 'Doc' Holliday. 'I'm more of a knights-in-shining-armor or Roman Empire kind of guy.'

'This is different,' said Rafi Wa nounou. They were sitting in the living room of the archaeologist's bright, spacious apartment on Ramban Street in the Rehavia district of Jerusalem. From the kitchen Holliday could smell the aroma of almond mushroom chicken, beef kung pao and soya duck as Peggy plated their take-out dinner of kosher Chinese food. According to Peggy the art of knowing which restaurant to order from was even more important than knowing how to cook, a philosophy she'd practiced since high school.

'All right,' said Doc. 'I'll bite. Why should I give up six months of my life to run around Ethiopia, the deserts of Sudan and the jungles of the Congo with you and Peggy when I've got a perfectly good job offer from the Alabama Military Academy and a chance to write my book on the Civil War?'

'Because Mobile is a sauna in the summer,' called Peggy from the kitchen.

'And the last thing the world needs is another book on the Civil War.' Rafi grinned.

'Okay, what do you have to offer besides malaria, fifty kinds of poisonous snakes and blood-crazed rebel hordes?'

'His name was Julian de la Roche-Guillaume,' said Rafi. 'He was a Cistercian monk, and he was a Templar.'

'Never heard of him,' said Holliday.

'I'm not surprised; he was pretty obscure,' said Rafi, popping a dumpling into his mouth. He chewed thoughtfully for a moment. 'He's usually referred to as the Lost Templar if he's referred to at all. He's basically been forgotten by history, and if he is referenced in some obscure footnote he's remembered as a coward who deserted his holy brothers.'

'Sounds like Indiana Jones material, doesn't it?' Peggy said.

'What is this *thing* you have for Indiana Jones?' Rafi said. 'He certainly doesn't use the appropriate field technique for a proper archaeologist.'

'You don't get it.' Peggy grinned. 'It's not Indiana Jones I have a *thing* for; it's Harrison Ford.'

'Tell me more about this Lost Templar of yours,' said Holliday.

'He was always more of a scholar than a real Templar Knight,' said Rafi. 'When Saladin entrusted the scrolls from Alexandria and the other libraries to the Templars when Jerusalem fell, Roche-Guillaume was one of the men brought in to evaluate them. He was apparently brilliant and could speak and write more than a dozen languages.'

'Sounds like an interesting guy,' said Holliday. 'What does this have to do with Ethiopia?'

'I found him there,' said Rafi. 'I discovered his tomb while I was excavating at Lake Tana last year when you and my dear wife were gallivanting around Washington getting yourselves into all kinds of trouble.'

'We weren't gallivanting,' said Peggy, bringing in the plates and setting them down on the table at the far end of the room. 'We were running for our lives; it's an entirely different thing.' She looked at her watch, then turned and used a wooden match to light the twin Shabbat candles on the old Victorian buffet. When they were lit she gently waved her hands over the flames, covered her eyes and said the blessing:

'*Barukh ata Adonai Eloheinu Melekh ha-olam, asher kid'shanu b'mitzvotav v'tzivanu l'hadlik ner shel Shabbat.*'

'Listen to that, would you?' Rafi said proudly as he and Holliday got up and went to the table. 'She's a better Jew than I am. She does the *licht tsinden* and the blessing like a pro.'

'And Granddaddy was a Baptist preacher,' said Peggy, sitting down. 'Who would have thunk it?'

'Thirteen twenty-four is more than a decade after the Templar purge by King Philip,' said Holliday. 'How did he manage to get away?'

'He never went back to France,' explained Rafi. 'Roche-Guillaume was no fool. He was in Cyprus after

Jerusalem fell again and he could see the handwriting on the wall. The Templars had too much money, too much power and they flaunted it to the king of France and to the pope. Not healthy or smart. They were politically doomed. Rather than go down with the ship, so to speak, Roche-Guillaume fled overland to Egypt. Alexandria, to be exact. He became a tutor to the sons of the Mamluk sultans.'

'Alexandria is a long way from Ethiopia,' said Holliday.

'You don't have a romantic bone in your body, do you, Doc?' Peggy chided, spearing a piece of duck. 'It's a *story*.'

'Sorry,' said Holliday.

'Roche-Guillaume was a historian, just like you, Doc, and a bit of an archaeologist to boot – you could even say he was a little like Peggy, because he documented all his work with sketches. Hundreds of them, mostly on parchment. Among other things Roche-Guillaume *was* a romantic. He'd become convinced over time that the queen of Sheba really did have a relationship with Solomon, and it was the queen of Sheba who showed Solomon the location of the real King Solomon's Mines. He was also of the somewhat unpopular opinion that the queen of Sheba was black. Coal black, in fact.'

'You've got to be kidding me.' Holliday laughed. '*King Solomon's Mines* is a fiction. A story by Rider Haggard from the nineteenth century. The mines are a myth.'

'Solomon existed; that's historical fact and so is Sheba. Some people think Sheba was a part of Arabia, perhaps Yemen. Given what I've uncovered I'd be willing to bet it was Ethiopia. Or at least it began there.'

'What makes you say that?' Holliday asked, picking at his food.

'Because of Mark Antony.'

'The "I come to bury Caesar, not to praise him" Mark Antony? Cleopatra and Mark Antony, that one?'

'That one.' Rafi nodded.

'He's involved?'

'Instrumental. It's thirty-seven B.C. and Mark's running out of cash. Cleopatra's paid for his wars so far but the cupboard is dry and his enemies are closing in.'

'Marcus Vipsanius Agrippa and his pals. I know the history, Rafi. I taught it at West Point for years.'

'Mark Antony's broke. He's got an army to feed, but like I said, the cupboard is bare and his mistress is nagging him. So what does he do?'

'Don't keep me in suspense,' said Holliday.

'He sends a legion up the Nile to look for the treasure of the land of Sheba and King Solomon's Mines.'

'What legion are we talking about here?'

'*Legio nona Hispana,*' said Rafi. He rolled a piece of steamed bok choy around his fork and ate it. 'The Ninth.'

'The lost legion?' Holliday laughed. This was getting more Byzantine by the second. 'They disappeared up by Hadrian's Wall. They were wiped out.'

'That's one theory,' said Rafi. 'The other is that they suffered heavy losses and changed their name when they were sent to Africa under Mark Antony. They became the Eighteenth Legion *Lybica* under Mark Antony and a questionable general named Lucius Gellius Publicola, who was inclined to betray you depending on which way the wind blew.'

'Says what historical source?'

'Julian de la Roche-Guillaume, the Templar turned rich kids' tutor,' responded Rafi. 'While he was in Alexandria he found the legion's records detailing their orders, equipment, stores, all kinds of things. The Imperial Romans were like Germans, meticulous about their records, but there's no record anywhere of their return. They simply vanished up the Nile.'

'Looking for King Solomon's Mines.'

'Apparently.'

'That's quite a rabbit hole you've got there, Alice,' said Holliday. He dipped a spring roll in a small dish of soy sauce and took a bite. 'What's next, the Mad Hatter?'

'Better,' said Peggy, grinning. Outside a light breeze gently ruffled the leaves on the olive trees in the courtyard. In the distance they could hear the arthritic creaking of the old stone windmill that had once generated electricity for the neighborhood.

'Better?' Holliday said.

'Harald Sigurdsson,' said Rafi.

'A Viking? The one who became Harald Hardrada, Harald the Hard Man? This is starting to get silly, guys.'

'Harald Sigurdsson was, among other things, the head of the eastern emperor's Varangian Guard in Constantinople. He also led the Varangians into battle in North Africa, Syria, Palestine and Sicily gathering booty. While he was in Alexandria raping and pillaging he heard rumors about the lost legion and sent one of his best men, Ragnar Skull Splitter, to lead a crew up the Nile looking for them.'

'When was this?'

'A.D. ten thirty-nine. About three hundred years before Roche-Guillaume.'

'So what happened to Ragnar Skull Splitter, or should I ask?'

'He disappeared, just like the lost legion.'

'So where is this going exactly?'

'Ragnar Skull Splitter took a scholar much like Roche-Guillaume with him to record the story of the journey. His name was Abdul al-Rahman, a high-ranking slave from Constantinople with a yen for travel and adventure. He was also useful as an interpreter. He also had his own artist to record what he saw, a court eunuch named Barakah. An eleventh-century version of Peg here.'

Peggy gave her husband a solid swat on the arm. 'I ain't no eunuch, sweet lips.'

'And they went looking for King Solomon's Mines, right?' Holliday asked.

'Not only did they look for them; they found them. Ragnar died of blackwater fever on the journey home but Abdul al-Rahman survived and made it as far as Ethiopia. While Roche-Guillaume was at Lake Tana he found al-Rahman's chronicle of the journey at an obscure island on the lake. He copied the parchments, which were buried with him.'

Holliday shrugged. 'Who's to say Roche-Guillaume didn't make it all up, a pleasant fiction? A Homeric epic. Where's the proof?'

Rafi got up from the table and went to the old Victorian buffet where the Shabbat candles burned. He took out an old, deeply carved wooden box and set it gently down in the center of the table. The carvings appeared to be Viking runes.

'Open it,' said Rafi.

Holliday lifted the simple lid of the dark wood box. Nestled inside was a piece of quartz about the size of a roughly heart-shaped golf ball. Threaded around one end of the stone was a thick, buttery vein of what appeared to be gold.

'That was in Roche-Guillaume's tomb,' said Rafi. 'If the thugs at the Central Revolutionary Investigation Department in Addis Ababa knew I'd smuggled it out they'd probably arrest me.'

'For a bit of gold in a quartz matrix?' Holliday said.

'It's not quartz,' replied Rafi. 'It's a six-hundred-and-sixty-four-carat flawless diamond. VVSI, I think they call it. I asked a friend who knows about such things.

According to him it's the tenth-largest diamond in the world. Fair market value is about twenty million dollars. The historical value is incalculable.'

'And this supposedly came from King Solomon's Mines?' Holliday said, staring at the immense stone.

'According to al-Rahman's chronicle that Roche-Guillaume copied there's a mountain of stones just like it. Tons.'

'Where exactly?'

'That's the problem,' said Rafi. 'As far as I can figure out the mines are located in what is now the Kukuana-land district of the Central African Republic.'

'Oh, dear,' said Holliday. 'General Solomon Kol-ingba.'

'Kolingba the cannibal,' added Peggy, eating the last piece of lemon chicken. 'The only African dictator with his own set of Ginsu knives for chopping up his enemies.'

Dr Oliver Gash drove the black-and-yellow-striped Land Rover down the dusty dirt road from Bangui at seventy miles an hour, the air-conditioning going full blast and Little Richard screaming out '*Rip It Up*' on the eight-speaker Bose. Since crossing the border into what had once been known as the Kukuanaland district of the Central African Republic and which was now known as the Independent Democratic Republic of Kukuanaland, Dr Gash hadn't seen another vehicle on the road. Every village he drove through seemed deserted, every roadside stall shuttered and dark.

The young black man behind the wheel wasn't surprised. In fact, the apparent emptiness made him smile. It was a demonstration of fear, and fear, as he well knew, was power. The bumblebee-striped Land Rover had the Kolingba royal crest on the doors, and news traveled fast in the new Kukuanaland about anything and anyone to do with General Solomon Bokassa Sesesse Kolingba.

Dr Gash was the minister of the interior in the Independent Democratic Republic of Kukuanaland, as well as the young country's minister of revenue and secretary of state and director of foreign affairs. Oliver Gash was not the name the man behind the wheel had been born with; nor was he a doctor of any kind. Gash had once been Olivier Hakizimana Gashabi of Rwanda and had left that country with his older sister, Eliane, during the genocide of 1994, traveling across the Democratic Republic of Congo to eventually settle in Bangui, the capital of the Central African Republic.

Three years after their arrival in Bangui, Olivier's sister had been chosen from an online catalog as a contract e-mail bride by an American named Arthur Andrew Hartman, who lived in Baltimore. Nineteen-year-old Eliane had agreed to the marriage only on the condition that Hartman formally adopt her eleven-year-old brother.

Hartman was in no position to refuse Eliane's proposition. As an acne-scarred, introverted, sexually problematic, onetime Section 8 discharge from the United States Army for an unspecified 'condition,' and an ex–postal worker now on psychiatric disability, Arthur Andrew Hartman had little or no opportunity for meaningful contact with members of the opposite sex and was far too paranoid about contracting a sexually transmitted disease to purchase relief from his lonely predicament.

Three years later Arthur Andrew Hartman was found with his pants around his ankles, his genitals mutilated and his throat slit in an alley behind a shopping center in the Gardenville district of Baltimore. For a brief period Hartman's fifteen-year-old adopted son was suspected in the killing of his 'father' but there wasn't enough evidence to prove the case, and the Baltimore state prosecutor's office declined to go forward. The successful murder of his despised and adopted father was Olivier Gashabi's first foray into the world of crime. It was not his last.

Eliane used her share of Hartman's postal life insurance policy and the money from the quick sale of his house on Asbury Avenue to purchase half interest in a mani-pedi salon. Olivier Gashabi, his name now legally changed to Oliver Gash, invested the fee paid by his sister for murdering Hartman into two kilograms of cocaine. That was in 2001. Ten years later Eliane Gashabi owned four mani-pedi salons outright and her brother had increased his original investment a hundredfold. He had also developed a number of serious enemies within the state prosecutor's office, the Baltimore Police Department and the extensive criminal network that ran between Washington, D.C., Baltimore and New York City. The twenty-five-year-old criminal entrepreneur was suddenly consumed by a passion to seek out his roots, and, traveling on his perfectly valid United States passport, he returned to the Central African Republic.

Criminal enterprise in Bangui was already controlled by a number of tribally centered gangs that enforced their rule with machetes, so Gashabi-Gash decided to travel into his own heart of darkness and went up-country by steamer on the Kottu River to the Kuku-analand town of Fourandao.

Fourandao had once been a French colonial town best known for its cocoa and tobacco plantations, both crops controlled by the old Portuguese family that had given the town its name. The town, a collection of one- and two-story mud-brick buildings with corrugated iron roofs, sprawled untidily along the banks of the Kottu for half a mile or so, and straggled into the surrounding jungle toward the distant Bakouma hills that marked the border with Sudan and Chad.

Oliver Gash arrived at the Fourandao docks early one morning to find the small city in the midst of a revolution. By the early afternoon, seeing which way the wind was blowing, he had allied himself with the forces of the KNRA, the Kukuanaland National Revolutionary Alliance, led by an upstart lieutenant in FACA, the Forces Armées Centrafricaines, named Solomon Kolingba. The actual governor of the territory, a doctor named Amobe Limbani, a member of the Yakima minority, fled into the jungle, never to be heard from again.

By late evening Oliver Gash had been made a full colonel by the newly minted General Kolingba, and by midnight Gash and Kolingba were celebrating the birth of the Kukuanaland nation with a bottle of Veuve Clicquot champagne liberated from the bar of the Hotel Trianon in the town's central square, now grandly renamed the Plaza de Revolution de Generale Kolingba.

The following day Gash and Kolingba got down to business. Due to various and sundry wars, political upheavals and criminal restructurings around the world, the normal trade routes for heroin at various levels of refinement were no longer available. Using his contacts within the United States, Oliver Gash suggested to Kolingba that Kukuanaland become the new Marseilles, acting as a refinement and distribution center for high-grade narcotics, then branching out into the small-arms trade, contract terrorism, blood-diamond marketing, large-scale money laundering and an assortment of other disagreeable but profitable occupations that would make the open city of Fourandao into the new home of Gangster, Incorporated. A 1930s Chicago for the twenty-first century. The American dream in the middle of an equatorial African jungle.

It worked beyond Olivier Gashabi's wildest expectations. Fourandao and the surrounding area had flourished. The airport had been refurbished with extended runways for private jets, and the ragtag army had been issued brand-new uniforms and new weapons, all donated by the General Armament Department of the Chinese government. The Chinese were also putting in a proper filtration plant for Fourandao and paving the surrounding roads. Oliver Gash had discovered a surprising talent for politics and diplomacy; as it turned out they had a lot in common with crime.

In Africa, as anywhere else, corruption and greed in the realm of politics was a way of life; the only difference was that in Africa it was expected and accepted.

Eventually the bumblebee-painted Rover reached the tumbledown docks of the town. A few barges were being loaded with fruit and bales of rubber for the long trip downriver but they were really no more than protective cover for the loads of drugs, weapons and other illicit goods distributed out of the harsh jungle country. Docked ahead of the barges was the single boat in Kukuanaland's navy – a donated thirty-five-foot river patrol boat from the Djibouti navy equipped with a fifty-horsepower Evinrude and a leaky cabin. Its only armament was a single Kord heavy machine gun left over from a Russian delegation that managed to offload it to Kolingba in the early days of his regime. When the general was in a particularly sporty mood he and Gash and a quartet of bodyguards would go fishing in the boat and hunt crocodiles with the machine gun.

The only thing worrying Gash as he drove along the waterfront was a recent meeting he'd had in Bangui with one of the more corrupt bankers in the city. The man had asked Gash what he thought about his future if Kolingba was no longer a factor. The man's meaning was clear – if Kolingba was removed, would Gash be willing to take his place? At the meeting Gash had been noncommittal – the banker could easily have been a trap set by Kolingba himself – but on another level the question had nagged. Gash hadn't survived this long by being stupid; he knew perfectly well that African dictators had the life spans of fruit flies, so perhaps now was the time to start considering an escape route if worse came to worst. He bribed everyone worth bribing and continued to do so, giving him an intricate web of ears to the ground within Kolingba's inner circle, but maybe he should be doing something more.

Gash turned the truck up the road to the center of town, passing tin-roofed shacks and open-fronted stores selling everything from bicycles to knockoff handbags and long Chicago Bulls T-shirts.

He finally reached the square and turned toward the compound that had once been home to the Fourandao family and was now the presidential compound. Kolingba had wanted to call it the Royal Compound, but Gash convinced him that although he was king, he was also the president, and calling himself that to the outside world would result in his being taken more seriously.

Essentially the compound was a high-walled fort, cement and straw under a layer of yellowing stucco with a wooden parapet and a pair of heavy oak doors. Inside the compound there was the presidential residence along one side, a barracks along the other and a mess hall, armory and jail cells along the back wall. Two guards who stood outside the gate carried stubby little Chang Feng submachine guns. Gash knew that the magazines in the weapons were empty, as were the weapons within the compound – all except those belonging to Kolingba and his two personal bodyguards, both of whom were his younger brothers.

Seeing the Rover come into the square, the two guards snapped to attention and the gates magically opened as he approached. A quick phone call from one of the dockside warehouses would have warned the gate guards of his approach and they would have been ready and waiting. A guard who had failed to open the gate quickly enough had been placed in the wooden strangling scaffold that had replaced the bronze statue of Ambrosio Fourandao in the center of the square, while the rest of the townspeople were forced to watch. A rope was threaded through holes in the neck piece of the scaffold, then twisted around a metal pole at the back, slowly and very painfully choking the life out of the man.

Kolingba had watched from the parapet of the compound as the executioner drew out the process over more than an hour, choking and releasing until a nod from Kolingba finally put the man out of his misery. It was the kind of thing that gave Oliver Gash the creeps but the money was too good to complain. Another year and he'd have enough to slip out of the madman's clutches and disappear forever. Like it or not, the king of Kukuanaland was as crazy as a box of crackers and, like any wild beast, he was capable of turning on you at any time. Dealing with the man was like walking a high wire over Niagara Falls. But the money just was so damned good.

Gash parked the Land Rover in front of the presidential residence, then went up the three wide steps to the covered veranda. There was a distinct colonial flavor to the porch, complete with wicker armchairs for the plantation owners to sit on in the cool of the evening with their tall gin drinks as they complained about the heat and the lack of civilized pursuits.

The two guards at the front doors snapped to attention as Gash went by, their eyes wide with terror. Gash went up the stairs to the second floor of the building and found his way to Kolingba's study, which overlooked the compound.

As usual Kolingba was at his immense desk, brooding over some document under his immense hand. He was wearing his full uniform: dark blue jodhpurs with a red stripe down the outer seam, a light blue shirt with black and gold shoulder boards, and a chestful of medals. A huge, steel-bound copy of the Old Testament stood between two wrought-iron lion's-head bookends at the front of the desk. A chrome-plated World War Two-era tank commander's helmet rested on one corner of his desk and an ornately scrolled silver-plated presentation Colt.45 automatic pistol lay close to his right hand. Gash knew that its mate was in the holster at Kolingba's hip. There was a narrow bookcase against one wall, mostly filled with books about General

George S. Patton. There was even a photograph of the actor George C. Scott on the wall, dressed for his role as the famous general. Kolingba's big head lifted as Gash entered the room. His eyes narrowed.

'"Now the weight of gold that came to Solomon in one year was six hundred and threescore and six talents of gold – beside that which chapmen and merchants brought. And all the kings of Arabia and governors of the country brought gold and silver to Solomon."'

'Truer words were never said, Your Majesty,' murmured Gash. He didn't have the faintest idea what the big man was talking about, but he presumed Kolingba was quoting from the Bible.

'The Bible speaks of my ancestor with great reverence,' rumbled Kolingba, the sound of his voice like the throaty growl of some immense beast, barely contained.

'Of course it does, Your Majesty.' Gash nodded.

'We must act quickly, Gash, before it is too late.'

'Of course, Your Majesty.'

There was no doubt about it; Solomon Kolingba was right out of his mind.